CW00431452

Visit my website at https://louis-park.com

Chapter 1

With a roll of the die and a grumble filled with
expletives, the Fates finished the game that would
decide my day. I was to grace a Hale Barns tea and
cake shop with my presence. Fortunate for me, as
they created the most fanciful and arousing cakes,
but not so fortunate for the shopkeeper and her
clientele, as the very sight of my squalid figure
would dampen their day.

The shop bell cheerily chirped my arrival. As
soon as I set foot in the shop, all conversations
quickly stopped and slowly, pair by pair, snarling
vicious eyes set themselves on me. They waited a
brief second to see if I would realise the error of
my ways and act the good sport by leaving. This
was not to be. As soon as I sauntered to the
counter, they all simultaneously fell back into their
conversations.

It was obvious what they thought; even their
old schoolteachers, who had so often tried to
hammer in the point not to judge a book by its
cover, would have joined them in their silent rage
at my intrusion. The SUVs, the litter-free streets,
the beautifully decorated houses, the artistically
groomed gardens and foliage, the pink faces and
the pavements without the smears of dog shit. It
was damn near treason that I did not realise that
these were the stamping grounds of superior stock;
only the most wretched would not take heed of the
hierarchy that for centuries had bled into England's
green pastures! To them, it was misspent taxes as I
clearly did not know that my place at the dining
table was beneath it.

I sauntered towards the counter with my eyes wide and a devilish grin that was jagged like a broken window. My mouth salivated with anticipation, so much so that drool crept out of the corners of my mouth and abseiled down to the floor. The cakes were all excitedly lined up and they paraded their sultry attractions behind glass as if they were in the red-light district of Amsterdam.

There were cakes dressed in colourful frilly icings like Can-Can girls; I saw cakes seductively positioned with only delicately placed creams and glazed fruits that barely hiding their most tempting of curves. There were terribly vulgar cakes that showed their perfectly layered insides. And the pastries! They were disguised to look so light and innocent that one would've never guessed their true, bestial nature. All of them waited to be ravished by my being — but only at the right price.

I was so close but as the shopkeeper was not to be seen, I was also tormentingly far. Like a child on Christmas Eve who sees his presents wrapped up underneath the tree, I waited miserably. I, of course, could have exploited the situation and had my way with these most sinful of delights without monetary recompense, but unfortunately, there would be consequences for such actions, as my face was witnessed and on show. That being said, I was still very close to giving in to these sirens that teased me. So, with a resolute will, I dealt with my predicament by forcing my focus away from the cakes and I decided to look around and listen to the clientele's conversations instead. Not the ideal escape, but I was not able to think of any other alternative.

I listened to a shrill conversation between two middle-aged women. They yacked about dieting; the sound was intermittently muffled by cake being shovelled down their gullets. Undoubtedly, they believed that by talking about dieting they were achieving some sort of healthiness. However, their bingo wings disagreed.

My ears moved on to a young lady and man who both spoke excitedly about the absurd TV soap they had watched the previous night. The episode involved a young female patient being raped by her overweight doctor whilst the patient was suffering from an epileptic shock. With great shock and awe, the assault came to an abrupt halt as her seizure had become so violent that it caused her to kick a nearby cupboard, which then shook a large crystal trophy off the shelf to career down and fatally fall onto the rapist's head.

I then switched my interest to two young ladies who fired out fact upon fact about themselves in fast Morse-code beeps. I barely understood what they were saying, as gigabyte upon gigabyte of information rushed out of their mouths and invaded my ears in a full-on assault. I was just about able to make out that they had said something about their university, strange exclamations about clothes and I swear to whatever deity would listen to me that they spoke in praise of unicorns. The information was just far too much and my brain glitched in error, so I had to give it a few good whacks to get it back in running order again. Listening to the public was all too much for me and instead of distracting me, it made my craving worse, as my need to devour the cakes became a way to escape such inanity.

A whiff of a heavenly Black Forest gateau took advantage of my wanton state and crept down my nose to caress my belly. I purred in response. I turned back around to stare forlornly at the cakes again. My lust became such a burden that my knees trembled with its weight. Drool soon flowed again, so I sucked the excess fluid in and quickly closed my gaping mouth, wiped it and then pressed my face hard against the counter's glass. I was but centimetres away from those temptresses! Control and good manners were being trounced by the gluttonous barbarian inside me. I then moaned and whined in frustration — and continued to do so — each moan and whine getting louder and louder. Suddenly the shopkeeper announced her presence with a shrill, out-of-tune violin of a voice.

"Excuse me, sir, can I help you?"

At first, I ignored this question that was riddled with scorn, but then it was fired at me again.

"I said excuse me, can I help you?"

It soon dawned on me who it was, so I quickly pulled my face away from the counter and stood bolt upright to see before me a chubby middle-aged shop attendant who I had not seen in this shop before. She wore a long pale purple cardigan that tightly drooped over her rolls and rippled low down so she resembled a fondue. Her nose was long, hooked, and decorated with red splodges that could not be hidden by her makeup. Also, her plump face resembled an overburdened bellboy carrying huge bags. The shopkeeper had finally arrived and a burst of euphoria shot into me as this, of course, meant *cake*!

Her face quickly became one of shock and panic when she saw what I looked like. If only it was my sense of fashion that caused such anxiety, as it certainly wasn't the height of vogue. My attire was simple, composed — as always — of a long tattered dark-brown leather trench coat, black combat pants that were kind enough to hide all sorts of stains, a black woollen turtleneck that was decorated with small holes and a pair of well-worn black steel-toe-capped boots. I also had my trusty tattered and torn rucksack on my shoulders, which was always filled with indispensable goodies and tools. But I felt her reaction was more down to what I actually looked like as a human being.

As regards to my actual self, I imagine that when Mother Nature was sprinkling the 'Y' chromosome into my primordial goo, the lid must have fallen off and the contents spilled in. After that, life spent a great deal of time and consideration chiselling violent marks onto me. My large and obscenely square head housed a heavy thick brow that was a twin to an Easter Island statue's. I also had long black chains of knotted hair and my greasy black beard was a writhing nest of snakes. Then there were my long muscular arms, which admittedly might have added to people's view that I was lagging behind in the evolutionary process. These arms were married to a large pair of thick callus and scar-ridden hands that were surprisingly nimble and delicate when the situation required. All this sat on a frame so broad that at times I'd have to enter doorways sideways.

It was my almond-shaped eyes and naturally tanned skin that made me a candidate for a far-right caricature of a foreign evil that had come to corrupt all that is holy in this land. There were also my scars. These were so numerous that it appeared I had been smashed to pieces and then haphazardly stuck back together again.

Because my face at that moment beamed with a delighted friendliness, the shopkeeper quickly reverted to her belligerent and condescending ways.

"Sir. This is a place for paying customers."

Without giving me time to respond she spoke rudely again.

"Sir. If you're not a paying customer, then I will have to ask you to leave!"

Those last words immediately caused my smile to disappear and my face to become distorted with anger. Terrible thoughts of actually being denied cake by this torrid woman tormented my mind. My heart pounded out a furious beat, my shoulders hunched, veins protruded on my neck, my fists became tightly clenched and my brow buckled down with the pressure of my rage.

"Sir—" she added meekly, as she saw what she had done.

I interrupted her with a growl.

"Now look here, I will call the—" she tried to say before I interrupted her again, with an even louder growl.

"Please will you—" Again, I interrupted with a growl and my mouth had also started to froth.

I carried this on until she was completely quiet and still. The shop had become deathly silent and all eyes were on myself and the shopkeeper. Most faces showed curiosity and a fear that terrible violence was about to occur. I really did not wish to carry on this silly charade any longer. So, with a contemptuous look, I reached into the inner breast pocket of my trench coat. The shopkeeper's gaze — and all of the clientele's dropped to that hand. Her brain must have formulated possibilities upon possibilities of unpleasantness, as her face anxiously contorted more and more while I rummaged around my pocket.

I suddenly ripped my hand out of my pocket and slammed it on the counter with thunderous force, making the shopkeeper and a few of the clientele yelp in fear. The old woman's lips trembled and her eyes moistened, yet she was not able to avert her gaze from mine. She must have read my face as that of one ready for bloody murder, as a faint whiff of urine mixed into the air.

I nodded down to indicate that she should look at my hand. The silly thing didn't quite understand. I again nodded down for her to look at my hand on the counter. This time she caught on and her eyes slowly drifted down. With slightly melodramatic flair, I ever so slowly pulled away my hand to reveal two crumpled twenty-pound notes.

"Why, my dear, of course, I am a paying customer!" I boomed with a chummy grin.

The shopkeeper slowly looked up at my face again, but she dared not look directly into my eyes. Clearly it was her brain that now malfunctioned, but I was not feeling charitable enough to give it a whack to help organise her thoughts. Confusion jumped into the rabble of emotions that was on her face.

"Well, now that you understand that I am a paying customer would you be so kind as to allow me a taste of the fine delicacies that you have on offer?" I asked jovially with a cheeky wink.

It took more than a few seconds of silence before she responded.

"Yes ... yes ... yes, you indeed are a paying customer ... I *am* sorry," the shopkeeper said, giving a sigh of defeat.

Tap. Tap. Tap. I tapped on the glass ever so lightly with my hand, but the sound still echoed throughout the silent shop. The shopkeeper's eyes slowly fell and saw the cake that I wanted.

"My dear, that one please." It was a Black Forest gateau provocatively dressed in cream, cherries and shavings of chocolate.

"The whole cake, please," I added politely.

"Yes. Er. Yes. Cake."

Even though her hands trembled and her face was ghostly, she still deftly served me the dessert. There the most provocative of gateau lay, on top of the counter, in an open pink box. The smell of the freshly whipped cream, the dark cherries and the chocolate sponge rushed up into my nostrils. It was heavenly and tantalising. The temptress gave me a look that begged for immediate defilement and to that suggestion, I was not one to say no.

I smothered my face with the Black Forest gateau. The absolute delight I felt from this act, the sensational tastes that exploded in my mouth — words could not do justice to what I experienced! I burrowed into the cake like a starved pig at its trough, occasionally coming up for breath and to give orgasmic moans. Then as quickly as it had begun it was over. I had consumed her! All that was left were the last remnants of cake on my face.

I slowly and methodically wiped the cake off my face with my finger and savoured the last morsels. At first, a part of me felt a painful sorrow for the cake's demise, but this was quickly taken over by a feeling of grateful contentment. I let off a rapturous belch in acknowledgement of the pleasurable experience, but the shopkeeper did not appear to register such compliments.

Having consumed a whole cake, I had become rather parched. So, I looked around the shop for an adequate drink to follow such a feast. The clientele averted their eyes whenever they met mine. My eyes eventually fell upon a delicate china teapot that nestled on a table where a young couple sat. I must admit I am a slave to a good cup of tea; it is an addiction that I have never conquered.

I sauntered over to this couple, who both tried ever so hard to pretend that I did not exist. The young man was quite a chiselled chap, blond, tall, smartly dressed and well built, what most would describe as good-looking. His lady friend could have passed as a sibling as she was similar to him but in a feminine way. She was blond, tall, attractive, fashionable and possessed the right curves in the right places.

"Hello, young man. I see that you're drinking tea there," I declared as I pointed at the intricate teapot and delicate cups.

The young man's eyes still faced downward and he did not respond. His lady friend had turned her head completely away, a common reaction to me from women. As one would rightly assume, I was someone who found being ignored rather rude.

"Young man, it is ill-mannered to ignore one that talks to you."

There was silence.

"If you persist down this path, I will take it as an insult. Such affronts against myself will always lead to consequences, consequences that I assure you, you will find most uncomfortable. Now, young man, please do not be so rude as to not look at me when I talk to you," I scolded.

The young man slowly and begrudgingly looked up. I could see the rage in his eyes, but that emotion was quickly extinguished as he looked straight into my face.

"Sorry … sir. It is tea," he quietly spluttered, like a reprimanded schoolboy.

"Tea, you say. Interesting. I am rather parched after eating so much cake."

Again, there was silence and the young man had failed to realise what I had insinuated.

"I said, I am rather parched."

The cogs slowly turned in this young man's head as he tried to understand what I wanted. His companion turned around sharply and enlightened him.

"He wants some fucking tea!"

"Oh. Um … would you like some tea, sir?"

"Why, thank you, young man, how kind of you to offer! Of course, I would."

I grabbed the teapot, took one of the dainty cups and filled it with the golden-brown liquid. I then added a smidgen of milk, just enough to complement the flavour.

"There is sugar as well, sir."

I gave him a little scowl of disgust in response.

As I held the small cup, I breathed in the mellow and smooth aromas, then sipped. It was divine! I then swished the beautiful English Breakfast tea delicately around my mouth. As I savoured the taste, it evoked a poetic calm throughout my body and even more so as it trickled down my gullet. Time was indeed relative and at that moment, it had almost stopped. One could almost forgive the British for their centuries of cruel bastardisation of the world, as without it such an abundance of tea on these shores would not be.

As soon as I finished the tea, I was brought back to reality and realised it was time for me to go. I thanked the couple for their gracious generosity and I also thanked the shopkeeper for her tremendous culinary skills. With a sunny smile and a spring in my step, I left.

The doorbell bade me a cheery goodbye as I left.

Chapter 2

It was a day where the sun was shining, the birds were singing happily and the trees were flaunting their fashion. I walked with a spring in my step; this was no metaphor as each couple of steps I did a little skip. There was wonderful music that reverberated through the leaves when the wind blew and the birds sang along with it. It all played in time to a beat that only I, for whatever reason, was able to hear. All passers-by seemed to ignore the music that surrounded them. Their eyes appeared glazed and empty, as their minds were far away treading water in a sea of thought. I, of course, did not care and was far too ecstatic about this splendid orchestra, so much so that I bellowed out a bass-heavy hum to join in. I paid scant attention to the scared faces that veered as far away from me as they politely could.

I was in Chorlton Water Park, one of the many parks in Manchester. As much as parks are a mutilated face of nature, they are places that I adore as they still give me a taste of that which I so love. I carried on with my merry stroll down into the adjacent Kenworthy Woods. Eventually, I reached a hidden corner that was mostly away from the public gaze. This corner was conveniently protected by large rhododendron bushes which I had planted, fostered and grown to hide a lovely garden of flowers that I had looked after since they were seedlings. I dropped onto my belly and shoved my rucksack underneath the rhododendrons and crawled beneath the growth. I was immediately embraced by a wonderfully comforting floral smell.

A steadfast and proud buddleia was the first to greet me. Its large purple tendrils were alive with hungry bumblebees and flowers that waved their hellos in a light breeze. I carried on my careful walk along a little pathway I had previously made. Next to give their greetings were a lively group of orange heleniums who happily coaxed many a bombus lapidarius and butterfly to pollinate them. Classy dahlias in white followed. As polite as they were in their appearance, they were provocative enough for the bumblebees to find irresistible. When I reached the middle of the little grove, I was surrounded by near luminous pink and bright violet penstemons that tried to hide their garish nature by drooping shyly. Of course, the bees were not put off by such an act. I flopped down in the little clearing in the middle of this orgy of wildlife and purred whilst enjoying the music that was all around me.

It was perhaps an hour before I perked up out of my tranquil state, feeling I had let myself enjoy such leisure for too long. I remembered that another hidden alcove of mine required pruning and tending, as it was filled with a different season's flowerage. Reluctantly, I pushed myself up onto my feet, grabbed my rucksack and set off to a different park where this other den lay hidden. I was a minute out of Kenworthy Woods and back in Chorlton Water Park when I came across a heinous act that required my immediate intervention.

What I saw was a pit bull terrier of a young man nonchalantly throw his chocolate bar wrapper into a bed of flowers. The music that I heard all around me screeched to a halt. As the wrapper floated to the ground, my jaw clenched, veins on my forehead and neck bulged, my breath became deep and heavy and soon all I could see was this young man and nothing else. He was very much the red and I was the bull.

The young man moved with an aggressive swagger. He was not the daintiest of creatures and he was certainly taller than me, with a large, muscular, six-foot frame. This macho front was paired with a peculiar fashion ensemble. He wore a tight black and floral short-sleeved shirt that appeared a couple sizes too small. He also wore a pair of white jeans that clung lecherously to his muscle-bound legs. All his prominent and protruding muscles begged for attention like a neglected child. He had a carefully sculpted crew-cut hairstyle and he clearly enjoyed the sunbed, to the point where he was a walking advertisement for how to catch melanoma.

I would not hesitate to say that it was quite fortunate for the young chap that I actually saw him commit the heinous act, as if I had not, the brain cells in his head would have continued to sign off approval of such churlishness. His wrongdoer's behaviour would then have remained and undoubtedly would have contaminated others to follow this terrible path. One day — or perhaps he already had — this chap would eventually fill some other just as deplorable life form's belly with his seed. Then another creature like him would be born, taking on his deplorable ways and the terrible cycle would repeat on and on until the whole world was nothing but a cesspit. Perhaps it is quite a big leap to make such assumptions, but I was not willing to take that chance with non-intervention.

As the young man walked off, I quickly looked around to see if there were any witnesses and fortunately, there were none. I was fairly sure that the young man had not noticed me hidden in the trees, which were a good forty metres away. Regardless, I took off my trench coat and left my rucksack, as they were the most identifiable items I had on. I pulled out my balaclava, put it on and then sprinted after the offending creature from behind. When I was about a couple of metres from him, I jumped and rugby tackled him right in the arch of his lower back. The young chap let out a high-pitched squeal as I lifted him into the air and slammed him onto the ground. I was quickly on top of the winded man and pinned him down. I thought I was going to have to do a "ground and pound" to tame this aggressive beast, when I noticed that his face was crinkled up in pain and tears were liberally leaking down both sides of his chiselled jaw.

"P-p-please don't hurt me. Please take all my money but just don't hurt me!" he whimpered.

The crying came as such a surprise that I was at a loss about what to do. Punching someone so pathetic almost seemed inhumane, so I thought perhaps a couple of good slaps would be more appropriate. The first slap caused the young chap to cry and whimper even more. It wasn't until about the fifth slap that the sobbing had started to go the opposite way and diminish. After a good eight slaps the young man had simmered down to soft whimpers. I jumped off the young fellow, who then quickly curled up in the foetal position and whimpered.

"Money isn't why I did this —" I tried saying, but before I could carry on, the young man interrupted me by bursting into tears again.

"Oh, God no! P-p-please don't rape me!" he wailed loudly.

The young man then made intermittent squealing noises in between each sob. If he could have seen under my balaclava, he would have seen a raised eyebrow. All the crying made the whole ordeal unnecessarily awkward.

"Sorry, young man. Rape really is not my cup of tea." I sighed.

The young chap momentarily stopped his whimpering but then broke out into a flood of tears again.

"N-n-n-no. No. No! I don't want to die!" he wailed.

"I am not here to kill you either!" I snapped at him.

I really had to speed this lesson up, as all the possible joy of a fight had been bled out by the cretin.

"If you try to run away, I will break both your legs. Now, get up!" I ordered.

I gave him a swift, hard boot up his behind to hurry him up. The young chap staggered to his feet, his head face downwards and his lips quivering like a reprimanded child.

"Move!" I said, as I shoved him forward.

The young man complied and lumbered forward with his slumped shoulders swaying slowly from side to side. An occasional shove was required to herd him in the right direction. When we reached the wrapper, I told him to stop and then pointed at the offending item that was crudely stuck in a bed of innocent gerwats.

"Rather than waste both our time with a lecture, I will make it clear that if I ever see you litter again, you will suffer in the most terrible of ways," I hissed.

Although the young lad was too petrified to bring his face, which had turned pale, to look into mine, I could tell he was rather confused.

"Now pick it up and throw it away properly," I ordered.

He hesitated at first, but another swift boot cajoled him onto the righteous path. The young man picked up the wrapper and threw it in the bin that was but three metres away. He then obediently came back to me and stood still with eyes cast down at my boots as he waited for further instruction.

"Now, piss off!" I snarled.

The young man didn't wait for a second to comply with my order. He bolted off and was soon out of sight. As much of a chore as that ordeal was, I did let myself enjoy the following feeling of pride that had pumped up my chest.

I sauntered off thinking it was very possible that I had scared the young man to such a degree that just the very thought of littering would bring back traumatic memories that would convince him to act otherwise in future. Alas, my pride soon evaporated as the reality became glaringly obvious:

far bigger acts of altruism were needed to make a noticeable difference. But before such black clouds in my mind could make me morose, they were blown away by the thought that I was soon to take my first meaningful steps into vigilantism.

I soon realised that the young man might have alerted the authorities, so I decided to leave my gardening in south Manchester until another day. I picked up my few belongings and headed towards one of my favourite alcoves in Heaton Park, this being in north Manchester, but before this plan could progress it was rudely interrupted by a very petulant and vocal stomach. It seemed a picnic was in order, so I swung by my humble abode and picked up what leftover food I had. I was then off on my merry way.

After a casual jog, I reached Heaton Park. I was near to my spot when I had to navigate past a portly couple having a picnic themselves. They didn't notice me as I walked by as they were too busy playing with each other's tongues whilst shovelling shop-bought swill into their mouths at the same time. Sodden, half-chewed boulders of food tumbled down and down on the ground all around them. I carried on, keen to get away from the vulgar sight.

The alcove was nicely tucked away and hidden by a small half ring of hedges and metal fencing. A friendly giant of an oak tree stood on guard near the entrance to this little nook. I had spent many an hour reading, lolling, sleeping, eating, meditating and procrastinating there. It was a lovely little getaway, priced at the reasonable cost of a small walk.

I fell to the ground and let out a sigh of pleasure as my head touched the thick soft grass. It was only a couple of minutes until my stomach loudly and incessantly pined, as it thought I had forgotten it. I quickly pushed myself up and then pulled out an assortment of leftover goodies from my rucksack. This was not a planned meal, so these scarce leftovers had to make do with each other. First came two tinfoil covered whole roast ducks. The ducks had been given a citrus marinade and were a leftover from the previous night. From a brown paper bag came a sourdough loaf that I had baked earlier that morning. I then pulled out some little plastic lunch boxes, all filled with leftovers from different meals. The smell of roast vegetables painted with garlic filled my nostrils when I opened one of these tubs. For my dessert, there was a plastic tub filled with a delectable panna cotta, layered with passion fruit jelly. Then, to top it all off, there was an assortment of cheese and crackers. One of the cheeses, a Camembert, was so runny that I damn near thought it was alive. Each time I turned my head it tried to silently creep off my cracker to get away. I showed it no mercy.

I ripped into the food fervently with my hands and teeth until there were only crumbs and duck carcasses left. I then fastidiously sucked any remaining meat and cartilage off the bones, licked the plastic containers clean and pulled out the final chapter of my meal: a flask of English Breakfast tea. After I had finished the divine nectar, I slowly fell backwards onto the floor with a satisfied smile lazily stretched out on my face. A thunderous belch rushed out of my mouth to tell the world of my contentment. I then closed my eyes to snooze as the sun's rays warmed me.

It must have been at least an hour before I awoke to the feeling of cold rain pattering down on my face and my clothes. Manchester's weather was, unfortunately, severely bipolar. I opened my eyes and saw that the sun had been chased away by a mob of angry grey clouds. I was not going to be able to fall asleep with the amount of rain that was falling and as I was not one to let the weather dampen my spirits, I got up to go for a stroll.

During my walk, Manchester's weather went through another change of mood: the sun came back swinging and chased away the fleeing grey clouds. I soon came across a friendly oak tree that stood with a few of its kind in a field and slumped myself down underneath it. As I sat back and took in the scenery, I spotted a grey squirrel who scurried down a tree to find food. It soon found some sort of morsel and sat down on its hind legs to munch away on it. I leapt to my feet and started to shout at the critter:

"BAH! BAH! BAH! YOU! BAH!" The squirrel simply ignored the racket I made.

"HEY! You boring, little grey git!" I shouted again.

This time the little critter turned its head to look back at me. I broke out into uproarious laughter. The squirrel was clearly not amused and went back to eating its food. When it turned away, I sprinted at it whilst making rasping noises. The squirrel dashed off before I could reach it and soon found a high tree branch. The critter then rained down a stream of angry squeaks at me.

I didn't have any intention of catching the creature, I was just playing with it, so instead of taking offence at its anger, I fell to the ground laughing. When I finally reined in my mirth, I noticed a family of four hurriedly walking away from me. The parents didn't even bother answering the children's questions about whether they could go and play with the "strange funny man and the squirrels".

There was something about grey squirrels that brought out the desire to be obnoxious to them. Perhaps it was because the little fellows had unwittingly caused the near extinction of their red-coloured brethren that I felt they all needed a good ribbing. Whatever the reasoning, I often chased, shouted and laughed at the fuzzy-tailed rodents until they themselves were red in the face with rage. On this occasion, it was an hour before I became bored.

I had a look at where the sun was in the sky and figured it would still be a fair few hours until my main course of amusement came. Suddenly my stomach strutted into my mind and made it obvious with a few rumbles that it wanted food again. I felt in my pockets to find a few pounds' worth of change. That small change wasn't going to get me the amount and type of culinary delights that the organ was accustomed to.

"Money, food and then fun," I mumbled to myself, as I went off to acquire a few more coins from a hapless Mancunian or two.

Chapter 3

It was a typical Manchester night and that meant the clouds completely hid the city from the gaze of the stars and the moon. All that could be seen up above was an abyss tinged orange by streetlights. And of course, no Manchester night was complete without a lecherous drizzle that tried to seep into every crevice.

The sound of old diesel-engine buses spewed out into the quiet night every few minutes. There was also the occasional noise of the odd roving pack of drunken youngsters. They tried to show both to the world and their own insecurities that they weren't insignificant, with their screams and shouts. One of these packs upped the ante and a short, sharp, smash of glass was heard. A victorious roar and hyena laughs followed. It was naivety of the highest order to think that they thought anyone beyond themselves respected such feats of destruction.

Amongst all this, I was impatiently lying on a poorly-lit concrete pathway in the middle of Whitworth Park. There was a thin mist that clung onto the ground all around me. I felt cold, wet, bored and tired. For whatever reason, I didn't get the nervous jitters and the screaming feelings of excitement that I usually had before such showdowns. Also, by that point, I'd usually have a giant grin on my face and my legs would be happily shaking.

Suddenly I felt anxiety shooting hot blood through my neck, back, ears and cheeks. A terrible thought stampeded through my brain: "What if my move into benevolent vigilantism were to fail?" I hadn't thought about the possibility of failure and it was an inconvenient moment for such a fear to reveal its monstrous self for the first time.

The fear found a friend in self-doubt and both then easily goaded me into thinking that the bumblebees would still die out, even if I were to succeed. The thought of those adorable fuzzy creatures that were filled with colour and delight careening into extinction violently tugged at my heart. I tried to force out such feelings of sadness with angry thoughts about the petulant, profit-driven entrepreneurs who considered such wondrous life to be negligible. However, that was not enough: such red quickly faded back into morose blue and the din from my rage could not stop my descent into despair. Soon after came a memory that I had long repressed. It was of my father stomping on a bumblebee's nest with sadistic glee whilst I looked on, powerlessly. I did not know how, but at that moment I was transported back into that same naked, bloody and bruised little boy who watched, helplessly, the only thing he ever loved at that house become brutally destroyed.

My face started to crack with such heavy emotions treading on it. Soon the tears formed and then snap, I was bawling with no sign of stopping. This, of course, wasn't the plan, as I was supposed to stay quiet, lying there on the floor. The idea being, that the police officers would approach me and get close enough for me to spring my trap. Instead, they found a balaclava-covered man in the foetal position sobbing his heart out. Fortunately, the six police officers that came to the park still approached me to find out what was going on.

"Where the hell is everyone? I don't see anyone else," one of the police officers exclaimed.

"Oi. What the hell you doing mate?" a different police officer asked me.

Previous to their arrival, I had called the emergency services to report that a couple of black youths were violently attacking a white male student-type and were doing it at this very spot. This was so I could have some sport with the police, but unfortunately, my own mentality had soured the mood.

"Mate. You need to tell us what is going on or you're going to get arrested!" one of them said after giving a deep sigh.

Such orders were of no use, as I was barely staying afloat in my melancholy. I simply carried on bawling, oblivious to the world around me.

"For fuck's sake. I think it's just another fucking loon! Think we need to get him sectioned."

"Mate, did you see what happened? And why have you got a balaclava on?" one tried to enquire sympathetically.

"No use, Tim. Telling you, it's a fucking head-case and he probably telephoned us to get us over here for attention. For fuck's sake, if he doesn't shut up, I am going to kick his head in," I heard an angrier voice respond.

"Oi, you retard fuck, I said get up, now, or I'll make sure you regret ignoring me!" the same angry voice barked.

Still I cried and still I was oblivious to such threats — that was, until one of them touched me.

"I said get up!"

Suddenly instinct took over when I felt the rough grip on my shoulder. My bawling stopped and I felt all of the muscles in my face relax to an emotionless state. My eyes opened to see a surprised-looking face. I quickly grabbed the offending officer's wrist from my shoulder and then grabbed his hand with my other hand. The police officer was only able to open his eyes wide before I sharply twisted his hand whilst holding his wrist still. A cracking sound was heard and a scream erupted. Next, I jerked my left arm back with enough power to throw the kneeling officer onto his back on the other side of me, and immediately after, I jumped up onto my feet. I saw five police officers, all looking rather anxious, a few metres in front of me. There was fear in their faces for a brief second, but they quickly registered their crying friend on the ground and soon their expressions became distorted with a desire for violent revenge.

I pointed at their compatriot on the floor, pouted, then mockingly pretended to cry — yes, I know, the hypocrisy! Suddenly, one of them reached for his taser. Fortunately, he was not the best quick-draw in the UK, and that meant I had ample time to side-step his shot. I quickly grabbed the insulated wires, gave a violent tug towards me and the police officer came tumbling forwards. His face ended up at the perfect level for a swift knee. Bleached white teeth rattled onto the concrete before the thud of his body followed.

I knew one of them had already circled behind me, whilst his colleagues came from the front. I swung my head back with perfect timing, heard a slight groan and felt a few splashes of warm blood on the back of my neck. Then, before he could recover, I ducked the flying fist from his colleague in front of me, fell to my knees and launched an uppercut straight into that officer's testicles. I followed through with such ferocity that I lifted him up above me into the air. The poor fellow was only able to let out a wheeze before he passed out and thudded onto the concrete.

I then felt a quick succession of punches. One went straight into the right side of my temple, another hit my other temple, and then one went right onto my nose. I quickly stepped back to regain my composure and face the culprit. I saw an uppercut heading to the underside of my chin, but I moved my head to the side in time. I then grabbed this one by the throat, squeezed my fingers almost to the point of snapping his windpipe, picked him up and slammed him onto the ground. There was no further movement from the officer, as he was knocked out cold.

The last one, who had not suffered any injury, tried to turn on his heel and run. However, I was quickly onto him and sent the heel of my boot into his ankle. A violent crack could be heard, he fell to the ground and I gave him another quick, bone-snapping stomp on the other shin. Instinct ordered me to turn around, so I did and faced a bloodied man charging right at me. I dropped low and jumped at him at the same time as he tried to rugby-tackle me. His face collided with the top of my head and I heard a muffled groan before he was silent. I did a quick press-up with enough strength that it flung me back up onto my feet.

I turned around in time to see the police officer with the broken wrist trying to get his taser out from the other side of his body with his one working arm. Before he could do this though, I picked up one of the unconscious officers next to me and threw him. It was a perfect hit and they both crumpled to the floor.

All the police officers lay motionless around me.

I noticed that I had a joyous grin on my face, while the adrenaline merrily pumped throughout my body. I took a deep breath and let out a sigh of pleasure, the like of which I also reserved for the time straight after orgasms. My chest pumped itself up and I slowly sauntered away from the scene. It was a rare and delightful treat to fight the police. Unfortunately, it wasn't an activity I could engage in too often, as the risk of being imprisoned was just too high.

I chuckled to myself as I now found my previous state of despair somewhat amusing and pondered whether it wasn't perhaps an inescapable human condition to always become anxious over what one held dear. Suddenly my memory let in the most fabulous of visitors and I remembered that there was — not too far from me — a twenty-four-hour convenience store that sold surprisingly delightful ready-made cheesecakes. Excitement took the helm as I remembered that tomorrow would be the first major step in my vigilante campaign. Of course, most people treated themselves to a little something after the denouement of their hard work, but I wasn't, unfortunately, the most conscientious sort. Also, I felt the campaign might lead to my arrest, or even death, so I convinced myself to go out to have some fun as it might be the last time.

I soaked up the mood for one last second and then quickly walked off the lit path into the park's enveloping darkness. After I was a good fifty metres away and had grabbed my rucksack from behind a tree, for some curious reason I had a sudden urge to look back. That was when I noticed a small black Scottish terrier merrily trotting by itself down the lit path towards the incapacitated police officers. As strange as it sounds, for some peculiar reason I could not help but feel that I had seen the little beast before. As if on cue, a pang of fear erupted in me and my stomach twisted into knots of every kind.

For a reason that baffled me, my gut sensed enough of a danger to scream, "RUN!". But the rational thinking that I held close to my very being calmly told me otherwise. It was simply a lost black Scottish terrier and my sudden feelings of fear were probably related to my anxieties about what I was going to do the following day. I turned around and carried on walking, but at a quicker pace, as I could not shake off the feeling of wanting to get away from the place as fast as I could.

Chapter 4

The police officer awoke to a Manchester rain that
lightly pattered on his luminous yellow coat and he
instinctively let out a groan. He didn't know why
he had groaned and didn't even know where he
was, let alone why he was lying outside in the rain.
Parts of him started to hope it was the consequence
of a heavy night of drinking, but then the events of
what had just happened slowly came together. Out
of nowhere, an excruciating pain very belligerently
screamed in his head and he looked down at the
mangled mess both of his legs were in. A pathetic
whimper crept out of his mouth.

A different pain coming from his testicles then
pushed through to join in. This new hurt helped to
remind the police officer that before his vicious
beating he had already been having a bad day. The
thought that DC Tina Bosworth had earlier brutally
shot down his romantic advances popped into his
mind. Tina was everything he wanted: she was
blonde, had a perfect smile with the cutest dimples,
hypnotic green eyes, perky breasts that ignored
gravity and a bottom so delectable that he felt the
urge to bite it every time he saw it. When they had
a drunken fumble after the Christmas work-do, he
felt it was going to be the start of a lustful
romance; however, she did not. Following this
drunken mistake, Tina thought she had made it
clear to the policeman that it was just a one-off and
that she had only gone with him because she had
drunk enough alcohol to kill an entire waddle of
nuns.

The police officer saw it differently and
thought perhaps persistence and a further flash of

his charm would be the way to make her his. Unfortunately, he was devoid of any actual charm and his actions quite easily fell into the category of sexual harassment. After what must have been a month's worth of such behaviour, Tina felt she had to make it very clear that she wasn't going to be his. She did this — a couple of hours before this recent call out — by making a number of clear and concise points whilst squeezing the officer's testicles to the point where he nearly fainted. She was not going to let "repeated sexual innuendo and outright fuck propositions", "lecherous groping" and the sending of "a multitude of dick pics" carry on. She then put it quite bluntly that, should he continue, she would first castrate him with her bare hands, then feed him his own testicles and get him fired for sexual harassment.

Even after being beaten and left mangled in the Manchester rain, the police officer still winced about the whole ordeal with Tina: he had never encountered such an unreasonable reaction before. It was not that such forms of romancing ever actually worked, it was more that the female officer in question would usually end up transferring to a different team or quit the force entirely — either way they were easily forgotten. But the officer didn't think he was going to easily forget Tina and felt that she had bruised his ego permanently.

The officer let out another groan as he remembered how he was so excited he was when the call-out about black youths in the park came through whilst he was nursing his testicles with someone else's frozen ready meal in the staff room. After the attempted castration by Tina, the officer found that his emotional state deteriorated to levels where he questioned whether he should even be a police officer any longer. Such dour trains of thought started with the feeling that he deserved more respect for the work he did.

He couldn't understand why people didn't realise that it wasn't easy hurting criminals. Sure, a few innocent criminals got in the way, but that was just the way it was. Well, that was what it *used* to be like before the advent of the smartphone. He moped in the thought that once that happened, a police officer couldn't even take a bloody piss in the bushes, let alone kick someone's head in, without some snotty teenager recording them. Suddenly an officer was famous for all the wrong reasons and their superiors then had to do something about it. He knew that there would be people who would consider suspension with full-pay whilst an investigation was pending quite a let-off for slamming a person's head into the pavement multiple times, but they didn't see the other side of it. Granted, the investigation was just a formality, but the boredom at home was intolerable, especially as it meant spending more time with two bratty children and an increasingly rotund wife.

But yes, the officer's mood had perked up out of his dark ruminations when that call-out came in about the black youths. It was happening in a park where he knew there was no CCTV and he also felt that that there would unlikely be any bystanders with smartphones ready to record every move at that time of night. At that moment, the officer had been filled with excitement and what had happened with Tina simply became fuel for passive aggression of the most violent kind. Of course, all that positive energy dissipated when a man wearing a balaclava broke both his legs.

"Tim! Tom! Matt! Fuck. You guys all right?" the officer called out to his fellow policemen.

The patter of the rain was the only reply. He reached for his radio but for some unknown reason, it wasn't receiving or sending any signals, even though it appeared fine. The police officer muttered a few expletives and thought it must have got damaged in the fight. He tried to turn over so he could crawl to one of the other officers, but the slightest movement caused pain so nauseating that he threw up all over his own shoulder and face. The police officer let out a roar of frustration at the skies, and then immediately whimpered. It popped into his head that, eventually, back-up would be sent to see what had happened and they would find the injured officers.

Whilst the policeman stared into the orange abyss above him, the thought of Tina was pushed out of his mind and he unwillingly projected the memory of the beating in his head, over and over again. It was as if he was strapped down and forced to repeatedly watch the savagery. Each time the reel got to the crack of his bones, it caused him to flinch and moan in pain.

Strangely, each time the events played through his mind, the officer felt a familiar feeling grow — he could not quite pinpoint why. Again, the reel played and he started to see something he recognised about the masked man. At first, he couldn't put his finger on what, but then he realised it was the masked man's eyes. He had seen those eyes, filled with rage and joy, before. It finally clicked: he had come across someone with those same eyes at the Youth Offenders Institute he was once a guard at — and it was someone who

33

had passionately loved the pain his rage had created. But before the policeman could organise the cluttered files in his head to remember who the culprit was exactly, a cruel laugh slowly and sadistically cut through the night. The police officer's skin crawled and tried to wriggle off him. One of the things that unsettled him the most about the horrible laugh was it sounded as if its pitch came from every octave, high and low.

"I say, you do have to commend the young chap. You bloody well do. He's tickling me through and through!" the peculiar voice exclaimed in a quintessential English accent.

The officer calmed himself and thought that he must have endured a head injury, which was why the voice sounded so strange. He grimaced through the pain, pushed himself up onto his behind and looked around, but only saw a black Scottish terrier sitting nearby. He could have sworn he saw the dog smile.

"Mate, where are you? We need your help. Please, you need to call the police and an ambulance for us, now!" the policeman ordered.

"Absolutely marvellous! The way he snapped your legs like twigs. That noise and the look on your face. My word, it was absolutely priceless. I think my favourite part was when he punched your friend right in the knackers. I can tell you something, your friend certainly won't be having children anymore!"

The voice then burst out into shrill, jovial laughter that horribly pricked the officer's skin all over. Half of the policeman was feeling disbelief and the other half was feeling something he had not felt since he was a child: abject terror. He gulped and felt that his day was going to get even worse, something of which he was quite right about.

"Oi! Listen here, you fuck. If you don't want to be arrested and later given a right good kicking, you better call the police right now! Well, the other police, I mean," the police officer screamed.

He then again frantically looked around again but only saw the little dog falling onto its back and then rubbing against the ground. The animal got up and stared right at the policeman. The policeman instinctively closed his eyes and, for a reason he could not explain, started to pray.

The officer was not a religious man, but he felt the urge to try and contact a higher power, as he could feel that something very terrible was about to happen. That was when he heard a few other groans from his fellow officers. The noise was the cue for the little dog to do what it wanted to do, especially as it knew that another group of officers were exactly two minutes and fifty-seven seconds away. Before the police officer could open his eyes and check on his comrades, he heard gurgles and muted screams from all around him.

The policeman opened his eyes and saw that all his comrades had disappeared and there, just in front of him, was a sneering black Scottish terrier. He could not help but to think that perhaps his brain was damaged far worse than it had seemed.

"Guys! Where are you? Seriously, where have you gone? I need you," the policeman meekly cried.

The little dog got up and trotted closer to the police officer, who was still frantically looking around. The canine walked up to one of the officer's legs where snapped white bone jutted out of his ripped trouser-leg, and then gave it a vicious little kick. The man wailed from the tidal wave of pain that crashed into his brain.

"Fucking little shit!" the police officer snarled.

He pulled a large metallic torch from his belt and went to swipe the grinning little critter, but it went straight through the canine and hit the ground.

"What the …?" Before the officer could finish his sentence, the dog's head melted into a rapidly growing and swirling sea of nightmarish black liquid that filled the air around it like ink dropped into water.

The liquid suddenly shot out and enveloped the policeman. At first, he closed his eyes in terror but when after a couple of seconds he felt that nothing had happened, he opened them to find that he was in a place where there was no light, only a terrifying and endless abyss all around him. It was as if he floated on a still sea in this haunting place. The sound of chattering teeth menacingly chimed all around him, and the man could only whimper in response. The sound grew and grew to a deafening volume and within a split-second, thousands of tiny mouths with jagged teeth suddenly came flying out from every angle and shredded him. The black abyss immediately and gluttonously drank up the bloody remains of the officer.

The little dog burped with satisfaction. Then the critter looked around and gave a little pout as it realised it had eaten all of the police officers and far too quickly. It thought to itself that it must remember to savour the meat and enjoy the flavour more next time. The little dog sighed; it deliberated whether to reverse time to have the meal again but decided not to, as that would have been breaking the rules to a degree that it would not have felt comfortable with. The cute animal gave a little shrug to itself and merrily trotted away, following the scent of its new-found toy.

Chapter 5

It was the late morning after my little jaunt with the police. I admit, even a vagabond like me can be quite the vain chap, so I went out to acquire a local newspaper to read about the fun I'd had the previous night. This meant a leisurely stroll in the park and a rummage through a number of bins to find that day's local paper. As it's customary for me to eat whilst reading the morning paper, I grabbed a lovely cappuccino and croissant from a passer-by. The menacing growl I gave extinguished any hard feelings the gentleman had. I then went straight back to my humble abode for a relaxing read.

A walk back to an abandoned Salford pub and then down into its cellar led me to a tunnel that was hidden behind decrepit furnishings. This tunnel was connected to a labyrinth that resided underneath the city. Underground Manchester was filled with abandoned air-raid shelters, shops, cellars, a failed subterranean transit system, public toilets, sewerage systems and tunnel upon interlinked tunnel. It was all wonderfully built up to a point, in the hope that thousands would regularly utilise this underground system, but for a myriad of reasons all further development ceased. These catacombs became my neighbourhood and down there a disused shop that was decorated with faded and dusty paintings of a sunny English countryside was my home.

Within the shop, I was able to rig up a source of electricity from a power box that was fortunately still active and had been put in place for the attempted subway system. It did mean a kilometre's worth of cabling was required for my home to receive electricity, but it was worth the effort as the energy allowed me light and heat.

The story was on the front page in big black emboldened letters, but it was not what I had expected. The story talked about the officers and the reason why they entered the park, but there was no mention of the fun I had with them. Instead, there was a story about how all six officers were missing without a trace. I was flummoxed; then the image of the black Scottish terrier merrily trotting along the path played through my mind. A pang of fear jumped out when, during this reel of memory, the dog stopped, looked straight into my eyes and gave me a cheeky wink. I shook myself out of my silly imaginings. Rather than further thinking about the matter, I decided to stay focused on my main goal at hand.

I went into my study, which used to be the storage room of the shop. I walked into a large room filled with stack upon stack of books, to the point where the entirety of the floor was a layer of books and the walls were covered by a layer of books, too. Even the furnishings were actual books haphazardly placed together. A large make-do book-sofa was in the middle of the room. The desk was simply stacks of books placed next to each other until they were a semi-uniform metre-high cuboid. The room wasn't as chaotic as it sounded, as each part was organised into genres and alphabetically placed in accordance with the author's name. I grabbed a couple of big black bin-liners that sat in the corner of the room and pulled out my plans from the bags.

On numerous bits of paper were cute, colourful writings at the top saying "Operation Fuzzy Freedom" and then the information I had collected about the multinational chemical company Oso. Scribbled bits of information from the company's social media web pages and their own publications (these came via the library computers as there was no internet down in my home) were the beginnings of my research. I grinned to myself as I came across the collated information from my phishing exercise on social media. I never knew being so duplicitous could be so gloriously entertaining. I was also quite dumbfounded about how much information I was able to acquire simply by creating fake profiles of recently divorced voluptuous vixens. The one unfortunate consequence, though, was that I had been sent at least a hundred pictures of erect penises. I had picked one of these deceived Oso employees for a more personal interaction by way of a home invasion — he was more than happy to provide me his home address when my false vixen expressed that she needed her lust quenched. From this, I ultimately ended up with the home address of Oso's Sales Director.

I continued to flip through a couple of months' worth of reconnaissance work staking out the Sales Director's property. I finally came across my perceived blueprint of his home in leafy green Wilmslow, which I had developed through said reconnaissance. I folded it and put it in my pocket. I then looked at a pocket-watch in my jacket and realised glumly there were still a fair few hours before it would be dark enough for me to put my plan into action. To take my focus away from the long wait, I opted to read and picked up a random book. Fortunately, a Dostoevsky novel found its way into my hand and I made myself comfortable on my makeshift sofa. Just as I finished, I saw that it was time to leave.

It took a few hours of jogging down back roads, through fields, wooded areas and alleyways in the increasingly dark Monday evening before I reached the Sales Director's home. His house was a small mansion that was enclosed by a tall and viciously pointy fence that separated it from the woods that encircled it. The architecture was a modern interpretation of a Georgian home and this created a certain peculiarity, as the large, modern bay windows behind the master-bedroom's balcony did not quite match with its traditional aesthetics. That being said, I could not complain too much, as the woods around the home were the most generous with regard to hiding my presence.

A difficult aspect of the mission was that there was a pair of German shepherd guard dogs stalking the grounds. Being a veteran of home invasions, I had encountered many a guard dog and like others before them, these two caused some issues. They prevented me from getting close for my stakeout and barked at me if I got too close to the fence. Fortunately, I was very well prepared for these two nuisances.

I waited in excitement until it was nine p.m., as that was when all of the housekeeping staff left like clockwork every night. Fortunately, today was no different. On most weekdays what would usually happen after this was that an escort or two would visit twenty minutes later; but for whatever reason, every Monday the Director opted to be alone. Even though this was the case, I decided to wait another hour to make sure there would be no visitors that night and for the sun to fully disappear.

I knew there were no other inhabitants, as I had learnt that his children attended boarding school and his wife spent much of her time in Italy, where she was originally from. However, there was one factor that did give me brief hesitation before I put the wheels in motion and that was the fact that, according to local news, the Director was quite the competent competitor in the amateur shooter's circuit and had a selection of firearms locked away.

Fifteen minutes after the housekeeping staff left as predicted, the Director opened his bedroom's bay windows. When the hour was about up, I threw a couple of large rump steaks over the fence. I had spiked them with a fair amount of ketamine in gel caps that were stitched into the meat. I went for the upper end of dosages as, based on past experience, contending with German Shepherds can be an exceptionally arduous task. Within the hour though, they fell to the ground giving odd moans of euphoria and confusion. I only had a short while left as it was around midnight every weeknight that the Director closed the balcony doors and went to sleep. It seemed that this means of entry was the only way in, as a security system was switched on when the housekeeping staff left. I had found this out a couple of weeks ago when I saw it being set off by a regularly used escort who went to open the back door when the Sales Director did not open the front door for her.

When I saw the second dog fall to the ground, I shot up and used a rope, a homemade hook, careful precision, an awful lot of core body strength and a gymnast's precision to get over a fence that looked far nastier than it actually was.

I headed straight to the Director's balcony and stood just underneath it pressed against the wall. The loud, mindless natter of a television obnoxiously cut through the silence of the night. From my rucksack, I took pieces of modified PVC piping and some small mirrors. Within a minute I had a two-metre periscope in my hand, that I used to spy into his room.

I saw the Sales Director lying down on his bed, snorting a line of what I imagine was cocaine and masturbating to what appeared to be a child's cartoon based on animated ponies. Although I had always found it fascinating what people got up to when they thought they were alone, this was quite a disturbing sight and one I didn't want to subject my poor eyes to. Unfortunately, I had to watch him like this until he left the room, as the rope and the hook would make some noise when used.

It took nearly half an hour of watching this horror show before he finally climaxed all over himself and his bedsheets. The Sales Director poked at some of his gloopy mess that was on him and grimaced with disgust. Much to my delight, he then got up and left the bedroom.

I dropped the periscope, but before I could throw my hook to attach it to the intricately patterned metal balcony, I heard the telephone ring obnoxiously. I stopped and quickly picked up my periscope again to look into the bedroom. I cursed under my breath as the Sales Director had come back and answered the telephone.

"Yes. What? Who are you?"

"What do you mean someone is standing underneath my balcony with a periscope?"

I saw his figure approach the balcony. I pulled the periscope in and flattened myself against the wall.

"What? He's plastered against the wall underneath the balcony?"

"What? The police won't answer my phone calls?"

"What? I am a bloody idiot that repeats everything you say?"

I then saw a bald, middle-aged head peek over the balcony to look underneath it. Its eyes widened and it mouthed the word "fuck".

"Hello, police! Fuck, fuck, fuck! Why isn't the phone working!?" he shouted a few seconds later.

I then heard the rapid thud of footsteps heading away from his room.

"Shit, why won't the alarms work!" I heard him scream from deep within the house.

I was frozen to the spot as wave after wave of conflicting thoughts roared into my head and bashed into each other for dominance. They soon melded into two distinct camps, one that wanted me to run away from the scene as fast as possible and the other that wanted me to finish the mission. All I knew was that whatever I decided, it needed to be done as quickly as possible. A smile crept onto my lips as I realised which course of action I was going to take.

I quickly ran to the other side of the house and saw a large metal ornamental table near the kitchen bay windows. I took a quick peek around the wall to see if the Sales Director was in the room — he wasn't. I picked up the table and flung it right through the bay door windows. The alarms had indeed been switched off and only silence followed the loud crash. I had almost stormed right through the kitchen but was distracted by the most tender-looking lamb chops that lay there naked and tantalising on a beautifully designed china plate. The meat was next to a plate with half of a gorgeous apple *tarte Tatin*. I quickly convinced myself that such food was essential energy for a hunt, so I grabbed all five lamb chops and gobbled them as I carefully started my search for the Sales Director. I did, however, look back forlornly at the *tarte* and promised her that I would be coming back.

I used a small mirror from my pocket to scan each of the rooms in the house without poking my head around the doors as I did not want it to be blown off. I was not a fan of the interior decoration of the house, which was dull, cold and abstract, with only a few scarce drops of lonely colour sticking out. I eventually reached a set of huge double doors that were obsidian-like but made of dark mahogany, with carved inset handles. They were hypnotising and I felt an urge to rub my face against the cold material. However, due to the possibility of a man with a large firearm on the other side of it, I felt it wise not to.

I went and lay on the ground on my belly behind the wall next to the doors and reached out to push one of them open. As the door swung, two loud explosions ripped through the house and small pieces of the door rained down onto my head and all around me. I pulled my arm back.

"You'd better get away if you know what's good for you! I am holed up in here and you'll only get about a foot in before I blow your fucking head off!"

I took out the small mirror and edged it out to get a better view. I was able to make out that he was a good ten metres away, defended by tables on either side of him in the far corner of the room. There were no windows nearby that I could use as a means of ambush; the only way to him was through the front doors. I was able to make all this out before I noticed the double-barrelled shotgun aimed directly at the mirror. A split-second after I let it go, the mirror exploded and debris flew all over me. A piece of marble floor flew right into the bridge of my nose. No blood came out but it smarted and tears streamed from my eyes involuntarily.

"AAARGH YOU FUCKING AMOEBA!" I screamed out.

My mind went into overdrive trying to figure out how I was going to get this man. I realised soon after that I still needed to keep my guard up, as the person who had called on the telephone may have been ready to outflank me.

Suddenly, taking me completely by surprise, a German shepherd drunkenly tried to launch itself at me, but instead went head-first into the wall right next to me. It was definitely down for the count. I looked at the wretched beast and it gave me an idea. I stood up, picked up the unconscious dog by the collar and swung it up past the door so its body showed in the room. I pulled it back just in time as two further explosions went off and parts of the wall and door again sprayed onto me. I had to be quick before he reloaded.

I ran in, still with the unconscious dog in my hands and spun around to give the dog plenty of velocity. Just as I completed the full three-sixty degrees I let go and ferociously hurled the dog at the Sales Director, who'd just finished reloading. The dog spun around like a boomerang and its skull smacked perfectly right into the Director's head. I heard the gun clatter on the ground and the man moan as I leapt over his makeshift barricade.

"Shit!" was all he uttered before I grabbed his head and kneed it a couple of times.

I then pinned him up against the wall by the throat with one of my hands. I knew I needed information quick.

"Who telephoned you? How long have you known about me!?" I hissed in his face.

All I saw was fear and confusion in his eyes.

"I-I-I don't know! I don't know who you are! I-I-I don't know what the hell is going on! My phones and security system stopped working straight after that call, so I thought that fuck was with you," he stammered out.

I felt confident that he was telling the truth. But with whatever was going on, I still had to be quick.

"I will have to summarise why I am here …"

"Is it the whore? Are you her pimp? I am so sorry. I was just so coked-up and she just wouldn't shut up, she just wouldn't. I didn't mean to hit her that much … please, I'll pay you whatever you want, anything you want at all, to make up for your loss of earnings. Just don't hurt me!" the Director begged.

I gave him a swift head-butt in response.

"Don't interrupt me. I am here because of the bumblebees!" I hissed.

Confusion took hold of the Director's face.

"You and the company you work for are killing them and driving them towards extinction. There is an abundance of evidence against you and the pesticide that you make."

The Director looked from left to right in the hope that something would come and save him.

"Since the banning of neonicotinoids, only Oso has been able to innovate a chemical similar enough to do the same damage but dissimilar enough to bypass the ban. Soon, others will follow suit. I am here to prevent—" I saw a flash of metal as the director's arm shot up after he had reached behind his back.

Before he could bring down the letter opener down on me, I grabbed his wrist with my free hand whilst still holding him by the throat. This time I pulled back quite far and head-butted him with such ferocity that his skull whipped back into the wall and cracked open. I muttered a few expletives and dropped the corpse.

A couple of minutes later, the bloodied and lifeless body of the Sales Director lay on the ground and the words "Bee AFRAID! Stay away from the bees!" were written in blood on the wall. I looked at it and couldn't help but feel that I had ended up with something that was quite silly and amateur. But I didn't allow myself any more time to criticise my own work, as the other unknown assailant was still around. I grabbed the Sales Director's gun, reloaded and that was when I heard the house telephone ring.

The ringtone had an overbearing menace that stabbed out through the silent house. I could not explain it, but my previous excitement quickly transformed into pulsations of fear. It was just a telephone ringing, but each jolt of its noise caused all the hairs on my body to stand on end. Beads of sweat populated my brow and my mouth went dry. Even though every part of me told me not to answer it and to make haste with my getaway, for some reason I felt powerless and carefully followed the noise, with the Director's gun in my hand. I soon found the phone in the hallway and apprehensively picked it up.

"HA! HA! HA! That was a bloody splendid good show, my boy! Well done to you. I especially love what you did with the dog. Bloody good job. I thought you had got yourself in a right old pickle, but then, BAM! You pulled it out of the bag. HA! HA! HA!" a most unnerving voice with a quintessential English accent laughed.

It was horribly spine-tingling, as it sounded as if its pitch hit every high and low octave at the very same time. I could not shake off my anxiety as it slipped into every crevice of my body and caused me to tighten up. The fact that the voice did this to me, given that I was no longer someone who felt much fear, made it that much more unnerving.

"Who are you?" was all I could hoarse out.

"You are such a delightful entertainer, my dear boy. I'll have to clean up the scene again for you, but it's the least that I can do. Don't you worry yourself about it. I'll see you shortly."

The phone clicked and went completely dead.

I couldn't believe what I had just heard. The phone and gun fell out of my hands due to the shock. Rather than stew on what had just occurred, fear ordered me to pick up whatever I had brought with me and run. Within seconds I was sprinting away from the Director's home as fast as my legs would carry me. The air began to feel like glass scraping against my lungs and throat, but even so I still ran. When I finally stopped and I regained some of my breath, I cursed to myself for not having brought the gun and also, I had not brought the apple *tarte Tatin*.

Chapter 6

It was not the best of ideas to head straight home, but it was the only place I could think of where I could clear my mind and think. I knew the operation had been a risk, but what actually happened was nothing I could have ever predicted. The very thought of being someone's form of entertainment gave me excruciating shivers all over. I tried to fight the shame and anxiety that followed me by setting light to powder-kegs of rage. Even with such explosions and a torturous thirst for revenge, I could not drown out the humiliation and fear I had just endured. I felt extraordinarily belittled, as this person had outplayed me to the point where I hadn't even known I was a piece in their game!

I tried to calm down by telling myself that, whoever it was, I would find them and make them suffer; but each time I thought of that voice on the telephone, it became alive in my ears and I'd fall back into a panic. I thought perhaps I was finally losing my grip on reality (something that I must admit was always a possibility, due to the amount of brain damage I have either self-inflicted or had inflicted on me throughout my life, through chemical hedonism and violence).

Aside from the sound of the voice being dreadfully peculiar, it also exuded such a confidence in its own power that I could not help but feel like an insignificant speck. It was a troublesome feeling, as the last time I had felt that way was when I was but a small child and at the mercy of sadistic parents.

Finally, I arrived back at the abandoned pub that led to my home. It was still dark and there wasn't a soul to be seen. I rooted around outside the pub and then inside, too, but found no sign of life other than the odd rat or two. I knew there was still a possibility that my home had been compromised, but I was simply not willing to go and sleep rough because of this new-found nemesis — I was not going to give up my home so easily! I slowly edged my way down through the tunnels that lead to my home. With each metre I stopped and listened for any sign of life larger than a rat. All I heard were the soft scuttles of small creatures and the dripping of water. Eventually I reached my humble abode and switched the lights on. I jumped and commando-rolled into my kitchen and emerged upright to find that no one was there. I then ran and jumped into my study, but again there was no one to be found. I checked the entirety of my home in the same speedy manner and was pleased to see that it was all how it had been before I had left. As soon as I slumped onto my book-couch, my mind fell into chaotic ruminations.

Different parts of me became disagreeable and unwavering as what I should do. As soon as I thought that packing up and moving home was the right thing to do, another part of myself told me I would be a coward to do so and reminded me of how important my home was to me. So, I thought about going out to try to lay traps for this new foe, but another part of me guffawed at the idea, as I had no clue who it was or how to hunt them. My mind convinced me that I should go and buy a gun, but then I no longer had connections with such people, and I was also reminded that I certainly didn't have the cash. I just about convinced myself that I should change my appearance, but that idea was quickly dismantled, as someone that good at playing me for a fool would not be so easily tricked by a shaved head, or new clothes. My mind then went back to wanting to run away and the same cycle of thoughts. I could only let out a frustrated sigh.

It seemed clear that I was going to get nowhere with my ruminations, so I felt that the only thing to do was meditate. I knew it was the only action that could bring me back to some form of equilibrium and focus. I locked and bolted the shop door. Next, I went back into my study, sat in the lotus position and started my meditation by focusing on the tips of my nostrils, where the air was brushing by. The cacophony of shouts and screams from the thoughts in my mind slowly quietened until all I processed was the feeling of my breath and the feeling on that tiny part of my nose. I simply sat and felt this focused sensation, nothing more and nothing less. When an hour or two had gone by, I switched to scanning my body, part by body part from top to bottom and bottom to top. I felt each and every sensation within me, all of which I observed with an equilibrium of emotion and without reacting to whatever feelings and visualisations the sensations brought to my mind's eye. The day's events played on and on like a film stuck on repeat, but my non-reaction to it told my being that there was no need to worry.

When my body scan reached my neck, an explosion of strange and intense imagery screamed into view. It seemed far more than a simple projection of the psyche: it was as if the spectator's seat was right in the middle of the whole annihilation. What I saw was a planet and its alien, humanoid population of trillions being consumed by a monstrous shimmering black sea from space that crashed into them like roaring rapids. The sea morphed into billions of connected tentacles with fanged mouths all of different sizes and all with different sets of insidious-looking jagged teeth. Each mouth then took swift chunks out of the planet and its terrified inhabitants. When the planet looked like nothing more than a peeled fruit, the black sea surrounded it all and shrunk inwards, devouring the planet until it was completely gone. I saw inhabited world after inhabited world consumed like this.

Although I could not hear it nor see it, I could feel the sadistic pleasure emanating from this being of infinite power. Oddly, I then sensed the being's joy turn into boredom and dismay about the destruction it caused. The being then appeared to up the ante: soon its destructiveness was taken to the level of whole solar systems and then galaxies. There were also visions of other equally terrifying creatures and technologically advanced alien civilisations putting up a fight against the beast. At times it seemed they had put the monster on the back foot, but it would then somehow gain the upper hand. Such fantastic battles all ultimately led to the beast's adversaries being consumed. Eventually, once again, feelings of boredom emanated from the beast, following its trail of galactic destruction. In its frustration, the thing took its violence to yet another level and the obliteration continued until the whole universe was consumed.

Even with the universe toppled on its whim, I felt once more that the being had become bored; it was as if it said, "Is that it?" Hence, it moved onto other universes. Universe after universe was eventually gobbled up but the boredom always inevitably set in, so it moved onto what I could only fathom were dimensions, as such chaotic physical sights did not make sense to me. It tore through what appeared to be dimensional membranes like paper and did this until the dimensions were but scraps that were easily licked up by its army of ravenous mouths. When the last shreds had been eaten up, the same feelings of tedium shot through the being and then suddenly I was back to what seemed to be my own psyche.

I was able to stay Zen-like throughout the whole ordeal by simply observing and my body scan continued to move on up to my head. That was when the day's events again jumped into view and tried to goad me into paying them further attention. When I started the body scan back down, rather than being propelled back into such cosmic insanity again, all I felt was a slight constriction around my neck, even though there was nothing there. It was a peculiar and off-putting sensation, but I stuck with my training and did not react. I simply carried on with my meditation. I then cycled between the body scan and the focus on breathing, every hour or so, until I finally felt confident that my mind had calmed down and I had regained focus.

I opened my eyes and checked my watch: it had been almost eleven hours of meditation. I was calm, serene and I was back to a very finely tuned self that was ready to plan its vengeance on whoever the person was that had sought to humiliate me. I was a sharpened blade ready to cut.

A sensation of cold shot up through my feet as they touched the concrete floor of the kitchen. But I didn't take heed of the message of discomfort and proceeded to the kettle. I felt each muscle grimace in pain as I moved, but again it was only messages that floated on by without my reacting to them. Five minutes later and I had a teapot with a loose-leaf English Breakfast tea brewing.

Five minutes later, I took a delicate sip of the tea as I sat at my kitchen table. The feeling of the warm nectar that swished around my mouth was sublime. I closed my eyes and slid down in my chair until I was near horizontal — just what I needed. The call for another swig of tea was swiftly acknowledged and I pulled myself back up. I lifted the teacup and gulped. Midway through the gulp my eyes shot open wide and I sprayed the tea out of my mouth onto a grinning black Scottish terrier that patiently sat on the table directly in front of me. It looked at me, raised its eyebrows, and then shook the liquid off.

"I thought it best to catch you after you meditated, dear boy, as I wanted you to be calm as calm can be. Quite a snug little place you have here. I must say, it's rather quaint," said that same terrible voice I had heard on the phone at the Sales Director's house.

Chapter 7

The common reaction towards a talking dog that claimed it was omnipotent would be to think that one's mind had been put in a parcel and sent to the Bermuda Triangle. But I didn't instantly jump to the conclusion that I was insane as over the years, I had steadily built an abundance of trust in my own senses and faculties. I had dedicated many thousands of hours attaching myself to reality through meditation and being mindful, so to become immediately sceptical of what had been put in front of me was a difficult thing to accept. Was I going mad? The alternative was believing that in my kitchen there was a supernatural being in the form of a black Scottish terrier, patronising me rudely.

Picking insanity would have meant that I could no longer trust any of my senses: any thought, any feeling — and every deduction — would have to be questioned. Alternatively, I could put complete trust into my being and accept that the astronomically improbable was occurring. Like a good politician, I held off from picking a side and I chose to go with the flow to see where it led me — ideally to a place which did not involve an existential meltdown.

"Well, my dear boy, you've taken this rather ruddy well," the little black Scottish terrier said with a mouth that moved eerily to enunciate the words.

The little dog then walked around the kitchen table whilst wagging its tail and looked all around the room excitedly. It then sat on its behind and wagged its tail from side to side as it looked me straight in the eyes.

"Apologies for the intrusion. I've never been one to wait for an invitation. I can imagine it's a bit of a shocking affair, talking dog and all. Well, I could have chosen a different form, but once you've gone through a billion different shapes and sizes, you can get a little bored with any further change."

Before I could respond the dog spoke again.

"Picking the right form isn't as easy as one would expect. I do remember I was once a cat, but oddly enough people don't seem particularly surprised when they see a talking cat. That was not what I wanted, as I do enjoy some surprise at the first introductions. Mind you, one doesn't want to go to the other extreme, like the one time I was an —" unintelligible high-pitched screech — "That just caused anyone I met to quiver in absolute terror. I won't lie, it was fun at first, but only for about a day. After that, it all got rather tiresome. Try holding a respectable conversation with someone who is so scared that they've clawed their own eyes out! Well, it took me a billion or two tries before I finally hit the proverbial nail on the head. For the time being, that is. What do you think, my dear boy? Do you think it's the right fit?"

The dog stood up, gave its little bottom a waggle and then merrily trotted around the table before it came back to sit in front of me again. Reason and logic gave in their P45s at that instant and left the helm to my baser instincts. I grabbed a nearby kitchen knife, lunged and stabbed at the dog. The knife went right through the creature and right through the table until the handle stopped it going any further. To my dismay, there was no wound and no blood. The dog casually strolled through the knife as if it wasn't there and carried on talking.

"HO, HO! Yes, that is why I chose you, my dear boy! Bravo. That attitude is so much better than the whole whimpering and begging thing. Anyhow, where was I? Ah yes, perhaps best to take a seat as it might be a while before I finish," the Scottish terrier said with a cheeky wink.

I was dismayed at what happened with the knife, as to me it was further evidence of insanity. Although disheartened, I thought that perhaps it was best to try to ride with the situation again to see where it took me. So, I sat on a nearby kitchen chair and listened to the dog merrily prattle on about the many forms it had adopted, the pros and cons of such forms, and how various beings had reacted to each guise. Surprisingly, given the circumstances, I had become quite bored and yawned.

"Well, my boy, I could have explained such detail within a split second if you weren't such a backward species," the dog snapped.

It then gave a sigh.

"I suppose I need to explain myself a little bit more, as you seem quite in the dark. I am not wanting to toot my own horn, but I am, shall we say, quite powerful. Let's say that if I was feeling a bit peckish, I could turn this whole world into a delectable three-course meal. Something I have done many a time to other planets before ..." The dog then let out another sigh. "But even with all this power, I still can't get past the one little fact that I do get a little bored. Of course, I could make it so that I don't feel boredom, but where is the fun in that?"

The canine moved its front paws forward and arched itself down to stretch its back. I quickly grabbed another kitchen knife and repeatedly stabbed at the dog, but again it was as if the blade went through nothing but air.

"Oh, I do love a trier. Where was I? Ah yes, the long and short of it is that I skulk around here and there looking for beings or objects to keep me entertained. I've tried damn near everything else to stop the boredom, but in the end, I found the personal, one-to-one touch to be the most enthralling. Not long before you, I had a whale of a time with a tiny black Zortan flea on a jungle planet in the centre of a violent little galaxy about ten billion light-years from here. Small fellow, but bags of character, absolute bags of the stuff. You should have seen how the little fellow tried obliterating all those giant Drotomon. He was a marvellously good sport. I did help it a little bit, but it was mostly down to the little chap."

I jumped at the dog and tried tearing into it with my teeth and my hands. Again, all I got was thin air.

"HA, HA, HA! Oh, do behave, or you'll hurt yourself. Anyhow, now we get to why I am actually here: I have had my eye on you for a while and I am finding what you're doing an absolute hoot. Of course, I am talking about your wonderfully violent people skills. However, I see even more potential in this show you're giving me. I am wanting more violence, more glitz, more pain, more chaos and, most importantly, more *you*. Also, I am afraid to say, such marvellous creatures as yourself often end up dead sooner rather than later and that would be such a terrible shame. So, my pitch to you dear boy, is that I help you — but just a tad. This will be so you can keep doing what you're violently doing and also so that you can entertain on a bigger stage."

The little black Scottish terrier waited for a response, but I gave none, so it continued its prattling.

"There are of course rules to this. I've had an eternity to develop and hone them. I've found that without the rules I end up in the most dreadful states of tedium. Two of these are that I do not let myself look into the future. I allow myself the odd crude guess, but that's about it. The other rule is that I cannot significantly intervene to make life easier for you; however, there may be the odd special circumstance that may mean I do otherwise. I do know that is rather subjective: the rules can bend depending on my own interpretations and the mood I am in. It certainly isn't a perfect system but it's the best I have." The little dog then gave a cough to clear its throat.

"So, my wonderful boy, this will allow you to pursue your vengeful quest and whatever other violent pursuits you may have with far more gusto."

The dog momentarily stopped its lecture and thoroughly licked its genital region, an area that was nondescript as there wasn't anything there to indicate sex. It then looked back up at me and carried on with its talk.

"My dear boy, let me explain why my help is needed. Your main problem is evidence. No matter how careful you are in your violence, you're leaving numerous breadcrumbs that can be traced back to you. You know, just because you have your balaclava on, it doesn't mean you've suddenly become invisible to the eyes of the law. I know that is rather flippant of me to say and, of course, you're more careful than that, but I can assure you that you're on the verge of being found out. I've already had to be a bit naughty and clean up some of your mess, so you were not discovered. True, if you were tracked down, your last stand would be a marvellous hoot to watch, but I am wanting far more than that. So more specifically, my deal is that I will make sure that any evidence of your wonderful romps will never make it back to your human law services. This does not mean you will have a walk in the park — but it'll allow you to be so much more the star than you already are." The little dog paused, having spotted that I did not look impressed by its proposal.

"Ho, ho! You certainly are a tough sell. I know your quirky plans for the bumblebees. Personally, I couldn't care less about the blasted things, but think of what you could do for them with such freedom. I've seen your frustrations in having to be a bystander as these silly creatures slowly fumble into extinction. This is your opportunity, my boy! This is where you can become the saviour, the hero. So, what do you say, my boy, do we have a deal?"

I leapt at the little dog and landed square on my kitchen table, snapping the poor thing into two. Rather than wait and see if I had hurt the beast, I got up and picked up chair after chair and smashed it where it was. I then jumped on top of the wreckage and pummelled the little dog with my fists. After a good five minutes of savagely punching the beast, I eventually fell backwards onto my behind with exhaustion, rolled onto my back and I took some huge gulps of air. As I panted, blood from my fists slowly trickled onto the floor and made a drip-drip noise where small puddles had formed.

Eventually, I regained my composure and sat back up. I stared at the little dog, who was sitting down on the wreckage with its head tilted inquisitively.

"Is that a yes, my dear boy?"

"It's a no. It's a *no,* little dog," I calmly replied.

The dog then gave a wry smile as it wagged its tail.

"Well, my boy, it's a response that I am not too surprised about. I can't say I am not disappointed, but regardless, the offer still stands. Whenever you want to agree to it, all you need to do is just say so. See you soon, my dear boy, see you very soon."

The little black Scottish terrier turned around and merrily trotted out of the kitchen. I jumped to my feet and sprinted out of the room after the beast, but it was nowhere to be found. I dashed all over the underground tunnel network, but I could not find the obnoxious critter anywhere. It wasn't that I had the urge to talk to it; it was more that I thought I would have another go at trying to kill the thing.

I went back to my study and lay down on the ground. As soon as my head hit the floor the neurosis immediately pounced and made its presence known by questioning my sanity. It told me that this little critter could not have existed and because of that I was most definitely insane. But such an allegation disagreed with every other sense I had: they all told me the creature was most definitely real and that I should be very fearful of it. However, my neurosis was able to quickly convince the part of my brain responsible for logic to agree with it. The prospect of a so-called omnipotent deity visiting my home to offer me a deal so that I could become its dancing monkey was preposterous, but my senses — and a good part of my mind — simply refused to change their feelings about what they had experienced.

To bring about order in the mind, my psyche declared martial law and the propaganda machine went into overdrive. It was immediately spread that permanent insanity and assured destruction would be the price I paid for accepting the little dog as genuine reality. It then said that I would have to accept my present mental deterioration and hope that I could repair it in the future. The psyche's regime then coordinated a brutal crackdown on any dissenters but came across a zealous angry rabble that would not give a single inch with regard to its faith in what the senses had presented. These zealots put up such a fight that a civil war of the mind erupted and the consequence was that reality started to seep away from my grip.

Further chaos erupted throughout my mind as the initial unity of rebel factions broke down into infighting. Soon, disagreements took place with regard to how to interpret the information supplied to me by the senses. One of these rebel groups felt that the little dog was real but abhorred the idea of any deal being made as it was demeaning and it could not be trusted. They detested the thought of being a sort of pet and my ambitions being trivialised as a form of entertainment. Also, a potentially very powerful being constantly watching over my shoulder and wanting its money's worth might try to cajole me into acts I did not agree with. For all I knew, it could be a sexual deviant and wanted me to stoop to repugnant levels for its own entertainment.

Another insurgent group believed in the deal with complete faith and wanted to use it as a means to save the bumblebee. Also, there was the added benefit that I could start other campaigns to help bring about a world that I wanted. Plus, aside from such visions of grandeur, the fighting would be terribly good fun. Whatever the little dog wanted would be a small sacrifice for such gain.

There was a faction of moderate believers in the deal who wanted to accept it but also wanted to know whether it would actually be kept by the little dog. They felt that I would be a fool to believe that the little dog was without ulterior motives; there were also clearly nuances in the dog's statements and both things suggested that the trust could only go so far.

The final rebel faction simply said no to the deal with the utmost rage, as it was terrified of the little dog. This group then splintered into another group who wanted a yes to the deal, as they were so scared of the little dog that they felt I would have to comply, otherwise I would reap terrible consequences.

During this first stage of neurotic meltdown, a surprise attack came out of nowhere and a faction that was pro-trusting of my senses hijacked the logic part of the brain and used it to try to create propaganda of their own. They spouted on about how I had spent innumerable hours honing my senses to become near infallible; how the senses knew what they felt and would not lie; how all the senses were in agreement and how I would rapidly deteriorate if faith was not put back into the situation. However, the regime was able to move in quickly and took the reins back to flood the mind with the insanity narrative and the idea that the path back was possible, but it would be difficult. For me to find my lost sanity, the rest of the mind would need to heed to show complete obedience.

Soon the regime's propaganda evolved into the theory that I had undergone a significant deterioration of mental health and there was no deity that spoke to me. It was all a delusion, probably brought on by my upbringing, former years of heavy drug use and the repeated traumas to the head delivered by various folk. All sense of self, all senses, all thought, all memories and all logic were no longer trustworthy. There was only one path to go down and that was to map out this insanity, to then understand it and then to figure out whether it was curable or something I could adapt to. So, I started to try to think up the mental tests that I could adopt to figure all this out, when I heard my stomach rumble.

Even with the civil war still raging, all of the factions of my brain were all easily persuaded by the savage tyrant that lived in the filthy pits below. Out of formality and politeness, it provided my mind with some half-baked reason that I would think far better with some energy from food. None of the factions wished to question this, so I got up off the floor and had a quick look around for anything to eat — but the kitchen was completely bare. I checked for money, but I had none. I let out a sigh, as there was only one option left. I trudged out of my home and onto the streets of Manchester to earn some income, all the while missing the comforts of a once sane mind.

Chapter 8

The little dog's level of cognition was at such an impossibly superior degree of complexity and intelligence that the English language can only very vaguely describe its thoughts and intentions. Its cognition was so powerful that it even knew when it was being written about. It found the experience all rather curious and entertaining, but it did admittedly have some initial concerns, especially as it was such a pathetic and feeble being that was writing this part of the little dog's story. The critter was quite glad that the author didn't attempt to write its part in the first person, as such an attempt would have definitely led to a falling out. It would have been insulting to even consider being able to formulate such fantastically advanced and magnificent thinking into words. If the author dared try, the little dog had made it known that it would jump into the author's universe and eat him.

Just after its conversation with the vagabond, the little dog teleported onto the sun as it fancied a little bit of warmth for a siesta. As the deity lay down on the violent, super-hot surface, it thought about how delighted it was to have found its new toy. It felt the sales Director's destruction was such a rip-roaring good show. Numerous times it thought about the hilarity of the German shepherd flying into the Director's head and the subsequent fatal head-butt. The vagabond had the type of chutzpah that it had not seen for a very long time and when you have lived for eternity, that's a lot of time. It was such a breath of fresh air for the deity to be able to watch this type of unpretentious and passionate violence. Especially as the little dog felt that far too many lifeforms fought without any actual joy or love of what they did.

Just before finding the vagabond and after the black Zortan flea had finally met its doom, the little dog was almost ready to give up on finding a truly entertaining individual and accept that the best he could find at that point in time was Xorax III — or as many quivering trillions knew him, as "Xorax The World Eater". The little dog hated to admit that at first, it was somewhat enthusiastic about Xorax. With a name like "World Eater", where could it go wrong? Also, Xorax, even at just ten metres high, had murdered billions with his many, many razor-clawed appendages, something that was quite a nice, personal touch. However, the more the dog watched the terrifying monster, the more it grew bored.

The deity felt there was no joy or passion in Xorax's destruction and plunder. Although it was certainly grand in scale and at times its victims put up a splendid fight, the way the monster disposed of his foes was so tedious. There was no infectious energy and pizazz in the murders, it was all rather mechanical. What made it even less bearable for the deity was that Xorax committed such genocides for some silly reason around a religious belief that stemmed from a misinterpreted command from an allegedly belligerent god from dimension 26.29183746.12yz.

The little dog knew that god from dimension 26.29183746.12yz. It was probably the nicest god one could ever meet and it wasn't best pleased about Xorax's level of fanaticism in its name. In fact, the god was incredibly embarrassed about

Xorax, as the message it had left in that dimension was about the importance of using a good sun cream when sunbathing. The god could not understand how that simple message had been so flagrantly misunderstood.

The little dog remembered that the dull life form also had a need for an incredibly long mantra that affirmed its dietary habits before, during and after wreaking its destruction. Xorax wasn't the most eloquent of sorts and he would drone on for a good millennium or two. The mantra went:

I ate a screaming Worbler from Prime 6,

I ate a crying Terez from Lacturn Zeta,

I ate a bleating Rampan from Alpha Centuria 12532.9181 ...

... and so on until it had listed all of the billion types of lifeforms it had consumed. The mantra ended with:

I will eat many more,

That is the universal law,

You are all food for my jaw.

Ordinarily, the little dog would have given up on Xorax long before a million years had gone by, but as Xorax was so painstakingly boring, the little dog actually found itself unhappily glued to watching the creature. It was like watching a car crash — perhaps the wrong simile, as the little dog found it quite comical watching people die in car crashes. It was entertainment so uniquely bad that the critter struggled to stop watching the monster. The little dog of course eventually came to its senses when by chance it came across the vagabond when taking a momentary break from Xorax.

Even with the discovery of the vagabond, the thought that such a magnificent being like itself had ever considered using Xorax the World Eater as its plaything started to aggravate it to no end whilst it lolled on the sun. The little dog felt it was far too superior to be that wrong, even though the critter had purposefully made itself flawed so this reality would be more entertaining. Of course, with quick rationalisation, the little dog determined that it was ultimately Xorax's fault for being such a bore and tricking the little dog into wasting its time. The supernatural being suddenly felt rather perplexed, as it realised it hadn't yet disposed of Xorax. Quickly, it made a few mental calculations that no human or mortal being could ever comprehend and then disappeared off the sun. A couple of minutes later the little dog reappeared on the surface of the sun with a satisfied smile on its face and a slightly larger tummy.

The little dog felt that Xorax had put up a better fight than anticipated, but ultimately it was just a feisty snack. It was a pleasant surprise for the deity though, that the World Eater tasted better than expected. The canine could feel the monster's mutilated remains pleasantly wriggle in its belly as it lolled back onto the violent surface of the sun. A ferocious solar flare snapped off the surface and lightly tickled the deity's back.

The little dog lackadaisically thought to itself that it had been a long while since it had felt this interested in a life form's ability to entertain. After Xorax, it had started to think negatively about life forms. They all seemed to have this obsession with painting their genetic code onto the whole universe and they seemed to have an even bigger ego than the deity. They all believed that they were perfect in some way and that usually some god or philosophy bestowed on them the divine purpose of spraying their bits of goo everywhere. This usually led to quite hilarious circumstances, as you can't have two different life forms thinking they are the ultimate specimen. The comical dismemberment of limbs naturally followed.

Having spent billions, or maybe trillions, of years (it was difficult to count the years when you'd exist for eternity) looking for subjects for its entertainment, the little dog had developed a keen eye for spotting potential. It knew straightaway when it saw the vagabond that with a little tweaking, he was going to be a splendid entertainer. The little dog's plan was to turn him into a star — not literally, although the little dog could actually do that if it wanted to. But when you can entertain the omnipotent, that is when you've definitely hit the heights of fame.

As its plan had been set into motion, the deity had a quick think about what other manipulations were needed for the vagabond. The dog then curled up and fell asleep on the sun's surface. However, it wasn't quite asleep, as in a way the little dog was still fully awake. It was just something it had started to act out a few billion years ago, as it seemed like a fun thing to do.

A minute after the deity's eyes closed, a tentacle grew from its back and although it didn't have eyes, it appeared to apprehensively look around. It saw that it was by itself and that there was no food around; but then on instinct, it straightened up slightly as it realised what it was supposed to do.

A portal opened up and showed within it a giant black server where an odd, colourful light flashed on it. It was in a huge air-conditioned room where no one was to be seen. Whilst still attached, the tentacle grew at will in length and entered the portal and the server room. It appeared to look around the room and then the tentacle touched the server to access all of its contents. There were firewalls and software security in place, but the tentacle didn't need to think twice to bypass these. Soon it had all of Greater Manchester's police data at its disposal. The tentacle noticed that there had been a recent upgrade to the entire computer system. A quick shuffling of files, and the information on the deity's new toy became too irreversibly corrupt to ever be accessed and it made it look as if the cause of this was the system upgrade. As soon as the tentacle had finished, the door to the server room opened. It quickly shot back to the portal and was just about to go back onto the surface of the sun when it changed its mind. Instead, it slunk down the corner of the wall until it came across an intruder: an obese IT technician. The tentacle thought that its master would appreciate a midnight snack, so it grabbed the man by the leg and, before he could scream, it snapped back through the portal. Unfortunately, the tentacle forgot that humans were not the most hardy of life forms and the IT technician was vaporised as soon as he was pulled through and onto the sun.

The tentacle sheepishly looked around to see if anyone had seen its mistake and turned back to find the little dog still asleep. The tentacle turned back around, closed the portal to the server and opened another. This time the entrance was right behind a pale, balding and near square prison guard sitting alone at a computer. The tentacle sneaked in behind the guard and then shot right into his neck. The guard didn't flinch, he didn't even notice that the tentacle was inside him. Millions of microscopic tentacles grew from it and these headed to his brain and hands. Through controlling the guard, the tentacle accessed the prison mainframe, bypassed all the security, deleted all files on the vagabond and prisoners that had been inside with him at the same time, switched off all firewalls and left it all wide open to malware. The tentacle then made the man access ream after ream of gay interracial gangbang pornography on virus-infested websites, all of which had a balding white male as the receiving star. The tentacle shot back out of the guard and back onto the sun when there was enough malware to completely destabilise the system.

The tentacle opened one last portal. This doorway opened right behind a gaunt rake of a scientist, who was studying collected data on her computer. Again, the tentacle sneakily entered the person to control them. This time it was to manipulate her so that she became far more discerning with regard to the data about bumblebees and pesticides on her computer. The tentacle shot right back after haystacks worth of information was efficiently and perfectly analysed.

Back on the sun, the tentacle looked around and appeared to wait to see if any of its brethren were going to join it, or if it had any more orders. As it realised its job was done, it approached the little dog, apprehensively at first and suddenly snapped back into the deity's body. Just before the little dog started to lightly snore, a small smile crept up onto its face.

Chapter 9

The slop they served in prison was a foul, toxic waste that masqueraded as food. The main course was a torrid-looking lumpy brown gloop that had a single, limp, brown, over-boiled carrot poking its head out of the nightmarish sludge. It must have thought it was in the seventh level of hell. The wretched vegetable only had the company of a trio of grossly dehydrated yellowish peas that lay on top of the food like shelled-out carcasses on a desert dune. There may have been other poor victims within the gloop, but I simply did not have the stomach to delve into the abomination to find out.

Flies hovered over the food, but as soon as they tasted the slop, they turned their noses up and sped away in disgust. The dessert on the food tray was what appeared to be a custard with such a high viscosity that it seemed impenetrable. Out of curiosity to see if this was the case, I grabbed the plastic spoon that came with the tray and tried to penetrate the armour. The spoon crumbled in my hand. I could make out the faint outline of something hidden underneath the protective top layer of the custard, but it was a mystery that I was never going to find out about. The only thing I consumed from these terrible meals was the small juice box, which I became rather attached to. When you've eaten nothing for two weeks, a juice box becomes the most divine nectar of the gods.

The cell itself was certainly not the homeliest of places. Cold, blood-stained concrete flooring reflected light from a bright but ghostly LED bulb that intruded the cell's every nook. A small concrete bed that was embedded into the wall stuck out and a thin, blue, plastic-covered mattress lay on top of it. A corner of the mattress appeared to have been gnawed, leaving chewed-up sponge that seeped out the hole like spilled guts. A grey, stained pillow that was more bobbles than pillow hid in the corner of the bed in fear of further maltreatment. The obligatory metal toilet sat in the far corner of the cell. Skid-marks encrusted the bowl, with white mould and bacteria battling for the leftover scum. The metal sink and tap stuck out of the wall. Both were armoured with rust and the tap pathetically dribbled water when turned on full. There was a small barred window about four metres from the floor that welcomed the cold in gladly. Certainly, the room itself was somewhat minimalist and not quite my cup of tea, but I had lived in worse in my time.

The prison guards seemed to be unable to comprehend the simple concept that if you put an aggressive animal in a small cage and taunt it, it won't be the best of ideas to then go into the cage without the necessary protection. Manners do not cost a thing, but not having manners cost them rather dearly. It was decided that for their own safety — and that of the other inmates — solitary confinement was a necessity. Of course, I did not let this change of cell be an easy task for them.

It didn't require extensive mathematical ability to deduce that I was going to remain in prison following my eventual trial for a very long time. If there was an equation to deduce how long it would be, X would have certainly equalled "fucked". Imprisonment was something that I swore never to return to and always put measures in place to ensure that the risk of capture was as low as it could be when I earned my income, had fun and carried out my campaign. And such methods were working all rather well until I became convinced that I was insane.

When your main form of income is from home invasions, theft and street robberies, a decent level of situational awareness, cat-like reactions and of course, a sane mind are required. When you've lost all trust in your mental faculties, then such work becomes a far riskier venture, something I learnt the hard way.

It wasn't the actual mugging that went wrong. The issue was that I wasn't cautious and witnesses soon came across the scene. This in itself wasn't the fatal blow, but it was the starting domino. Without the trust of sanity, I was easily spooked, meaning that rather than gauge the situation, I sprinted away at full pelt with my balaclava still pulled down over my face. Whilst running away, neurotic thought after neurotic thought rumbled on by about my mental volatility, drowning out my common sense and environmental feedback.

During this ill-thought-out escape, due to the jostling, the hair under the balaclava unkindly moved around to cover my right eye. Rather than rectify this, my mind found itself trying to determine whether the world around me was actually reality. Without looking, I ran onto a road and a double-decker bus smashed right into my side.

I was knocked out. A fair few stitches were required and my face grew to the size of a watermelon, but aside from that, no breakages. The doctor said it was a miracle that I survived and so relatively unscathed. He was quite a nice fellow and he seemed sincere about helping people, so I do somewhat regret biting his finger off as he was doing a quick check-up when I awoke. What can I say? I wasn't in the best of moods. I was handcuffed to a bed in a strange-looking place and I had come to the horrific discovery that they had shaved my head, as "there was a significant infestation" that resided in it. So naturally, I resorted to such reasonable action. To be fair, I am sure he had it re-attached and it would probably become a funny story around the dinner table in a week or two.

I was originally denied bail and at first, I was only going to be sentenced for two counts of robbery. But these minor offences quickly escalated, due to what I had done to the doctor, the prison guards and the prisoners. Also, unfortunately, in the eyes of the authorities, the fact that I had only *mildly* tortured the prisoners and guards wasn't going to work in my favour. I, of course, saw it differently, as such dislocations would surely have invigorated them in future to act with more appropriate etiquette. Anyhow, even a con-artist fortune-teller of the most bargain-basement kind could have predicted that I was going to end up in solitary confinement.

There was certainly a silver lining to the whole solitary confinement ordeal though, that being it allowed me to spend a good seventy-two hours continuously meditating. This was in part due to having nothing else to do, but there was also enough sanity left in me to force myself into that act of self-medication. The epiphany that came from this was that I could put faith back into my mind. Such deep thought and self-analysis simply could not find any significant deterioration of my senses or thoughts; each neuron and synapse was up to the correct specification.

I started to grasp that the experience with the black Scottish terrier was simply a glitch in my programming and one that hadn't affected the system as a whole. However, there was no denying that it was significant and would require further investigation. But that aside, I felt confident about putting near-complete faith back into my mind. That being said — and as improbable as the little dog may have seemed — the more instinctive side of me was still erring on the idea that some sort of supernatural being had indeed engaged in communication with me. That feeling was a stain that I could not wash from my mind. Paradoxically, it was deeply linked to my trust in my own self and I simply could not reject such a notion. Instead, I simply chose not to react to these confusing feelings. This meant that such thoughts would be allowed their place and stage, but like a madman shouting predictions of Armageddon in public, it would not be taken seriously.

Within solitary confinement there was certainly a lack of stimuli, this being a factor that could easily drive a sane man to irreversible ill mental health. However, for my part, it had helped me to force the mind into introspection and allowed me to ultimately quieten it. There was a worry about doing too much meditation, as this could lead to a permanent disintegration of the ego. Then again, perhaps with constant meditation, I could reach higher planes of thought? Yet, even if I sought such a divine purpose, I knew that there was one chain that I could not break free from and I would be dragged down from the heavens kicking and screaming. The tyrant that held this chain had been passively putting up with the fact that it had not been feasting on the treats that it had become accustomed to. It was not one that would lower itself to eat the prison slop that was served, but it was not going to silently accept the present situation.

I toyed with the idea of escape from the prison, but that prospect was shot down. It was not because I would be relentlessly hunted and be forced to lie low. It was not because I would have had to have run away to somewhere as isolated as the Highlands of Scotland. It was not because the prospect of sex would have vanished like a puff of smoke. It was because there would be no more venturing to delicatessens for a slice of Munster that stank with a foul hedonism. It was because there would be no more morning partakes in a patisseries' decadent viennoiseries. The beast below was not going to let such a horrible future take place.

My stomach knew that if I escaped, my spice rack would deteriorate to whatever I could forage. The horrifying blandness of the food I would be forced to eat would shock it to its core. Fresh game would be delightful at first, but then I would be damn near degraded into a meat and potatoes man. Nightmares could not be made of worse.

No more Keralan fish curries, no more pho, no more gyozas, no more Iberico pork, no more chorizo, no more ackee and saltfish, no more jerk pork belly, no more gelato, no more homemade pasta, no more bibimbap, no more beef bourguignon, no more Sichuan hot pot, no more vignotte, no more freshly made sourdough, no more Brie de Meaux, no more chorros, no more gambas al ajillo, no more chicken mole burritos, no more Parma ham, no more buffalo mozzarella, no more seafood linguine and the list went on and on. It was a list that never ended and it was a list that the tyrant below kept on reading out night after night as I lay in bed. I easily succumbed to such torture and became agreeable to whatever plan it had hatched. Although it didn't tell me what it was, I could feel it deep down in my gut and I knew that I would know what I'd need to do when the time was right.

I was in the middle of meditation when that right time struck and the door swung open to reveal prison guards outfitted in riot gear, holding riot shields, each armed with batons. As they rushed in, a little smile crept onto my face as my instinct excitedly cracked its knuckles. Just as the first two guards rushed in, I jumped to my feet, turned around and jumped with one foot on the edge of the bed. In a flash, I leapt off the bed and onto the wall where the small barred window was and used the other foot to push off that wall into the adjacent wall near the corner. I then pushed off that wall so that I had enough height to grab the bars of the window. I held the bars with both arms and pulled myself up into a tight ball with both my feet pressed against the wall.

Six of the eight prison officers were already in my cell when, like a swimmer, I launched myself at the back two of the six. I was able to spin around and put my forearms in front of my face as I crashed into the two who stood in front of each other blocking the entrance of my cell. They went flying out of the cell with me on top. The two prison officers who were outside the cell looked on in horror.

I rolled off the two crumpled guards beneath me and yanked both their batons from their hands. I put one of the batons up to protect my head and stood up at the same time, as one of the nearby guards in the corridor swung down at my head. I then used the pointed end of my other baton and stabbed it right into that officer's thigh with enough force that it penetrated into the flesh. Before the guard could scream in pain, I took advantage of his compromised position and ferociously stabbed at the side of his ribs with the other baton a couple of times. A loud snapping noise followed each stab. The guard fainted from the pain and collapsed. As he started to fall, I ripped the baton out of his leg and gave him a violent front kick, so he went flying back into the four guards that were trying to get out of the cell.

I felt a baton strike my temple, but as I had so much adrenaline pumping through me it might as well have been made out of Styrofoam. I turned to the culprit in the corridor, charged him right in his shield and pushed him until he was pressed against the wall. Then, like a boxer picking apart holes in his opponent's defence, I stabbed at every opening all over his body with the pointed ends of the batons. The guard screamed out in pain, both of his arms slumped down and he dropped his shield. I put both of my clenched hands around his helmeted head and pulled it down into a knee so ferocious that it caused his head to fly back into the wall. Shards of his helmet scattered across the corridor as he slumped to the floor.

One of the two guards that I had previously went flying into had got up. The other was halfway up from the floor when he felt my foot come up into his face. His visor broke and smashed against his face, causing blood to splatter against it as his head shot around the body as if it was in orbit, pulling his whole body onto its backside to smash into the ground. I then ran at the guard who was up on her feet. She put her shield up at her side to protect herself. I jumped right up into the air and landed an overhead elbow right on the top of her helmet. The helmet buckled and a large elbow imprint was left in it as she crumpled to the floor. I spun around and saw that one guard from my cell had been able to get out over the body of his unconscious colleague and was now in the corridor with me. Behind him, a fellow guard was trying to get out of the entrance with two more trailing her. I threw my batons at the guard trying to leave the cell to cause a split-second distraction, then I sprinted at her and flying drop-kicked her. She went flying back into the two guards behind and smashed into them as if they were bowling pins.

The guard that was outside the cell started to whack at me whilst I was on the floor. He only got one strike to my head and one to my back before I was able to roll onto my back. The next strike I stopped by catching his wrist with my left hand, grabbing the outside of his hand at the same time, twisting it whilst keeping his wrist stationary, then pushing the hand down forward until it was flat on his forearm. As he screamed in pain, I pulled him forward and lifted up his plastic visor. The briefest look of surprise and then dread filled his face as he figured out what was going to happen next. I grabbed the sides of the helmet and forced him down to be head-butted. One for damage, one to make sure he was out cold and one for good luck. I pushed the unconscious guard off me and sprang to my feet. I picked up two batons off the floor and placed myself just outside the entrance of the cell. The three guards were now up and ready. Two of them did not look particularly enthusiastic about their current situation. The more confident one in the centre turned to either side to encourage his compatriots.

"Come on! Let's get him," he pleaded to the other two. Both the other guards turned away from his gaze in embarrassment.

"Die, you fucking Chink cunt!" the braver guard roared as he charged at me with his shield in front and baton behind him, ready to swing.

I took a few steps back, so he ended up out in the corridor, more exposed. Just before he reached me, I side-stepped him, tilting my head so the baton just missed it. The guard had too much momentum and as he passed me, I gave a rapid stab to the side of his exposed ribcage. The guard gasped, stumbled and then fell to the ground. I quickly went up behind him and stabbed the other baton with enough force that it went through his trousers and became deeply lodged in his rectum. The man let out a sharp squeal and passed out. I turned around to look at the two guards left standing. Before I could even take my first step, they both dropped their shields and batons. I gave a little pout, as I was looking forward to the fight.

"Please take off your helmets," I ordered.

Both quickly did as I asked and both kept their gazes firmly at the ground. To make sure they knew their place, I gave one a quick thrashing until she was out cold. The other I left unharmed, as the plan was to seek help from him with regard to the navigation of the prison. I felt that he understood what would happen if he didn't give me what I wanted. As he started to talk, the prison alarm erupted. Based on what he said, though — and even with the prison being on lockdown — I would still be able to go through with my plan. What I might do after that was, of course, a different story.

Even with all the adrenaline pumping through me, I could feel that my body was experiencing the side-effects of that sudden burst of exercise. Self-care was important, especially if I wanted to be at my fighting best, so I did a few dynamic stretches. I rolled my shoulders forward, I rolled them backwards; I swung my arms around forwards and then backwards; I jogged on the spot swinging my heels back to hit my rear end; I jogged with my knees going up as high as possible and then I twisted my body from one side to another. Unfortunately, I didn't have time to do a full set as the police would be on their way.

"What?!" I snapped at the confused-looking guard when I finished my stretches.

He quickly looked away. I then looked for a pair of boots that would be my size. It only took a couple of tries before I found the perfect fit. I quickly tied up all the unconscious guards around their wrists and ankles with plastic cable ties from their pockets. I put a cable tie around the neck of the one guard who was still conscious, connected it to another cable tie, which was connected to another and this went on until it formed a chain that was like a leash. I needed him to lead the way and also to open the gates.

I then ripped up all of the guard's clothes, twisted them into ropes and tied them around the unconscious guards so that they were bunched together like bananas. I then criss-crossed the remaining fabrics to become another makeshift rope that I threaded in, out and around all of their feet.

"Lead the way. I am sure you can imagine that any untoward behaviour will leave you quite the unhappy chappy," I told the guard.

I gave him a shove and we meandered down the hallway whilst I held his leash and dragged the unconscious guards behind me with the makeshift rope. The hallways flashed with red lights whilst the sirens blared out and that meant the walk wasn't the most pleasant. We reached a couple of abandoned gates, both of which the guard was able to open. Surprisingly, there were no other guards to greet me. I asked the conscious guard why this was and he said that staffing had been reduced greatly due to funding cuts, so there weren't that many guards in the prison in the first place. He then said — matter-of-factly — there were probably only a handful left who had sealed off the prison and were waiting for police support.

Unfortunately, we had to cross through two prison wings. The conscious guard was probably thinking that I was going to let all the prisoners out, but that certainly wasn't on my mind.

"HA! HA! Nice one. Oi, mate, open the doors for me. I said open the fucking doors! OI! YOU FUCKING CHINK PAKI CUNT!"

"Let us out, blood. Blood, I'm talking to you. Oh shit, I know you! You the Chink? Gaz, it's the Chink! Remember me? Remember what you did? WHEN I GET OUT OF HERE, I AM GOING TO FUCKING KILL YOU!"

"Fuck me! It's The Chink. Mate, we took out the Hardy Boys' crew together. Remember? Come on, free me, mate. FUCKING GET ME OUT OF HERE!"

"*As-salāmu alaykum,* my brother. Open the door, brother and set me free. Come, do what is right for me brother…".

"I'm wanting some of that. The one on the leash, he looks so pretty."

I moved through the wings ignoring the pleas and the threats. I had to stick to the plan; if I'd stayed any longer, I probably would have spent too much time taking out my aggression on those behind the cell doors, as they weren't the most respectful of sorts. I also spotted a few characters from my distant past I certainly wasn't fond of.

When we reached the dining hall, it was a bit difficult trying to manoeuvre the guards through all of the chairs and tables. They occasionally got trapped under a table, something that caused me a fair few frustrated sighs. We then reached a large red padded steel-reinforced door at the end of the dining hall. The leashed guard put a key in to unlock it, then another key to unlock another lock and then finally one more key to unlock the final lock. The conscious guard then opened the door.

"Here we are," he mumbled meekly.

I was glad that we had finally reached it. The other guards at that point announced they had awoken by giving the odd muffled scream. I am not the most patient of sorts when hungry, so I went over and gave a few kicks until they quietened. I then dragged them into the kitchen and instructed the leashed guard to open up the locked drawers, cabinets, larder rooms, fridges, the cooking-utensil cage and the freezers. I then ordered him to lock the main kitchen door and took his keys off him.

I was a child in a sweetshop! Mind you, it was like a shop where the sweets were stale or stuck together — but when you have not eaten for two weeks, then such things are still fit for a king. I tied the rope into the end of the leash and then excitedly went to look at what feast I might make.

Chapter 10

It wasn't an easy task trying to conjure up a feast. The prison kitchen was filled with a disjointed mixture of ingredients, half of them being of exceptionally poor quality. There was blasphemy after food blasphemy within the cupboards. Low-fat cheese made out of rubber, skinless pre-cooked chicken breasts, only four spices available, low-fat yoghurt, completely skimmed milk and other such bland heresies. It wasn't a complete lost cause as I did find a treasure trove of uncooked chicken quarters, but they did require defrosting. There were also various tinned beans, marginally edible vegetables, eggs, butter, salt and a few other ingredients. Each time my mind came up with an answer I realised that I was still a few jigsaw pieces away from a complete meal. And while I was trying to conjure up the impossible, an incessant whiny voice kept on trying to interrupt me. On and on it kept bleating and pleading for me to speak. When I switched off the walkie-talkie, the voice then resorted to speaking on the prison tannoy system; there was, unfortunately, no escape. My brain had been starved of food for the past two weeks. It was clear that I needed at least something to give me some energy.

It was a few litre cartons of custard later, with my brain now comfortably whirring, that I was able to think up a plan.

I decided to have a go at the hostage negotiation thing, so I picked up the walkie-talkie. Admittedly, this was something I had never done before, so I was initially quite awkward.

"Er. Hello. I am the hostage-taker, yes, that is what I am. Um. I suppose I read out my demands now, don't I?" I asked with hesitation.

"Hi. Thank you for reaching out. You started to have me worried there. So, what is your name? I am Ted," the voice responded warmly.

I ignored his question and went straight to reading out my demands. At first, I was excited about the whole negotiating thing, but it soon became rather drab. I thought it might become a battle of minds and wits with the negotiator, but all he did was keep trying to act as if I was a long-lost friend. Also, initially, I just couldn't seem to create the drama in my voice that I wanted … perhaps it was simply stage fright?

Politely, I asked the negotiator to stop his chummy charade, but he just wouldn't and all I got in response was, "OK, OK. I can sense you're upset, it's a difficult situation that you're in. We can change it and make it better together." I told him to stop again and he gave a, "Yes, I can see where you're coming from. I'll see what I can do and then we can solve this situation together."

Such positive encouragement started to cause me to long for the opportunity to dislocate a number of his limbs. Instead, as many a fellow Brit would do, I resorted to passive aggression.

I gave the tied and bunched-up guards a few kicks and kept the walkie-talkie on so the negotiator could hear the screams. The far more sombre response of the negotiator helped my understanding of this hostage-taking business to click into place. From here my confidence grew and I started to have fun. The haggling was especially entertaining. It was a: "I won't torture and kill if you do this and this," sort of thing. I started to daydream and thought perhaps I should have got into sales or purchasing, as I seemed to be good at this negotiating business. I had never been the sort to seek a bargain, but I started to understand why so many apparently enjoyed it.

"Yes, yes. No one comes near or I am executing the lot of them in ways that will make your stomach churn," I stated coldly.

"That's the last thing we want. So, what do I call you? If we're going to be working together, we might as —"

"Bloody hell. If I knew I'd have to deal with someone like you I wouldn't have taken hostages! It has been non-stop mindless drivel, all this 'Can we be friends?' I am starting to think I might as well just execute the lot of them just so I don't have to deal with someone as tiresome as you," I interrupted brashly and then giggled when I switched the communicator off.

To try and get what I needed, I told them that one of the guards appeared to be in a coma. I suggested that the baton must have gone far too deep into his rectum. However, I didn't realise how funny this would strike me and couldn't help but chuckle straight after. They didn't seem to see the funny side, though and urged me to hand him over so they could provide medical attention. I tried to carry on with my haggling, but I ended up giggling again. Their concern just added to the hilarity of it.

"If you want the guard with the baton up his ..."

"Yes. The guard ... rectum ... bloody hell ..."

"Look. If you want this anally impaled …
you're going to have to give me a minute …"

It was at least a couple of minutes of heavy,
belly laughs before I was able to get myself
together. I explained how the exchange would take
place, what I wanted for the possibly dead guard. I
also made it quite clear that any funny business
would mean all hostages dying.

"OK! OK! I'm sorry, I'm sorry. Don't get
hasty. We've heard your demands. I'll see what I
can do," the negotiator said to end our little
chinwag.

It was evident that the police were all set up
just outside the main kitchen door, as there was no
other entry point into the kitchen. I opened the
door slightly, enough so that whoever was outside
could see the near-naked leashed guard with a
kitchen knife close to his throat; this being just
another threat so they understood my position. I
made sure I stood far enough so that if there were
any shooters, they wouldn't have the right angle. I
then pushed him out but held on tight to his leash. I
sat behind the door and pulled out a piece of mirror
glass attached to a fork with rubber bands. I poked
it out with the door still ajar. I was able to make
out numerous police officers with guns drawn and
floodlights focused on the doorway. I also saw the
large shopping bag placed a couple of metres away
from the door. The leashed guard obediently —
and without hesitation —picked it up. Then he
appeared to wait for a second to see if the police
were going to do anything to save him. They did
not and before the guard got any bright ideas, I
yanked the leash viciously. The guard staggered
back into the kitchen with the shopping bag. I

locked the door, grabbed the bag and checked inside. It had what I needed: ingredients to make a jerk spice, gloriously ripe plantains, a six-pack of malt fizzy drinks, sea salt flakes, black peppercorns, a pepper mill, an assortment of Scotch bonnet chillies, bird's-eye chillies, a fair few cuts of belly pork, chicken stock and a large tub of vanilla ice cream.

"Now it's your turn. Hand over a hostage," the negotiator commanded.

I was quite impressed by the order. He was able to demonstrate an authority I hadn't known he had in him, but I still ignored him and quickly moved the bunched-up guards in front of the door again. I then put my set of keys into the locks from inside so I'd know if they tried to unlock it from the other side, then went to go cook up my feast. Time certainly flies when you're having fun, as my chicken quarters had all defrosted. The thrill to be back in the kitchen and cooking again was such a beautiful feeling. The prospect of being fed hung over me seductively and aroused me with the aromas that emanated from my cooking. I thought my skills might have been rusty after such a long hiatus, but I was able to whiz through the preparation and cooking without a hitch. I was in a Zen-like focus and it felt as if no time at all had gone by when I produced a delicious two-course meal that sat in front of me seductively. Admittedly, I didn't make a starter as I was far too hungry to even consider it.

For the mains, I made eight jerked chicken quarters, eight jerked pork belly cuts, jerk gravy, a big bowl of coleslaw, a chilli sauce, rice and peas and a pile of fried battered plantains with a sweet chilli dip. My dessert was a couple of plantain tarts with the litre tub of vanilla ice cream. To make sure the food they gave me wasn't poisoned, I fed the leashed guard a portion first. It was an incredibly difficult ten seconds. The jealous rage I felt at that moment was indescribable. But after only one bite I felt there was enough evidence to suggest there was no issue with the food.

My first bite took me through the universe, straight back to the Big Bang, to the beginning of time itself and carried me onward until I had reached a purity of cosmic self that I could only describe as Nirvana. When I swallowed, I was rushed back through this space and straight back into reality. It was but thirty minutes later that I had finished every last crumb.

After the meal, I sat on the kitchen floor, propped up by the wall, my belly poking out from under my top and a content smile stretched lethargically across my face. My plan was complete and it had gone without a single hitch. I couldn't have asked for any better. I sipped and sipped on the malt drinks as I relished in the afterglow of the meal. The drinks were beautiful and sensual as they cooled down the spices on my tongue. The incessant voice still pierced the silence to try to harass me into answering the walkie-talkie, but I was far too relaxed to bother.

"Was this your plan all along?" a meek and puzzled voice asked.

I was in a good mood, so the prospect of conversation didn't seem daunting.

"It was a good plan, was it not! I am fed to the brim and now I can relax," I replied drowsily.

"Relax? You know there's a load of armed police officers out there waiting to pull the trigger?"

"Ah yes. A minor inconvenience," I said, whilst shooing the worry away with my hand.

The leashed guard's confusion was easily seen on his face.

"But you'll be shot dead or thrown into prison for the rest of your life …". The leashed guard stopped talking and a look of panic came over him, as he thought such inquisitions were going a step too far.

He was wrong, though, as I was feeling rather chipper. The wonders of how a mood can so easily change after a good meal!

"I don't plan on being put back in a cell. Of course, I know what the alternative is. If I don't follow this path, I will be tortured in those horrible little cells until I have keeled over dead. It is an inevitability, as even if I escaped, the sad reality is that I would eventually be hunted down and returned. It was my stomach that figured this out long ago. It knew that I would not be one for such a vapid existence. So now I am here, feeling heavenly after eating my last meal."

"Aren't you afraid of dying?"

I let a minute's silence go by before I responded.

"Well, it doesn't matter if I am afraid. Death comes to us all so I might as well have things end on a high note, rather than with a broken soul and in despair."

I took another sip of the malt drink and then gave a loud belch. I tasted the fumes from my stomach and it brought back the memories of how wonderful it all tasted. I then opened up another bottle of malt drink. A peculiar urge that was definitely from a foreign land came out: generously — and surprisingly — I rolled a bottle of a malt drink to the leashed guard.

"Drink," I ordered.

The leashed guard gingerly picked up the drink and opened it. At first, he took a light sip, but then drank it all down greedily.

"Thank you for the drink. I am Jack, by the way. So, what do I call you?" he asked with a bit more confidence.

"To have a name you need other people to use it, otherwise you lose it. I imagine you've heard what some of the prisoners called me. That's a name from a past that died long ago. I suppose these days the most common thing people call me is 'scruffy cunt', often before I end up putting a boot in them. So probably best not to call me that. No name is needed, there won't be any confusion about who you're speaking to."

I didn't quite understand why the guard wanted to know so much about me, but he carried on with his inane questions and, surprisingly, I responded.

"Okay. So, where did you learn to make the food you made? It smelt amazing."

"Cookbooks. Trial and error. Well, also that meal's influence came from a home invasion of a bloody fantastic Jamaican chef. I must confess it is a hobby of mine to do home invasions of those who are talented chefs and to politely encourage them to cook me a meal or two. I learned a few tricks of their trade that way."

The leashed guard looked away and then sheepishly changed the topic.

"So how did you learn to fight like that?"

I let a short silence follow his question as I reflected and breathed a heavy sigh, as it was not something I had spoken about before to anyone. But I thought, as I was soon to die, I might as well continue the conversation.

"I am sure you can gather that I did not have the most loving of upbringings. My father, to put it very lightly, was quite the sadist. Although this was the case, for some peculiar reason he did not want me to be what he thought of as weak. Perhaps he thought it would be an embarrassment to the genetic code that he had passed on to me. So, he took it upon himself to train me in ways of inflicting and understanding violence, from when I was a small child. A part of me suspects that he also did this due to an admiration of the Spartans, as there were quite a few similarities in his methods to theirs."

I let out another heavy, deep sigh.

"My violent neighbourhood further ensured that such skills were continually fed and grown until many years later I became … well, I do not wish to be immodest, but quite the notorious and successful underworld enforcer. There is, of course, much more to it, but it is a long story and I do find such history boring."

"Yes, I am sorry. I only asked because I've always wished I could fight; but as you've probably seen, I am not the most capable."

As the leashed guard carried on talking about his own insecurities, I looked him up and down.

Having eaten, I started to feel that my libido had woken up from its hibernation and now wanted nothing else but to hunt. I hadn't been one to voluntarily sleep with men before, but perhaps due to the situation I was in and the prospect of death being so close that I could feel its breath, for some reason, this glistening lithe man sitting cross-legged, wearing only rather provocative, tight briefs, brought about an arousal in me. He was soft-skinned, slim, shaven-headed and athletically built. I looked him up and down again. I glanced at the mild bulge in his crotch and then stared at his firm behind. The urge to pin him face down, pull down his cute little white briefs and have my way with him whilst pulling his leash played in my mind. The guard stopped talking as he noticed me leering at him. My gaze caught his and he quickly turned away. His face turned red and I noticed he'd definitely became a little excited himself. As I imagined that it was probably going to be my last fuck ever, I thought it a good idea to give men a go.

"Do you want me to fuck you?" I was straight to the point.

The leashed guard blushed to an even darker shade and now it was palpably obvious what he wanted. I was quite surprised that he even had the urge, but I wasn't going to question his motives — well, definitely not when I had that much blood rushing down below. I tugged at his leash and then let my legs fall open. The leashed guard crawled over compliantly without looking up. Just as he was only half-a-metre away from me, I heard a soft crumbling noise of gravel and stone. I didn't even bother rationalising what the sound could be and stupidly ignored it. I grabbed the back of his hair and then roughly pulled his head back. He let out a little moan of pleasure. Just as I was about to move things forward, a much louder crumble of concrete cut through the silence.

I shoved the guard out of my way and jumped to my feet with my arousal still very much visible in my trousers. I saw the larder door start to open, so I grabbed a heavy cooking pan and hurled it with a thunderous backhand at the door. As the door fully opened, the pan went straight into an Armed Response Unit officer's face and he immediately crumpled. I then leapt onto the kitchen counter and launched myself across the room at the officer following through behind him. I was inches away from reaching him when I saw his gun pointed at me. I then saw another armed officer behind him with *his* gun pointed at me and that was when I heard a quick-fire round of bullets. Straight after this, all became pitch black.

Chapter 11

A middle-aged Mestizo lady with a sharp, square jaw and black hair tied in a tight bun sat behind an enormous mahogany desk in a large, ostentatious, red-leather office chair. The desk was so large that it made her tanned, scar-ridden, yet lithe frame, look as if it belonged to a child. Her face appeared to bear a menacing scowl, but this was because of a scar that cut through her top lip and into her cheek. It was a face with clear, soft skin that barely had any wrinkle lines, partly because she rarely ever expressed any emotion. Such cold mannerisms were odd, juxtaposed against her fashion choices, which often involved bright colours and intricate patterns. On this day, she kept it very casual with colourfully patterned yoga pants, bright yellow trainers and a matching sports bra.

The lady's sense of fashion also chimed oddly with her office, which was spartan and practical. The windowless walls of the lady's office were covered in mahogany panels and there were no decorations on the surface of these. There were also minimal ornaments on the desk aside from a few items and a small built-in computer that could swivel in and out of the furniture. Next to the computer was a framed picture of an angry-looking black cat, who stared down anyone who looked at it. There was also a large dirty white mug filled with cold black coffee and an ashtray that brimmed with used cigarette butts.

The lady sat back and put her feet on the table as she listened to Mozart's Piano Concerto No. 21 playing softly in the background. She looked at the picture of the flat-faced Persian cat and sighed. It was fifteen years to the day since her wonderful little Attila had lost his life. The lady couldn't stop comparing every new cat she'd had since to her beloved. They were always too grumpy or too nice, never the right blend like Attila was. She'd loved every part of him, even when he was being a little madam about his food. The tantrums her little darling made when he was not given his favourite Kobe fillet steak tartare were adorable to the lady, although not so much to her guards as Attila would often take his aggression out on their ankles.

When Attila was on the grumpy side — which was near all the time — he would take to swatting, scratching, biting, chasing and hissing at her guards. But he, of course, knew better than to ever do that to her. When he was with her, he was a little cute ball of fur filled with purrs and cuddles. As he was only this way with the lady, it made him seem so much more special to her. Her love of the little feline was at a level that others might interpret as worrying. For example, on one occasion when the lady was in the process of dining and bribing a Brazilian senator, little Attila — without provocation —attacked the politician's ankles. The politician was unfortunately not the biggest fan of cats and clearly saw it as too much of a big deal, as he then kicked Attila. The next morning the politician's head was found on the steps of Brazil's National Congress. Although grotesque, this act was in fact quite charitable compared to what the lady did to the people who murdered her beloved pet.

As the megalomaniac fell into her memories of that terrible day, she winced. The culprits were some silly Colombian cartel who thought that they could easily muscle in on her territory; one of the unpleasant things that they did after they ambushed her at her home was decapitating her poor baby. Obviously, she wasn't fond of the gang rape either, but when you were brought up as a child prostitute in the slums of Lima, rape wasn't the worst ordeal in the world. They had left her for dead: clearly a fatal error. If they hadn't killed her beloved Attila, then she would probably have been happy with meting out just, say a month's worth of torture and mutilation, before a brutal public execution. But instead, the cartel leader and his family had the most gruesome and perverse deaths imaginable.

The torture required some of the greatest minds in medicine and psychology to develop. Such great minds were of course kidnapped and with guns to the back of their heads, they developed a near-perfect combination of intense psychological and physical pain. Following their help, they were all disposed of.

The memory of the torture that went on for almost two years brought a sweet smile to her face. It was a very personal affair because it was mostly done by her own hands. At first, she was amateurish and accidentally killed a family member of one of the cartel's leaders after only a couple of days, having got carried away. After that, like a true professional, she went about the task with patience and an obsessive meticulousness. However, all good things come to an end; the joy she first derived from it disappeared and it all became a chore. The facial contortions of terror and screams of pain became tediously repetitive. The finale unexpectedly came when she forgot to change her shoes and blood squirted out all over a pair of brand-new white Manolos. As soon as that happened, she stormed off and returned with her favourite weapon — a platinum-plated and sapphire-encrusted revolver — and executed them all.

Of course, the Peruvian megalomaniac didn't stop there with her revenge: she set about putting the sword to as many members of the cartel as possible. The death toll went into the thousands and unfortunately, this meant a fair few of her own died as well. But, as she was such a formidable tactician, her ultimate victory was inevitable. There were no regrets about the amount of blood that was spilled: just by looking into Attila's eyes in his picture, she could tell it was what he would have wanted.

Fiorella put down the picture of the only love she ever had and went back to her computer, as her empire would not pause for her own sentimentality. As soon as her screen switched on, she was invaded by a horde of notifications. It was only thirty minutes ago that she had cleared her emails and system alerts. She went onto the system database to see that her AIs had completed basic health checks of all the divisions from the less-than-legitimate side of her empire. The reports came from the Cartel Consultancy Department, Dark Web Distribution Team, Novel Psychoactive Research Division, Contract Killing Department, Accountancy Department, Bespoke Drug Production Capital Manufacturing Division, Cartel and Organised Crime Contract Enforcement Team, Pathogen Research Division, Medical Research Department, Malware Research Team, AI Research Division, Financial Market Manipulation Team, Extortion Team, Cyber Enforcement Team, Operations Department, Costings, IT, HR, Well-being Team and, of course, Prostitution. All came back with green markers stating that there was no evidence to suggest ill health or significant risk.

Even with such newly developed AI in place — and as progressive as she was with technology — she still felt the need to scrutinise every part of her empire because a part of her simply did not want to relinquish much control. It was a couple of hours of rooting around records, case notes, firing off emails and reading the replies before she was content that the black market side of her empire was in a fit state. Once such essentials were complete, the megalomaniac looked into one of her own personal projects. She went through the case file within her Operations Department and saw that there were updates. The smallest of smiles crept onto her face as there was confirmation that every member of the London Doyle Gang had been sealed alive in oil drums and thrown into the North Sea. As soon as she read that, her bruised ankle throbbed to remind her that a stumble was the reason why she was still alive.

Fiorella read the case closure summary attached to the file. It described the assassination attempt by the Doyle Gang and the reasoning being that they weren't happy with her "foreign interests" moving into their territory and taking the majority of their business. The megalomaniac shrugged to herself and felt that it certainly was not her fault that they provided low-quality product, namely drug-riddled, beaten and traumatised prostitutes. She felt it was an obvious fact that a happy and healthy prostitute was a profitable one. Fiorella just did not understand how so many of the British were so averse to competition and to actually providing a good service or product. She read further. The report described the British gang's response as unexpected and, like so many previous attempts on Fiorella in the past, it was a close call. It was only her ankle giving way on a poorly laid pavement slab at the right moment, which meant that she was not given a bullet hole in her head.

The megalomaniac closed the case and signed it off. She let out a sigh, as it seemed that even though she had grown to become so much more than her drug cartel origins, she still constantly seemed a hair's breadth from being brutally murdered. She had originally hoped she could rid herself of this Sword of Damocles by diversifying her empire's portfolio and also by adding into its legal international conglomerates. But even with such acquisitions buying her further political influence in the legal world, she was still having to stay at least three steps ahead of her competitors to ensure that she survived.

Suddenly the email icon 'blinked' and she was brought back to the tedium of running her empire. In her inbox was a report about a contract her organisation had brokered between two syndicates being broken and one of her people being murdered in the process. As high-stakes as many may perceive such infractions, Fiorella barely spent a minute thinking about the appropriate response. She typed up her orders and then sent it to her Operations Department. The email went to a colourful and wonderfully comfortable office. (If this work environment was compared to a Silicon Valley tech giant's, the observer would find them indistinguishable.)

"Sorry, guys, but it's going to have to be a late one. Don't worry, there will be double pay for the overtime and we'll pay for whatever food you want to order in. Yes, Ted, even food from Mr Yamato's Sushi Parlour … I know, I know, that sashimi is to die for! Also, I am sorry. I know you've all got your own little projects going on and it's going to be a bummer putting a halt to them, but we do have a bit of a problem …

"Yes, Becky, I know you're just about to go through with a hit on that Colombian lawyer but trust me that can wait. You see, a Volgograd mob have broken the contract we brokered for the Afghans. They've done this by trying to take over their heroin production and distribution …

"I know, Steve, you'd think the Russians would have learnt from their history books about invading Afghanistan! After raiding a factory, they murdered half of its workforce and what's worse, when our inspector went to check up on the matter, they murdered him, too. They returned his decapitated body with a note written in blood that our beloved leader was a c-word and that she would be next, if she dared interfere …

"I know, Andy, it's horrible to resort to such misogyny in this day and age. Anyhow, the order from up top is that they want the whole mob's leadership dead and that a clear and brutal message is sent. Our beloved leader has personally requested that their genitals be ripped off — whilst they're alive, of course — and shoved into their mouths before they are executed. Okay, people, so that's the end product, it's down to us to get to that point. Personally, I think it sounds like it's going to be quite a fun one. I'll give you a couple of hours to come up with your own ideas and then we'll go through them all."

It was but seconds later when multiple email notifications again blinked on the megalomaniac's screen. Fiorella sighed as sometimes it felt it was an impossible battle and that with each email she read, another three quickly appeared to take its place. It was six more hours before she reached an email that read:

Dear Honourable Leader,

I have attached the plan we have developed in regard to the Volgograd mob. I have also attached a contingency plan.

I hope they are satisfactory.

Nev

Fiorella slumped back in her ostentatious red-leather office chair and swivelled around as she had a think about the plans she had just read. After three full swivels, she had come up with a decision and immediately emailed a reply to her Head of Operations. Just as she felt ready to call it a day and had finally cleared her inbox, another email notification blinked onto her screen. She sighed and said to herself that this was definitely the last one.

It was an uninteresting request seeking approval for a critically injured prisoner, who was awaiting sentencing, to be sent to one of her private high-security prisons so that this individual's death could be faked and he could be medically researched, as it appeared he had a unique ability to heal. She quickly gave approval and cc'd in her operations department so they could make it so.

Just as she took what she thought was a final sip of coffee, another email notification blinked. Fiorella stared at the screen for a couple of seconds and told herself that this was *definitely* going to be the last one.

Chapter 12

It might have been aeons or seconds, I was none the wiser, but from the centre of this nothingness, a faint drop of colour grew. Drip by drip the colour pooled and eventually formed into a dream and a memory from my childhood.

It was a beautiful, clear, blue sky summer's day and I was a nine-year-old child again. It was a day that wasn't particularly different from any other. My parents were out and I was locked in my bedroom. I was only able to look out at the alluring warmth and the bright green chaos that was the garden. Within my locked bedroom, which was without carpet, there was a variety of punch bags and gloves, a dirty mattress and bedding in the corner of the room, a plastic bucket that was half full and books upon books stacked in another corner.

These books weren't stories of heroism, love, friendship or fantasy that hid the reader away from reality. Each book had a purpose and that was to build the mind's understanding and skills of inflicting violence. The topics were martial arts, military strategy, chess and historical wars. My father had the belief that such analytical development would improve my ability to fight. Anything other than these books he believed would make me weaker than I already was.

I had stopped my training and opted to apathetically watch the goings-on outside. The sun's rays shone directly into my eyes from the corner of the window, so I had to put my hand up to block them. It was a while absent-mindedly staring out of the window at the anarchy of the garden below before a strange feeling bubbled up to the forefront of my mind. At first, I did not understand what it was and what it wanted. It was odd, as when it took over, the absolute fear of my father became quite easily ignored. With this feeling of curiosity, I set about trying to break free from my prison.

I checked everywhere in my room for anything that could help me. I looked under and within my books; I explored the cracks in the floorboards; I looked around my training equipment. It wasn't until I finally peered under my mattress that I found a small teaspoon. I quickly used the thin handle like a screwdriver to unscrew the safety locks on the window to get it open.

Without thought and only being guided by an instinct to get out and explore, I pushed the window open and climbed up onto the ledge. It was quite obvious to me that there was only one way down the two floors: by the drainpipe that went down from the roof next to my window. Without hesitation, I grabbed it, pulled myself close to it and slowly eased myself down. It wasn't a difficult task and it wasn't long before my feet touched warm concrete paving slabs.

The small platoon of these green mossy slabs kept the chaos of the large garden at bay from the house. I had lived in this house my whole life and before this point, I had never explored the garden. It was off-limits because, according to my father, there was no reason for me to go into it.

The garden was the kind where an all-out war between thistles, grass, nettles and other such weeds took place. You could not walk through this battlefield without becoming a victim of collateral damage. As I was already quite desensitised to pain, I did not worry about my naked and bruised body getting hurt by this small patch of nature. I casually walked into the chaotic growth to explore. The nettles lapped up the opportunity to lash at my bare legs. I was somewhat intrigued by the turmoil and the complex patterns from the plants that grew there but, ultimately I was not satiated. I felt there was more that I wanted and needed.

I was about ready to leave and climb back up to my bedroom when I heard a buzzing sound that reinvigorated my waning interest. I followed the noise and spotted some odd-looking black and yellow creatures on some knapweed. It was love at first sight, as I had never seen anything so silly and adorable in all of my then short life.

A strange sensation took hold of my face and I felt it stretch and my teeth become bare. What was even stranger was the gurgling, shriek-like noise that leapt out of my mouth. I jumped back in fear and excitement at the sight of the strange creatures. I could not fathom the strange emotions that were growing out of my chest. More odd gurgles and giggles came. I slowly inched closer to the silly creatures as they flew from flower to flower. I rasped at them, leapt back and giggled again. I edged closer to them again and sat my naked behind on a large tuft of nearby grass. With a tilted head, I watched in amazement.

I soon got up the courage to reach over to try and touch one of them. My hesitation meant that the first time I did this I missed, as the bumblebee had flown away to go to another flower. I huffed in frustration and looked for another target for my affections. I was quicker off the mark now, but as they appeared so dainty, I was mindful to be gentle as well. I lightly stroked the insect with my index finger. It didn't respond and simply carried on with its farming. I, of course, found absolute joy in this, as it didn't react to my affection with violence. More excited gasps and giggles came.

I spent hours watching and lightly stroking the bumblebees in the garden that day. Midge and flea-bites gathered all over my arms and legs, but the obnoxious loudness of the bites could not take me out of my enthralment with the bumblebees. I didn't quite understand what was going on, I just simply felt that I wanted to be around these fuzzy, silly things.

Bit by bit the light started to fade in the garden and one by one the bees became less numerous. As the light slowly faded, the garden started to appear more and more ominous. Also, a familiar instinct became louder and louder, imploring me to go back before it was too late.

Suddenly, in one blink of an eye, I was back in my bedroom again, except this time I was a couple of years older and curled up in a ball in the corner of my room. I was doing something I had not done since I was a toddler, and that was cry. The mucus, tears and blood from my wounds all mixed together to drip into a little puddle on the hardwood floor.

Again, it was a clear, blue-sky June day, except this time the sun contemptuously stared down at all those below. Eventually, I stopped weeping, which meant I was able to hear the odd expletive coming from outside. A dread gripped my stomach and chest as I realised what I was going to have to do. I slowly and wearily pushed myself up to look. A quick wipe of the mucus and blood from my nose left a trail down my forearm. Even with the sun blazing through the window, my naked body felt cold and I shivered uncontrollably. I shivered so much that I nearly fell to the floor, but I persevered and carried on to the window.

There, standing in the half-dug-up garden, leaning on a shovel by the palm of his hand, was what appeared to be my father, except all that could really be seen was a lanky shadow with piercingly cold blue eyes. These eyes immediately set upon me with accusatory rage. I quickly dropped down to my knees to hide. I heard many a word being hatefully said but I could not comprehend them, although I knew it all related to further punishment as I had refused to destroy the bees' habitat.

Then, for some reason, five of his words cut right through the haze and chaos in my head:

"All your fucking fault, this!"

That was when I came to.

Chapter 13

I, of course, wasn't the happiest when I came out
of my coma. I awoke to an old, familiar feeling of
chemicals depressing my nervous system. At first,
I was convinced that the talking black Scottish
terrier and the prison had all been a dream. I was
actually back in a horrible reality, where I
regularly got high to the point where I couldn't
move. However, I soon noticed the sensation of
handcuffs and this jarred against such notions. I
forced my eyes open to see where I was but all I
could make out was a mixture of blurred lights and
dark shapes. It took a few minutes before my eyes
adjusted and I was able to recognise that I was in a
small, dark room, surrounded by medical
equipment, some of which was hooked right into
me. I was trying to understand whether this was
part of my high or whether I was actually in a
hospital bed. Eventually, my mind did land —
quite hard, I must add — and what had happened
came crashing back to me.

I remembered my hostage shenanigans, the
final part of which was my getting shot. I tried to
get up to have a look at myself, but my body was
far too weak to let me move my arms up more than
an inch. Also, my mind was much too hazy to
focus and to check my body to find out how
injured I actually was. The drugs in my system
certainly didn't help. It wasn't until a couple of
days later that I was able to establish that I had
fifty-one stitched-up bullet holes riddled
throughout my body.

I suspected that the Armed Response Unit were more than a bit trigger-happy. I suppose it is understandable, as I was a high level of threat, but even with that in mind, fifty-one shots was going overboard. Clearly, they wanted to make sure I was dead, but they very much failed. They were probably quite disappointed when they found out I had survived, this being a little thought that did bring me a modicum of joy. It was the first time I had ever been shot and I must say, it was something that I wasn't keen to repeat. Although I'm not one to generally complain about pain, fifty-one bullet holes were no easy thing to get over. None of this would have mattered if I had simply died, but clearly my body didn't get the memo that that was the plan.

Bed-ridden and restricted, there wasn't much else for me to do but think and meditate. Whenever the hospital staff came in to check up on me, I pretended that I was still unconscious. The doctor who regularly checked on me was quite the disturbing sort. He had a habit of talking to me and to himself during his rounds, in what I guessed was a Danish accent. When I heard his straightforward and matter-of-fact manner with the nurses and myself, I felt I was correct.

On one check-up, he expressed absolute disbelief that I had survived. He said that when they found me, it was as if I had gone into a state of catatonic hibernation. My breathing and heartbeat had become near deathly slow. He hypothesised that this was what saved my life. He then went on to say that my circulation slowed to the bare minimum to keep my brain oxygenated, while preventing as little blood leakage as possible. He also explained that whilst the bullets had hit vital organs, they had caused only superficial or insignificant damage; other bullets seemed to have hit bone and then stopped and the last remaining bullets simply became lodged in my muscles.

On another round, this same doctor had joked that he hoped that I would die soon as my autopsy would be "supremely fascinating". He was still in disbelief that my bones had only slightly fractured when they were hit by the bullets and that there were minimal signs of infection. He kept on saying with great disappointment that I was a spectacular specimen that required study and it was a shame that I was due to be shipped off soon for a court hearing. I guessed he wouldn't have said this much if he'd realised I was very much awake and only playing possum.

Even with my supposedly miraculous ability to survive and heal, I was still the resident of a very broken body. Each night I tried moving and each night all I could manage was to lift my arms an inch before my body gave in. During one of the days at the hospital, I heard what must have been a police officer ask the doctor when I would be fit enough to be moved for the court hearing. The doctor bluntly replied that it depended on what state they wanted me in and that if they wanted me to die in court, then they should take me there now. The police officer nervously chuckled that I had only needed to be conscious and that I was not likely to die in court.

It was not long after that I was confronted about my play-acting. On the day this happened I awoke to the beautiful smell of a sweet potato rosti, spinach, bacon, salsa and poached eggs. My stomach whined at the smell. Unfortunately, it was but a few seconds later that I gave in and opened my left eye just a smidgen for a little peek. There I saw a tall, skinny doctor with immaculate blond slicked-back hair. His bespectacled blue eyes were inquisitive and curious. They sat behind a long nose on a bright, clear, thin face. A polite, closed smile came my way and I got the feeling this was about as expressive as he could be.

"Sleeping Beauty awakes. You do realise I am a doctor and it isn't difficult for me to tell if someone is pretending to be unconscious? Anyhow, that isn't important; I really wanted to talk to you about your body's amazing ability to heal. What you have is … how should I say — yes, a *wonderful* vehicle. The very fact that you became conscious so early on is a miracle itself. If I had my way, I would cut you open right now and look at every cell in your body," the doctor casually intoned as he sat at the bottom of my bed.

I saw the breakfast he had on a portable hospital dining table next to him. The doctor, with a little bemusement, looked at my wide-open eyes and then at the food. Next, he lazily cut into the sweet potato rosti, bacon and egg, heaped the generous bite onto his fork, piled some spinach and salsa onto it and then, ever so slowly, ate it. Each chew was precise and his face showed that he savoured every morsel.

"I do not intend to flatter you, but I thought after what I read in your media stories, it was clear you were a man who enjoyed his food. Today was not the first time I used this knowledge to try to coax you out of your little game. I did initially try the standard hospital swill, but that, of course, didn't work, as it is terrible. I tell them all the time, but they do not change what they offer. Anyway, I had to cook up this meal myself in the hospital kitchen."

Again, with the precision of a surgeon, the doctor distributed an equal amount of the various parts of the meal on his fork and took another bite. The only part of me that was capable of expressing the murderous rage I felt for him were my eyes.

"You are quite the fearsome one. I am glad to see that you have not suffered any brain damage, which further adds to how wonderful your vehicle is. I don't *need* to tease, but I get very bored with pretending to care for patients in this hospital. I am a researcher, you see. I have only come here as a locum doctor so I can do some experiments. These are, how you British say, hush-hush. I came across you through sheer good luck." He gave a little sigh.

"It is such a shame that you are so weak, as I'd like to see more of what your body can do. Look, I can even do this and you cannot do a thing." The doctor pulled out handcuff keys and undid my cuffs.

"I am … quite resourceful," he said whilst jangling the keys.

I tried to get up, with a rather simple plan in my mind: kill the doctor and eat his food. Admittedly, I wasn't too sure in what order. I was able to get my arms and neck a couple of inches up before I fell back down.

"I wouldn't be disheartened by that attempt. You did a fantastic job to lift yourself up that much, especially as you should be dead right now. Barely a sign of infection, no major trauma to your organs and you're not even brain dead after being shot fifty-one times. Yes, your vehicle is very splendid."

He then grabbed my right cheek and pulled it. However, it did not feel as if this was to mock me but seemed he was checking to see how elastic it was.

"I look forward to the day I get to tear you apart piece by piece," I was just about able to rasp out.

"Your anger is understandable. I think I would be the same if I were in your shoes … but I am not."

The doctor then went back to meticulously eating his breakfast whilst I watched impotently. My stomach angrily hissed but it soon fell back into giving loud whines.

"It's rather surprising that you have a court date. Especially as no one even knows who you are, since they can't find you on the systems. Oddly, one of your hostages did say he might know who you are but he has suddenly disappeared … Anyhow, they think you must be a foreigner, give that you cooked Jamaican food when you took those hostages and because you're a tanned man. I do wonder how people reach such high levels in their organisations with such simple thinking."

The doctor stayed silent for a few seconds and stared at me absently.

"Anyhow, these idiots are unashamedly proud and powerful bureaucrats with an insatiable lust to stick to their needlessly complicated processes and they clearly think that for them to truly squash you, they need you in court to make it all above board.

Apparently, they have a judge all ready and waiting for whenever you're fit to go to a hearing so you can be officially sentenced and legitimately locked up. A part of me feels that they are a touch scared of you and see your weakened state as an opportunity to rid society of you for good, without the chance of you running wild as you did before."

The doctor then stood up, looked me up and down and gave a heavy sigh.

"Such a shame, though. It would be a waste for you to be left to rot in some cell. Anyhow, I've delayed all this as long as possible and sent a request to the upper echelons of my employers to intervene. Hopefully, they will take heed so we can become reacquainted before it is too late," the doctor said with the faintest of smiles.

He then deftly handcuffed me to the hospital bed again before he left the room. I thought the doctor had gone to alert the authorities and that it was going to be that very day or perhaps the following day that I was wheeled out to go in front of a judge. In fact, it was four more anxiety-filled days before police and security came to take me away. During that time of waiting, as I had given up my charade, I opted to eat.

Although it was infinitely more palpable than prison food, hospital food was one of the greatest displeasures I had ever experienced and my stomach only just coped. Having eaten the food and having a little more energy, I was pleased to see that my libido was still in working order. I noticed this when I was given a light sponge bath by the nurse. However, there wasn't much that I could do with regard to helping my proud fellow, as I didn't have the romantic charisma to convince the portly and elderly nurse to befriend it. She carried on with her work as if it didn't even exist, something that I found quite hurtful.

On the day that I was wheeled into court, the portly nurse came in to do her rounds. This time, after she completed her checks, she found a chair, sat down and switched the television on. She watched a daft soap in which a gangster's daughter had fallen in love with a man (who had been born a woman) and this man also became pregnant with the gangster's child after a drunken fumble. It was absurd, but the nurse looked enthralled. When it finished, she got up and left the room without switching off the television. More nonsensical shows came on, one after the other. I watched mindlessly, as part of me was curious about what people actually found interesting about this world of TV. Eventually, just before I was about ready to fall asleep, the news came on. The initial headlines were about a frivolous squabble between the Prime Minister and one of her cabinet. The subsequent story was just as dreary, as it was about some musician or actor who had died a wonderfully peaceful death. The story after that, however, was a damn sight more interesting. This one was about bumblebees.

A group of scientists had provided near irrefutable evidence that certain pesticides were decimating bee populations, pesticides that were being produced by the chemical company Oso. It had taken a continuous stream of evidence and years of decimation of the bees before neonicotinoids had finally been banned. Clearly there was going to be a repeat of the same lengthy process before this new pesticide was banned as well. This new evidence and the government opting to refuse to say anything at all about the subject was further confirmation of my belief. They clearly didn't want to change the status quo and the only reason I could come up with was that they were somehow in cahoots.

Within the news story, there was a backdrop of scientists providing reams of reams of information pertaining to the potential consequences to humans. I, of course, didn't care about what happened to our species, but I became morose at the thought of all those bumblebees dying because of capitalist greed. Such thoughts added fuel to an old rage that wanted to burn and destroy them all. These feelings led me towards fantasies of becoming the destroyer of all that was so-called "civilised". In this realm, I pillaged, plundered and caused the streets to run red with blood. It was a rather melodramatic reverie, but I was far too weak at that moment in time to do anything else.

Involuntarily, I refocused back onto the fact that the bumblebee was on the verge of tumbling into extinction. Guilt came out of nowhere and punched me right in the gut. I was winded and nauseous with the realisation that I had completely failed in the campaign I had set out to accomplish. The thought that I had become so callous and neglectful of something that I had supposedly loved tore at me. All that preparation and work wasted and all because of my own fears and gluttony.

I started to feel that it was ultimately my insatiable lust for food that had got me into so much difficulty. My accursed love of succulent meats, for one thing — not just any meats, but perhaps a boneless, butterflied leg of lamb, also marinated, perhaps in lemon, Greek oregano, salt, pepper and garlic, the meat seared to perfection so it seductively dripped juices and was cooked to a state where tender morsels fluttered off the bone and into my mouth, its savoury goodness hitting every perfect note of pleasure. My stomach let out pathetic moans and whines as images of this piece of lamb floated just out of reach in my mind.

My desperation for such food almost reached the point of complete delirium, as I was also seeing hocks of Parma ham dangled above my head and whole roast ducks sitting on my belly. I forcibly stopped such torture, as I realised it was stemming from the schemes of that tyrant below, who wanted to take over. I had to focus on other, more pressing and more benevolent thoughts, such as how I was going to escape and kill every Oso employee I could find. But I realised immediately that this was also just a fantasy brought on by the state of my body. The feelings of guilt swiftly returned and mercilessly took their time torturing my broken self.

I was powerless and I was to be sentenced so that I could be thrown into some dungeon and left to rot. What made this even worse was that, in this future, I was destined to be a starved and guilt-ridden husk of a man. I knew I could wait until I had healed and that eventually a window of opportunity might appear so that I could make my move to escape. Of course, I'd be hunted down and that prospect no longer deterred me as there was the possibility that I could carry on with my campaign. However, such an opportunity might not come until many years had gone by and I simply didn't have that much time or patience. Every day I wasted, the closer the bumblebee came to extinction. Also, the thought of living on prison food for years sent terrible shivers down my spine.

There was, of course, suicide, but guilt simply told me that wasn't going to happen. My emotions had got too much of a hold on me and I knew they would not let me take such a way out. Their plan was to force me to rectify the mess I had caused and get back to my campaign. I was also able to tell that my stomach was going to do whatever it could to ensure that I was going to eat the food that it thought it deserved. At first, I thought there would be civil war between these powerful internal factions, but they seemed to come to a quick and simple agreement over what they would make me do. I had thought there was simply no way out of this situation — they felt differently — and before I even had a chance to contemplate things, they made me make my move.

"Little dog, we need to talk about this deal," I meekly rasped out.

Before I had time to regret my decision or to ridicule myself for even trying, I heard a sinister chuckle in the eerie voice that touched every octave.

"That sounds like a wonderful idea, my dear boy, do carry on," the voice said.

I turned my head and saw the little dog sitting on a nearby chair. Its tail wagged and its tongue lolled out of its smiling mouth as the beast panted.

"I will agree to this deal, but only on one condition," I responded with a grimace, as it hurt to speak.

"Why, what is that, my dear boy?"

"Don't call me boy," I was able to spit out.

"HO HO! You are so wonderfully feisty. I am sure we are going to have a terribly good time, my good chap," the canine laughed out before disappearing into thin air.

Chapter 14

I sat handcuffed to a wheelchair, crippled to the point where breathing seemed to be the only function I could successfully manage. I was in a courtroom lined with polished wood panels and where all the public gallery seats were empty. Somehow, they must have successfully wrangled that the court being open to the public would have frustrated the process of administering their so-called justice. Obviously, for whatever reason, the powers that be wanted this to be a hush-hush affair rather than a media circus.

Even though I was debilitated, they still had a few security officers within the courtroom. However, they appeared to be the penny-a-dozen private security types. They certainly didn't look the healthiest of sorts, with their pot bellies clinging on for dear life as they hung over their trouser belts. Each security officer wheezed and sucked in large breaths, since even the act of standing seemed strenuous for them.

Of course, even before the charade started, I knew I would vehemently dislike the judge and the prosecutor, but it did come as a shock when I found that I wanted to hurt my own barrister the most. This was due to the fact that he appeared keener on getting me locked up than the prosecution themselves. Which meant it was a courtroom where it seemed every person was taking relish in what they thought would be the inevitable outcome.

Prior to the court hearing, my barrister had briefly met with me to discuss the proceedings. As

I was barely able to talk, he simply talked at me and informed me of what was going to happen.

"This is a strange one, especially as no one has any idea of who you are. Anyhow, I have made it so that you have already pleaded guilty today, so we're just having the sentencing hearing. It will be a quick and painless process — well I imagine not so painless for you. But none of us wants to waste our time. Of course, what we're doing is somewhat illegal, but you'll be locked away in seclusion before you have the capability to raise any allegations about our conduct. Also, it would be a cold day in hell before anyone believed you," he said with the slightest Yorkshire twang.

My initial instinct was to try and rip his throat out, but I was a long way away from being capable. Instead, I kept calm and grinned at the barrister. I then gave him a cheeky wink. The barrister was taken aback.

"You really are chuffin' tapped in the head. Certainly, makes an awful lot of sense," he scolded.

A brief look of embarrassment appeared on his face after accidentally revealing too much of his Yorkshire upbringing. Still, with a grin on my face, I motioned with my hand for him to get closer so he could hear me speak. At first, he hesitated and then shrugged.

"I am going to kill you first," I just about whispered.

"Yes, you are definitely quite mad. I suppose you'd have to be, to do the things you did. Anyway, I'll see you in the courtroom. Goodbye."

Perhaps the barrister was quite right in regard to the sanity part, as I had had this feeling of intense mania since the little dog popped in for its visit. Nothing had actually changed since I agreed to the deal, as the little dog disappeared straight after our conversation. I should have seen this as a confirmation that my sanity had indeed vacated its home, but for some peculiar reason, I felt rather confident that something that worked in my favour was going to happen in court that day.

Hence, I was wheeled into the courtroom with a supremely wide smile on my face. One of the guards, the most overweight and obese one, kept on looking at me, and then grimaced.

"Creepy bastard," I heard him mutter.

The judge who presided over the case spoke with the most formal and aristocratic accent that spoke volumes about his class and upbringing. Such communication was to demonstrate that he was from the country's most well-bred stock, even though he looked the opposite. Big floppy ears, a long, thrombosed nose, dull grey beady eyes and crooked teeth on a wrinkly, gaunt face said that he was the runt of the genetic litter. Regardless, he was a man of power and it certainly sounded like he rather enjoyed it. Upon entering the court, the judge's beady eyes fell on me and the disgust and hate were not concealed on his face. I imagine, as there wasn't a jury nor any members of the public present, he was far more open to revealing his true self. It wasn't until the report of the guilty verdict and the reading of the offences from the prosecution that the judge made his first swipe at me.

"I suggest that the defendant wipe that juvenile and hideous smile off his face. Does he not know where he is?!"

"Your Honour, I am afraid the defendant's nerves have got the best of him. Please let me have a quick word with him," my barrister responded.

"Wipe that smile off your face, you muppet!" he whispered in my ear.

"Or what will either of you do?" I just about chuckled out.

He glared at me and then turned to the judge.

"Your Honour, I am afraid the defendant will not stop his silly game. I do not believe that we can ask the guards to forcibly stop the defendant from smiling, so please may we continue?"

The judge glared at me, clearly trying to bring me into line with the power he wielded. I simply stared back and waited. It wasn't long until the process started again and the offences were discussed by the prosecution.

I wasn't paying attention to the long list of charges that I had been accused of, but I did notice that it took quite a fair few minutes before she was finished. I was busy fantasising about how I was going to dismantle everyone who had caused me offence. It was only the court usher and clerk who seemed to have any semblance of professionalism. The prosecutor then went on some spiel about me being so heinous that I swear she was on the verge of calling me the Anti-Christ. I did notice that they tried to attribute a murder to me. It was quite rich that they did this, as the guard died in the hospital due to an MRSA infection. The rapidly descending quality of the increasingly gutted healthcare system was not my fault at all. I zoned out for the rest of the speech, as it was unnecessarily long-winded — what took fifteen minutes could have taken two. It was clear that the barristers and the judge were people who got masturbatory joy from hearing the sound of their own voices.

The prosecution finally came to something marginally more entertaining and read out statements from the victims. To do this, she pulled out a heavy, thick batch of papers from a briefcase. The weight of the statements caused an almighty thud on the desk where they were dropped. This was probably done for dramatic effect and to cause shock; instead, though, I felt a slight beam of pride. I also thought to myself that I hadn't actually done that much harm to anyone, as most of them had survived the ordeal with injuries that would heal. Clearly, I didn't realise how terribly sensitive some people were.

One victim talked about continued psychological trauma, how it was going to be a year until he could walk properly again; constant sleepless nights; that he had to go on long-term sick from work for intensive therapeutic support for his injured mind and body; that he was suffering from crippling anxiety and so on. I raised an eyebrow and then chuckled a little bit to myself due to the absurdity of what was readout. It was, after all, no more than a good beating that he had endured.

The next victim statement reported pretty much the same thing, but they added that this person now struggled with impotence. I chuckled to myself again: at this rate, it would not be long before they blamed me for the problems in the Middle East. My defence barrister turned around and glared at me. I stared back at his scowling face until I won the competition and he turned back around. Then the prosecution said that, since the hostage situation, this guard had also suffered from urinary and bowel incontinence. When that was read out it could not be helped, I had a right good laugh. Even though it must have ripped a few stitches, the thought of a prison guard on the verge of tears running to the toilet with his hand over his clenched bottom made sure I was as good as gone. I don't feel any shame in admitting that such slapstick comedy is my cup of tea.

"There will be no such disgusting and offensive behaviour in my courtroom! Do you hear me?" the judge snarled.

I, of course, carried on chortling away and ignored the old gnarled root.

"I will dissolve the court and you will be taken away, do you hear me?!" he said, almost in a shout.

Still, I roared with laughter, but also grimaced in pain after every few chuckles. It was clear that even without the deal with the little dog, whoever was running the show had a plan for me and they weren't going to deviate from it. My sentence was certainly not going to be reduced with any forms of good behaviour and it was obvious that the sentencing needed to be completed as soon as possible. So, I carried on with abandon until eventually, my body told me it could take no more. As soon as I had quietened down, the prosecutor continued reading out the victim statements whilst the judge sullenly stared at me. Unfortunately, there was no further material that brought a repeat of such mirth.

My defence barrister, in response to what the prosecutor had presented, simply said that there was nothing to add. No background information was available and there were no circumstantial considerations, as no one knew who I was. It didn't take long before the sentencing began. An evil and hideous grin that showed each crooked tooth in its disfigured glory erupted onto the judge's face.

"I have heard both sides with regard to the defendant. Without a doubt, it is clear that this man is a significant danger to society. There is no remorse demonstrated and it is felt that only his injuries prevent further acts of dangerous and morally repugnant behaviour. The sentencing will be of the harshest severity within the current guidelines and I can assure the court that due to the number of his offences, the defendant will not see the light of day until the oldest of age or death. I do not —" the judge snarled out before being interrupted by laughter.

It wasn't me returning to my merriment, it was that familiar voice which somehow hit every high and low note.

"I will only do this once. It's only because it's the start of our arrangement. Anyhow, please do enjoy your revenge on this corrupt theatre!" I heard the voice say.

Everyone else in the court looked around trying to find out where this voice came from.

"What? What? What? How dare you suggest corruption! Find this dreg that is making such a racket in my court! I will make sure they are charged with contempt!" the judge shrilled.

One of the guards walked around the court and then stopped at the public gallery.

"Bloody hell, Your Honour, someone's left their dog here," the guard exclaimed.

As the circus continued, I felt a peculiar tingling sensation emanating from all of my wounds. It was quite an odd sensory experience, quite pleasurable but also very painful. Then it felt as if each wound became glued shut and within seconds there was no more pain. Out of curiosity, I looked down at my shackles, which appeared to be melting as they had turned into what looked like milk chocolate. A quick shrug of the shoulders showed my acceptance of the impossible and then I went about eating my delicious new bonds. The silkiness and the creaminess of the chocolate were in perfect harmony with the cocoa. I was able to eat the whole of my shackles without anyone paying me any notice, as they were all distracted by the little dog. The fat guards were waddling after the deity, who was easily and casually trotting away from them.

When I had finished my snack I stood up, jumped over the dock and landed right next to my defence barrister. He immediately turned around and gave me a look of surprise.

"My apologies, but this will hurt quite a bit," I said whilst sneering.

My arm shot out, grabbed his throat and lifted him off the ground. That was when everyone else realised that I was free.

"GUARDS! GUARDS!" the judge shouted.

The defence barrister tried clawing at my wrist and shook his head, trying to convince me to stop. By the time the first guard reached me, there were four finger-sized holes in the dead barrister's throat and blood profusely gushed out. I dropped the body and swung right round to connect a left hook square on the fat guard's chin. It was the perfect strike and a fair few teeth flew out of his mouth as his body crumpled. I then sprinted across towards the judge and jumped to pull myself up onto his stand. I heard the little dog's spine-tingling chuckle follow.

"I am afraid your corruption is treasonous and the sentence for that is, of course, death," I spat.

The quivering judge closed his eyes and the smell of urine flooded the air. I grabbed his silly little wig and flung it away. In one quick action, I smashed his bald, freckled, sun-spot covered head sideways down onto his desk. Next, I grabbed his pen and stabbed it right through the temple until hit the other side of his skull.

"Haha! Marvellous, old chap, absolutely bloody marvellous!" I heard the little dog cheer.

I looked around. None of the guards were approaching me; they were huddled with everyone else trying to open the courtroom door to get away. However, for some reason, it was locked and they were all trapped inside with me. I sauntered across towards the four guards that remained, the court usher, the clerk, the solicitors and the prosecuting barrister. One of the guards thought he would try his luck and ran up to me, but in the process tripped over his feet and cracked his head on the corner of the public gallery. The blood leaked all over the courtroom floor. When I reached the prosecutor, she thought that perhaps her ability to persuade might save her.

"Listen, if you stop now, we can make a plea bargain. We can get you the best deal possible, I'll make sure of it ..." she pleaded, just before I wrung her neck like a chicken.

The prosecutor crumpled to the floor. I looked at the rest of the quivering court. There wasn't an incentive to dispose of them and it felt wrong to hurt those who wouldn't fight back.

"No? Perfectly understood young chap, they're a bit pathetic, aren't they? Also, I imagine you're wondering what I will do about getting rid of the evidence? Well, of course, someone like me has a fair few options but I'll show you the one I enjoy the most," the little dog teased with a wicked grin on its face.

I turned and saw that the deity was now right next to me. Slowly, the little dog's head turned into an unnerving, floating black liquid that defied gravity, grew in size and floated up. Then from this liquid that light could not penetrate, five monstrous grinning wolf-like mouths with jagged teeth appeared on the end of five tentacles and these immediately shot out. The mouths sank into the screaming, crying survivors. As the deity devoured them, another couple of mouths were shot out of the body to spit some sort of acid, which completely dissolved the corpses and spilt blood. A nervous grin grew on my face as it dawned on me just how powerful this creature was. My mouth went bone dry and my head cleared itself of all other thoughts as it tried to figure out what to do.

"I could have just wiped their memories, but where would the fun be in that?" the little dog chuckled.

Chapter 15

"Yes, I must say the flavour is much better when they're alive," the little dog said after he burped.

Rather than letting me reply, the supernatural being carried on talking.

"Humans are quite the tasty lot, you know. You should give them a go one day. That sedentary lifestyle of theirs leaves the flesh all rather plump and tender. There is no need to put a human in a box and force-feed them until they're ripe for the slaughter; most of them already pretty much do the work themselves. Absolute genius, so much so that I do wonder sometimes whether it was me who created your species or whether it actually was just chemical chance."

I looked at the little dog blankly. I had only just started to process what had just happened.

"I could try to remember that fact but you know, when you have existed in an infinite amount of universes and an infinite amount of dimensions for eternity, memories about such a small speck of dust like your race take a little extra mental steam to work the cogs, something, admittedly, I can't be bothered to do," the canine chortled out.

I was still frozen with confusion and indecision. It wasn't because I was scared, as quite frankly I was; it was more that I hadn't the foggiest idea of what to do. I would have grasped at straws, but my brain didn't have any for me to grasp. Also, the constant yammering from the canine didn't help. The little dog answered another imaginary question that I'd had no intention of asking or interest in.

"Yes, I could go wild and have a little party by eating a billion or two of your kind, but I think that would become far too much of a good thing and I would become bored of such lovely flavours. I must remember to be patient and savour each little morsel ..." The little dog paused for a few seconds.

"Did you know that when humans are eaten alive the adrenaline and cortisol bring out an aromatic flavour of the meat? Just a pinch really does enhance the tastes to a level that is so much better than snacking on a regular rotting corpse. I must say that you're looking a little peaky, my dear chap."

I turned my head and looked the critter in the eyes. This time, the little dog answered the question that I *had* wanted to ask.

"If it makes you feel any better, I don't play with my food. I don't see the point at all in doing all that torture business. I won't lie: I tried it once with a particularly aggravating planet-sized fleshy monster thing. The most grotesque thing you would have ever seen. The bloody thing kept offering me sacrifices and prayers. What's wrong with that? you might think. But it wasn't just the one or two, it was millions nearly every bloody day. I couldn't get anything done as my focus was constantly drawn away." The critter let out a sigh before speaking again.

"At the time, I was trying to watch the most delightful Zozkof robot assassin that had gone rogue against its programming, but I simply couldn't pay it any attention with that idiot constantly babbling on about how amazing I was. So, naturally, I vented my grievances on the planet-sized buffoon." The canine interrupted itself to scratch behind its ears.

"I did some of the most heinous and painful things to it for at least a thousand years, but it didn't take long for me to realise that it was an incredibly time-consuming and dull activity. Also, I ended up missing out on watching the Zozkof assassin's laser and explosion filled death. The amount of moaning and whining that comes from torture as well, it's just absolutely unbearable. From that point, I became an absolute believer in the idea that if anything is that frustrating, then just eat it and be done with it."

The little dog then winked. I felt somewhat better after hearing that. It was one on a long list of points of concerns that had been furiously written out onto my mind. If I was going to cross this beast, then at least the very worst would be that it would just eat me.

"That being said, how tasty whatever I've eaten is will influence how long they are digested for. That pathetic sycophant I just told you about, well, it had the most delightfully meaty texture and rustic flavours, so I digested the old fellow over a good million years. If you remember what I said before, the more alive the food, the better it tastes, so although it had been torn asunder, my digestive tract has this amazing ability to keep my food quite alive and quite in pain until it has all been fully dissolved at the molecular level."

An evil grin erupted onto the little dog's face as it looked at me. My concern was immediately written back onto my list.

"Ho-ho! But do not worry, young man, you are probably much too stringy and tough. Too much exercise, far too much! Also, it is not my plan to eat you, as you're far too entertaining and I wouldn't want you to become a bore because you're constantly worried about being eaten. I want you to be able to be *you*. Anyway, we must get going. As they say, the show must go on!" The little dog laughed out whilst wagging its tail and jumping in the air.

This was not a position I was used to. It is an impossibility to prepare oneself for such events, as such events should never happen. There were many choices in the matter, but regardless of what the little dog said, there was a strong possibility that almost all of them would lead to me being eaten. Death wasn't such an ordeal but being slowly digested alive over aeons admittedly frightened the hell out of me. A part of me tried to comfort me with the thought that I would probably get used to the intense pain, but that wasn't a prospect that I was willing to try out. It was clear that the waters were furiously heading in one direction and I simply could not swim against such currents.

"What do I call you, little dog?" I asked reluctantly, after I'd let out a heavy sigh.

"My name is so complex that it would take your primitive brain five billion years of processing to even comprehend the first syllable. So, it's probably best to just to call me Little Dog. I actually quite like it; it has a cute ring to it. Don't worry, I know what your real name is, although it really doesn't suit you. So, I'll call you … Cain!"

Little Dog then ran around me barking happily and jumping up. It then jumped against my leg with its tail wagging. This time, I felt the critter and my hand became thoroughly licked when I gingerly moved it closer to inspect the creature. Oddly, to me, there was no difference to any other dog I had touched before.

"Fine. Call me that, I don't care," I muttered.

I thought that although the critter was clearly quite powerful from what I'd seen, it didn't mean it was as powerful as it claimed it was. Also, the creature was quite petulant and arrogant, so there were hopefully weaknesses to discover.

"What about the CCTV?" I asked.

"The deal is the deal. I wouldn't worry about such silly things."

I was just about to open the door, but Little Dog interrupted.

"Hold on one second," it said.

The critter quickly teleported to various different spots in the courtroom, in split second after split second, all the while looking at me. It then reappeared right in front of me.

"I felt like there was something missing in that fun little hoo-hah you just had and I think it's because I am not a fan of this new look that they forced on you. Hmmm, okay. Look over there, my dear man and you'll see a little present," the canine said as he nodded at where he wanted me to look.

I saw my tattered trench coat and fusty clothes neatly folded on one of the public gallery's chairs. Underneath these were my rustic and well-worn boots. I raised an eyebrow, as clearly there were some perks to this new-found — and twisted —

relationship. I went over and picked up my trench coat and shoved it into my face. The stale cabbage and leather smell were still there. I looked it over to see how it was doing. There were some new bloodstains noticeable on the inner lining … these were probably from the bus hitting me but aside from that, it all seemed relatively intact. I could not help but show that I was ecstatic, as it felt like a little part of me had come home. I smothered my face with my clothes again for a good few minutes until I realised that a malicious supernatural being was waiting for me. As soon as I pulled my face away from my coat, I noticed my neck and my face being tickled.

"Sorry, my good chap, but your new hair is without the varied wildlife that it had before. I am sure it won't take long for you to get a new habitat up and running in there."

I lightly stroked my hair lightly and it felt off-tune as it wasn't as greasy as before. But it still felt heavenly having the length again.

"Thank you, Little Dog," I mumbled out to it.

I quickly ripped off my blood-stained overalls and almost jumped right into my clothes. Whilst I was getting changed, a tentacle suddenly appeared and spat some sort of acid onto the clothes I had just discarded.

"Much better. We don't want you hurting and killing in the fashion faux pas that you had on before," the critter chuckled.

"Before we get going, Little Dog, I must say that I have seen the most fantastic happenings when it comes to your abilities. Please don't take this as rudeness, but one cannot help but be curious. The curiosity is not about your proven ability, but more about where it ends. I do apologise if this offends you, but could you actually show me the true extent of your power?" I politely asked.

"Well, young man, you just have to have faith. HA! I am just being silly. I can give you a quick demonstration, yes, but then again, a sceptical and adept mind might still assume that some trickery is afoot. You just wouldn't know if what I showed you was actual reality or not. Especially as you don't have the instruments to adequately test what I could show you. For all you know, I could simply be a more technologically advanced species that appears this powerful due to how primitive you humans are. Also, I am afraid that the human brain's computational power is far too small to produce a relevant deduction. You try explaining the notions of power or demonstrating your capabilities to an ant and see how far you get. But if you still wish to be bamboozled by such levels of energy and truth, then I am more than happy to show you — and indeed to tell you my name."

I frowned in response. Little Dog was quite right: for a more powerful and technologically advanced creature, it really wouldn't be that exceptionally difficult to make it appear that it was godlike to humans. Hell, it was even quite easy for humans to trick other humans into such outlandish notions without *any*demonstrations of actual power; the numerous churches that have popped up over the past few thousand years was a testament to this. Essentially, all that I would be able to deduce was that the critter was still far more powerful than I was, I wouldn't know what the extent of this power was. There probably wasn't any point in asking the canine to go through whatever demonstration it had in mind. Then again, I thought it might help me identify a potential weakness.

"Okay, Little Dog. Show me."

It was what felt like a second later when I came to and found myself on all fours on the ground, profusely vomiting. My vision was warped and fuzzy, my ears rang loudly and all I could vocalise was gurgles. Every neuron was jumbled up together in tight, tangled knots, and the sensory information crashed into them like angry wave after angry wave. It was as if I had just been born into a world and a body of which I had no understanding. I could not tell how long it took, but eventually, the nausea, the feelings of absolute chaos and my senses settled to a point where I was able to realise that I was still in the courtroom and that Little Dog was sitting on a nearby chair, lolling on its back.

"I am afraid, my dear chap, your noggin couldn't quite process everything you've just experienced. Far, far too much sensory information for you to handle. I did tell you my name, but by that point, you were frothing at the mouth, your eyes had rolled back and you were babbling like a little child. I know, it's quite convenient that you can't remember a single thing and I imagine it didn't do much to convince you. I suppose all you need to know is that I am substantially more powerful than any person on this planet. Keep the picture within that frame and I think you'll do just marvellous."

When my brain solidified a bit more, I tried to remember what had just happened. Suddenly I started to feel an intense sense of vertigo as all the colours around me warped again and I was sucked back down into a bottomless void. I could feel my body retching and trying to vomit, as it thought that was the answer to my current woes.

"Yes. Probably best not to think back to what just happened. To ensure you survived, I had to compress your memory of the experience into a size small enough that your brain can store it. Don't worry, it's in a file so small that it won't hinder any of your cognitive abilities or brain's systems. However, the issue, my dear chap, is that you simply can't access it, as if you tried your head might explode. If you don't believe me, you might want to give your eyes a wipe."

As I wasn't in any state to disagree, I complied. I looked at my hand and it was red with blood.

"When you're bleeding from the eyes, it's safe to assume that whatever you're doing, it probably isn't going to end well. *Now*, do you believe me?"

"If you can so easily compress it to such a small size, why didn't you just delete the memory?" I rasped out.

"HA! That would be far too much interference in your reality and I must confess, it sounded like quite the funny thing to do. It will certainly keep you on your toes, you know, the ever-looming prospect that your head might explode," Little Dog chuckled.

I stared right back at the supernatural being and I was glad to notice I had healed to a stage where I could feel rage again. Thoughts of murder were abundant, but it was clear that such feelings were all talk in my mind and no action. Suddenly Little Dog appeared like it was trying to look sheepish but was getting the attempt quite wrong. It looked down and seemed to pine and then it looked up with big beautiful wide eyes that accompanied the most blood-curdling and bass-ridden growl that I had ever heard. The sound of it echoed throughout the courtroom and my head. A second later the critter gave a whine and followed that with an ear to ear smile.

"I know it's quite the inconvenient time to ask such a silly favour, but I can assure you that we won't be interrupted. You'd think that, being this powerful, I wouldn't even hesitate, yet here I am rambling off from what I want to ask. Anyhow, I've seen what I want being done to many an actual dog and I want someone to do this to me, as it looks like jolly good fun … So, without further delay … My good man, if you would be so kind, please would you rub my belly?"

"What?"

"Yes, you heard me correctly, my dear chap. As strange as it sounds, it's something that I must give a go, at least once. Canines make it look so delightfully entertaining and as you little people say, when in Rome …"

I looked at Little Dog apprehensively but couldn't quite come to terms with the fact that something so powerful wanted me to actually treat it like a dog.

"Oh, please be a good sport, Cain!" it implored with a grin on its face.

I sighed and walked forward, as it seemed I didn't have a choice in the matter. I went to touch the canine's belly, tentatively, as the first time I sought contact with Little Dog my fists went right through it. This time I felt fur and bodily warmth that was identical to every other dog I had touched.

"Oh, bloody hell. Ooh, bloody hell! That certainly is ruddy good. Marvellous, my dear chap. Marvellous. Oh yes!"

I quickly swung at the critter with my free hand, as I thought it was worth a try. My fist went right through its head like before, even while my other hand was still rubbing its belly and the canine was still moaning with excitement. I then tried squeezing my hand around its belly as hard as I could, but it made no impact at all; the beast actually panted even harder.

"Okay, okay, that's enough. If you do anymore, you might end up proposing to me!" The critter shot up and skipped towards the courtroom doors.

"Come on, young man, let's go and do what you do best," it almost sang out.

The doors of the court swung open as Little Dog approached them. I let out a heavy sigh and followed it out of the room. We both walked down the stairs and pathways off the crown court in silence. There wasn't a soul in sight until we reached the entrance. There stood two overweight, and middle-aged private security guards, idly waiting. They didn't appear to have heard or know anything about what had just happened up above. Rather than give them a chance to notice me, I sprinted up and gave one of them a jumping punch straight on his chin. He went straight to the ground with a loud exhalation of air.

"What …?" was what I heard as I did a backhand like a tennis player with my fist on the side of the other guard's chin. He went stumbling a few feet to the side before he hit the ground and rolled a couple of feet. I turned around to ask Little Dog a question but stopped when I saw the left leg of the other guard sticking out of its mouth. That answered my question. The leg was then sucked in as if it was a piece of spaghetti. I raised an eyebrow and as I turned around, I heard loud crunches of snapping bone from where the other guard was.

"I know I keep on banging on about this, but really, you humans are such a tasty lot. If you get a good one, the meat is so eloquently marbled with layers of luxurious fat," the canine teased.

I ignored the comment and walked through the building's revolving entrance doors. I was back in city life, where streams of people flowed by. There was no mass panic, no screams or shouts; it was as if the usual rat-race was in progress and the usual averting of people's gaze from what they perceived to be a homeless man and his dog.

"I thought there was going to be at least some press outside, Little Dog?"

"Well, apparently one of your species' most famous of celebrities has conveniently had his soft drink spiked with MDMA, GHB, methamphetamine, LSD, diazepam and a large dose of sildenafil. He is currently naked, quite observably aroused and grazing on the grass of Piccadilly Gardens. They have all rushed over to cover the story."

I responded to that with a wry smile. My stomach took advantage of the silence that followed with a whine and a rumble.

"Are you going to magic me a little bit of money? I'm quite peckish, you see," I asked.

"I am afraid not, young chap. That isn't a part of the deal."

"All right then. You'd think your eating antics would have put me off food. So, first things first: I've got to get to work, Little Dog. Obviously, you're welcome to watch."

The canine gave a jolly bark in response.

Chapter 16

Fiorella let out a gasp and a moan as her body shivered all over in pleasure.

"Aye! Si. Si ..."

Her body jolted a couple more times as her guard continued with the cunnilingus.

"Stop," she ordered quietly.

Immediately, the guard stopped. Fiorella took a few seconds to sit back and bask in the afterglow of the experience, then scooted herself up her office chair. Leaving the guard underneath her desk, she lit a menthol cigarette. It was only after a few long drags that she decided to roll her chair backwards so that the guard could get out from underneath her desk. A brutish-looking man with a near-perfect square jawline, a brow that was an overhanging cliff and a look that was cold as death itself crawled out. He then stood to attention, his face still glistening and awaited further orders.

"Thank you. That was most appreciated. Go and clean yourself up and make sure another takes your place, as you deserve the day off for that. Go to Lisa at HR and tell her that you have earned yourself a bonus, let's say a level C," Fiorella ordered in a hoarse *limeña* and West-coast U.S. accent (she learnt her English from American businessmen when she was a child prostitute and later on, from kidnapped American businessmen who were being ransomed when she ran a cartel).

The man who had just demeaned himself was ex-Mossad and had a very extensive history of successful assassinations. The fact that he was such a brutal murderer added to the eroticism for Fiorella, as being able to command someone so lethal into such sexual servitude was a thrill. Also, he would not have been in the position he was in if he was not capable in such areas, as making sure Fiorella climaxed regularly was a job requirement for her elite guards. This was certainly no easy task, as sometimes it was a near impossibility for her to reach the heights that she demanded. There had been many a time that she had three or four of her most loyal and deadly taking turns in providing oral pleasure for hours on end until she reached such plateaus.

Like many other megalomaniacs with an abundance of power, Fiorella's had an insatiable lust and a varied palette of desires, such as taking substantial pleasure from being on the receiving end of the rougher types of sex. This added a difficult dynamic for her elite guards, as her joys of being sexually degraded conflicted against their absolute fear of Fiorella. They knew that if they pushed it too far and their leader actually felt degraded beyond the realms of her own sexual perversion, then there would be some terrible form of torture, or worse, waiting for them. It was only last week that one of her elite guards pulled her hair much too hard, talked too dirty to her and she made Fiorella gag more than she would have liked. This ex-CIA spy was subsequently executed five minutes after the consummation finished. Quite unnaturally, this perverted leader enjoyed the fear that her guards felt when they were manhandling her and it was a true testament of their willpower to actually stay visibly aroused during the rather confusing ordeal.

Of course, Fiorella wasn't a complete monster and knew she had to placate them somehow, too, as they were all vicious killers. To do this, the men and women who were successful at such sexual services received the most lavish of gifts in return to alleviate their feelings of humiliation, an example being that the ex-Mossad guard who had just pleased her orally was to receive a supercar of his choice or a hundred-thousand-pound bonus. Such opulent gift-giving and such a high libido meant the personal bill that she had racked up had reached the hundred million mark for the year. However, such costs were a drop in the ocean of the money she actually made.

When the afterglow had waned, Fiorella put her white silk dressing gown on, and her white, fluffy, mink fur slippers and went to log on to her computer. It was back to the mundane reality of checking emails, an essential aspect of empire-ruling these days. The first email she opened was about the identity of a particularly annoying hacker who had been revealing the financial irregularities of the super-rich. Not that she cared about any of those one-dimensional idiots who only thought about acquiring more money and hedonistic pleasures; it was more that her businesses were getting caught up as part of the collateral damage and she didn't want any further scrutiny of her activities. In a way, she thought the hacker was quite noble, risking his skin for such a worthwhile cause, but a threat was a threat.

She replied to her email to her Operations Department, thus:

Yes, please take immediate action. I suggest short-term surveillance to identify any co-conspirators and when all information is collated, frame the perpetrator for a humiliating crime (e.g. child pornography, but only to a level where bail can still occur). The framing will need to be done in a way that means friends suspect that he is being targeted. Then a week or two later, once he has been bailed and is awaiting trial, eliminate him, but make it look like a suicide. Let his co-conspirators live for a month, so they can spread their fear, and then eliminate them in whatever gruesome fashion you see fit.

Fiorella

Her next email read:

Yes, I do agree that the coral colour on that cloth will suit nicely for the décor of the new reception area. I want it to be welcoming and put people at ease. Also, that custom-built sofa-chair that you sent ... YES! That will need to be in the reception, too.

Fiorella

Fiorella had the tendency to send her emails in chunks, as she often would often remember other things that she had forgotten to put in the first message.

Oh, I forgot to mention. Please chase up the police to see how they are doing with regard to our missing Oso sales director. The police have had a fair few weeks and I have not seen any updates. I want to know if the destruction left behind was due to a struggle, or if he had simply gone mad due to his significant cocaine consumption and disappeared into the ether. Although he was Sales, he did have some worth to the organisation, so I do want to find out what happened.

Fiorella

She then came across an email that was worrying enough to cause a raised eyebrow on her face. She even went as far as to print the email and its attachments. Like all issues that required a bit more thinking for Fiorella, she jotted down the key points on paper, so they were right in front of her. She could barely remember that she had okayed the Operations Department to have this now-missing person's death faked and then to have him experimented on in one of her medical research labs. She even had to go back to her old emails to double-check. What happened had definitely caught her interest.

She felt it was apparent that whatever organisation was behind this was so professional that they were able to get rid of any and all evidence, even to the point of making all the dead — and possibly alive bodies — disappear. That the act had taken place within a U.K. court in broad daylight added to the level of professionalism required. Not only this, but no genetic matter was anywhere to be found. Even in today's run-down courts with their ineffective privatised security, it was surprising that whoever had done this was able to do it this well. The police officers that she had on her organisation's books reported that not one iota of evidence was found and the CCTV simply did not record for the duration of the incident, after the man was brought into the court.

What added to her belief that this organisation did not want this man to be known was that any photographic or CCTV evidence of him in any previous hospitals, prisons, or anywhere else that might have recorded him, simply did not seem to exist. It didn't stop there, as the media at the court had all conveniently gone elsewhere to cover a drugged celebrity exposing himself. Clearly this target was quite an important man and Fiorella wanted to find out why.

The only people that Fiorella believed could have committed an act with such professionalism were her own. It would have cost her tens of millions, but it would have happened if she had really wanted it to. She quickly deduced it couldn't have been her known competitors as her spy-network was that good she would have easily found out such actions in advance. This gave her cause for concern, as it meant that an unknown organisation was potentially as lethal as hers. Also, she thought that these people may have acted in the knowledge that her organisation was targeting the imprisoned man, which concerned her, as it meant that there was a possible mole or moles in her organisation.

Fiorella felt that, as good as these people were, there were definitely flaws in the covering of their tracks, none of which made sense.

"They went about getting rid of all visually recorded data on the man," she pondered "leaving not one trace of their tracks, but they let all the medical records of the man survive. Perhaps the medical significance of the man was of no importance, but it also meant that the most unbreakable link for identification still existed: his DNA. There was also the fact that although the witnesses in the court were clearly eliminated in an effective fashion, witnesses from the previous hospital and the prison are still alive."

Fiorella then mused, "If these people were that good then why didn't they eliminate those witnesses as well?" Fiorella's back suddenly shot straight up and she quickly dialled her Operations Department.

"Hi, Steve, so you're on call today. It's an urgent one, it's about ... Oh, you already have your people on it. That's wonderful, Steve ... What? Our man is the only witness that is left ...? Even the prisoners? *Puta madre* ... I know you already have our finest people watching, but you need to increase the surveillance to the point where we even know when he blinks ... We can't make it too obvious, so the doctor isn't to be notified. I want at least one of these people captured alive, as we need information about this new organisation."

Fiorella paused for a few seconds before she spoke again.

"Update me if you find anything more about this man that escaped from the court and if there is anything interesting about his DNA. Thank you, Steve."

Fiorella sat back; she had a strange feeling, the like of which she had not felt for a long time. It was fear of the unknown and fear that this new hurdle might actually pose a threat to her and her plans. Like all obsessives and control freaks, she went back to the information at hand to repeatedly analyse it, hoping to uncover a new idea.

When she delved deeper into the man's slender file, she saw that what led him to be arrested and put in the hospital was that he was apparently running away from a mugging gone wrong.

"Obviously it can't have been that. There's a possibility that he was trying to escape from this unknown organisation. Clearly he is someone with specialist training as the way he easily dismantled so many within the prison would not be achievable by someone with ordinary skills." This train of thought took Fiorella to other known facts, none of which led anywhere and eventually it all came to a stop when she realised there was nothing more to add. She reluctantly decided to plan for how to limit further damage and repair the damage that had already been done.

The main cost of the incident was that the organisation had lost a judge and two barristers that were on their payroll. In many countries, acquiring new — and corruptible — representatives of the law at that level wasn't a difficult task, but in the U.K., it did require a great deal of time and effort. Of course, ultimately, the organisation would find replacements and Fiorella had every confidence, as there was always a way to bend people. This convincing took a substantial amount of resources, however, as many an investigation for blackmail was required and also a lot of money was needed for generous bribes.

Fiorella sighed and gave herself a little reprieve from her work by spinning around on her desk chair. With every few spins, she alternated the direction. Then suddenly, she stopped, spun back so she was in front of her computer and wrote an email to Human Resources with the Operations Team cc'd in. It was a simple order saying that she has authorised initial funding of five million pounds for the recruitment of a judge and two barristers. If further monies were required, then they would have to request them directly from her. As lavish as Fiorella was with her employees and her organisation, she was stringent about any waste that went into operations. She was lavish so that her henchmen were effective and loyal, but not wasteful. To ensure efficiency, an all-seeing eye was used and this meant every penny was accounted for through her AI system, which was ever-present, sifting through the tiniest pieces of data.

As Fiorella was only one person and always wanted to have complete control of her empire, she embraced such technological advancement that allowed micromanagement of thousands of her henchmen. Her AI gave her the terrifying ability to control all her black-market staff, as it was learnt from her own behaviours and intruded into every facet of their private lives. Access to deeply private information and her AI meant that nearly all irregularities in behaviours, potential predictors of disloyalty and significant risk factors were brought to her attention. This allowed her near-complete knowledge and control of the entire fabric of her organisation.

After spending around twelve hours working at her desk, Fiorella felt her stomach rumble and tell her it was time for her dinner. She pressed a green button underneath her desk and a couple of seconds later her office door opened. In walked a well-dressed man with a bulge under his suit jacket where his gun was holstered. As soon as he walked in Fiorella's lust became aroused. She admired her guard's soft, chocolate-coloured skin. He immediately stood at attention. After ogling his shoulders, buttocks — she'd had had a mirror installed on the other side of the room so she could do this —, and the large bulge at his crotch, Fiorella noticed his hypnotic green eyes. She was torn: did she want food, or did she want to devour this alluring man? As she sat with her legs crossed, she swung her chair from side to side and looked the guard up and down. Not wanting to be forgotten, her stomach responded with an angry rumble.

"My very beautiful man, I am ever so hungry," she said.

"What do you desire, Ma'am?" he enquired whilst looking into the distance behind her.

Fiorella responded with a smile.

"I'm sure you can tell what I desire ... but I'll need the energy first as I think you are the type who will last and last. Yes, tell our chefs to make me something ... Japanese," she drawled before she shooed him out with her hand.

Chapter 17

In a way, the company that Little Dog provided did not affect my nerves as much as I first thought it would. The canine didn't get in the way at all and in fact, I found it somewhat uplifting that after each slap or blow I gave someone, the supernatural being gave a happy yelp of approval. Admittedly, this meant that I did go a little overboard compared to what I would usually do, as I had this new-found urge to impress. Such feelings were all new to me and it actually didn't feel as degrading as I initially thought it was going to be.

Once I had my money, I shot off and bought five wood-fired pizzas from a takeaway. I plonked myself just outside the restaurant's wall and messily ravaged the lot of them. Little Dog had disappeared by this point, but, as if by instinct, the supernatural being reappeared as I was venturing out to earn more money — this time for other reasons — as my libido had been reinvigorated. When I had acquired enough pennies and provided Little Dog with some further entertainment, I headed to the red-light district, visibly on full mast. Even with a trench coat on it was obvious what was on my mind. This time the supernatural being tagged along and even watched the sex. At times, when I looked over whilst having my way, I noticed the clear interest on the canine's face. One of the prostitutes thought it disconcerting, but I assured her that Little Dog was not going to join in and that there was nothing to worry about.

Finally, after these two needs were filled, I was able to think again with a clear head and that was when I thought it appropriate to see if the supernatural being had fulfilled its side of the deal. This meant a trip to the library.

"Forgive me, Little Dog, but it's still quite a difficult prospect to grasp. Also, trust is of course earned and not simply given," I said as we walked.

"Have you not earned the trust of your own senses? It really isn't a difficult concept, my dear chap and you saw it for yourself. If it makes you feel better, though, let's go down to the library, as you desire, although I haven't the foggiest idea what you will find there," Little Dog replied, with some incredulity.

There was a considerable walk to the closest library as there were increasingly fewer and fewer in Manchester. Access to knowledge was slowly becoming the privilege of the few. When I reached it, I immediately sought a computer to check the internet for all news outlets that might have reported on the court case. There were many news stories about the court, but only in relation to the missing staff and that no one knew how they had disappeared. It was also noted that the violent criminal that was *me* was missing. Then there was the related public uproar about how the authorities had "let this happen" and how there was absolutely no visual evidence to describe what I, the mad, violent fugitive, looked like. I repeatedly refreshed the internet browser over the space of a couple of hours, but still no significant evidence of what had actually occurred within the crown court appeared.

Even with this clear-as-day proof, I was still apprehensive about Little Dog's offer. Of course, there were natural anxieties about the fantastic situation, but there was a feeling that there was going to be a *con* in the deal … was I going to be left twiddling my thumbs as malevolent forces sought retribution against me? I was just about to further question the self-proclaimed deity when a librarian suddenly appeared and berated me in the quietest way possible.

"Excuse me, sir. I am afraid you're not allowed any pets in here," she hissed.

The librarian turned to Little Dog and gave it a compassionate look. She then looked at me with a disgusted and disapproving face.

"Poor little thing," she muttered.

Little Dog, who had been lying down on the desk, perked its head up, slowly got up, stretched and then looked around to see if there was anyone else about. It then licked its lips as it looked the old, plump librarian up and down.

"My dear, you smell absolutely delightful," Little Dog chuckled with an almighty vicious grin on its face.

The briefest look of horror erupted on the librarian's face, but it quickly returned to a disapproving scowl.

"Quite the juvenile joke, that. I am afraid the rules are the rules and you must follow them."

"Look at the way that fat wobbles on your jowls as you talk. Looks so very succulent … but I really shouldn't. I mean, I dread to think of the number of calories that you are. You'll go straight to my hips."

This time it was clear to the librarian that I hadn't said a word.

"W-w-what? D-d-don't be daft. Is this a prank? Is this some kind of robot?" she stammered.

"Well, clearly you want me to, as you keep on strutting your meat right there in front of me. I suppose it's quite understandable, as it is a privilege to be eaten by a god. Anyhow, I would hate to be rude and refuse you."

The dog's jaw and mouth rapidly multiplied in size as its head melted into a floating black liquid with the one viscous snouted mouth attached. The mouth grew until it was just a bit bigger than the librarian. The colour completely drained from her face.

"It's j-j-just a silly prank. V-v-very silly prank," she said as the jaws and sharp teeth surrounded her. A muffled scream came just before the first chomp. A split second later, Little Dog's head shrank back to its regular self and the sound of crunching bone could be heard as the canine slowly chewed its snack.

"Must always remember to eat slowly and savour. Otherwise, the moment is simply gone too fast," the canine whispered to itself just after it swallowed.

I raised an eyebrow. I had watched the events in mild discomfort. It seemed that a great deal of my previous anxiety from watching such brutality had turned into more of a morbid fascination. I suppose I felt that it wasn't every day that one gets to watch an alleged deity devour people, so there was some interest there and I didn't really have a choice in the matter. Soon after, a confused-looking member of the public came into view.

"Sorry, I thought I heard a scream," he said before disappearing after I gave him a scowl.

"I know, I know, I said my role was to just observe and ensure that no evidence leads back to you, but sometimes I simply can't control myself. I do get rather peckish at times. I suspect, my good chap, that I have opened the floodgates and I'll have to chomp on a few more, as that librarian really was quite marvellous. I really do recommend that you give human meat a try," Little Dog mused.

I turned back to the computer and checked a few other news websites. As obnoxious as Little Dog was, it appeared that it was sticking to its side of the deal. I turned back to the canine and stared at it as it vigorously licked at its nondescript crotch. It felt rude to interrupt so I waited until it noticed me.

"Yes, yes, my good chap?"

"I suppose it is a silly question, but for some reason, I am curious about this: do you feel remorse?"

"What do you mean, Cain?"

"Well, for me to harm or kill I need a good reason. I don't think I have ever committed violence without a good reason. If I did what you just did there, I think I would probably regret it."

"Did you not hear me before? I was *peckish*. Bloody good reason, that. I could paint you a million and one fanciful explanations of why I don't feel remorse and fill them all with impervious legitimacy, but that would not be me. Perhaps you would think differently if you had a taste. I can save you a bit of thigh next time, if you want?"

"As curious as I am about how a human would taste, there is a part of me that just wouldn't let it happen. So, thank you, but no thank you. I thought a being as powerful as you are wouldn't need to eat to sustain yourself?"

"HA! You sly little rascal, you're still trying to find a weakness, I see. Of course, I don't need to eat humans or anything at all, to be honest. I suppose if you want the most basic reason for it, then it's just to pass the time, as it's quite a fun thing to do. Perhaps in a few hundred billion years I'll get bored of it, but for now, it's a bit of a hobby and by Jove, I can't give it up when humans are such a tasty lot. Any more questions?"

"I suppose, as you have just mentioned Jehovah and with the supernatural now seemingly the norm, it has given me more of a curiosity with regard to religion again. I might as well ask whether a monotheistic God that encompasses all, exists?"

The supernatural being gave a yawn before it replied.

"It depends on what your understanding of existence is and what a God is. Unfortunately, you only have one life and it would take far more than that for me to truly explain such concepts to you. Also, I couldn't provide you with a reply that you would understand since it isn't a yes or no answer. I would need to speed up your evolution and then teach you a completely new language; English is much too clumsy to even express the most basic of points. Your mathematics and physics are only slightly more expressive, but they still negate the most complex fundamentals. So, unfortunately, with your languages and your level of comprehension, I can only answer with a Yes, there is and a No, there isn't."

Blood rushed to my head and my fists, as I was still not use to such condescending interactions. I knew there was no point in being aggressive, so in the end I only huffed.

"By all means continue with the theological or philosophical questions, but you will find that you're simply not capable of understanding many of the answers. Not that you are a stupid; compared to other humans you are relatively intelligent; it is just that your species is quite dim overall. Anyhow, now that we have nattered about theology, how about you tell me what your plans are, Cain," Little Dog said with slightly more tact.

I let out a sigh, as I didn't feel that the alleged deity would give me any meaningful answers to my questions.

"I suppose there is some difficulty in deciding where to start, Little Dog. There are, of course, a lot of people on the list whom I want to die, but now that I am put on the spot, I can't seem to decide on a single one. I feel that although my campaign is on the go — and we will certainly get to that — I still need to test the waters some more, just to get the feeling of which direction the current is going."

"For all my bluster, I am quite an easy-going one, Cain. I will let you decide and we can go from there. If it helps, perhaps think of those who wronged you when you were young and less capable."

The first person that popped into my head was my father, but I did not have the foggiest clue of his whereabouts, or even if he was still alive.

"There is always a police station. It could be quite a joyful romp," I said, though without much enthusiasm.

As fun as it sounded, it seemed an idea that just didn't suit the occasion. The former idea had far too much emotional resonance and the latter had far too little. There was, of course, a middle ground somewhere in all this.

"I am sure that is an idea that would entertain, but I am sensing it isn't something that you're particularly enthused about. Perhaps something for which you feel a bit more passion? As you said just now, you need a good reason for such violence," the canine goaded.

I had only begun to pout for a brief second when my mind struck gold.

"Ah yes, Little Dog. I had forgotten about this most wretched of places."

"Oh, please do tell, Cain."

"It's a horrible little pub that I actually set fire to once when I was somewhat younger. Unfortunately — and surprisingly — it was a pub that had adequate fire escapes, so no one perished. The clientele of this most deplorable of places was a type of crowd who took a disliking to people like me for not being a few shades paler."

"Ho-ho! You humans are such a funny bunch. Any excuse to hurt others. It's so very entertaining. Sorry for interrupting. Do tell me more."

"Well, I decided to set the pub alight because the patrons weren't the friendliest of sorts. They had opted to ridicule my fashion sense and what they perceived my race to be as I walked by. As I was far too concerned about scoring my next heroin fix, I merely responded with a few expletives and went on my way. They didn't take too kindly to that, though, so they attacked me by surprise. As there were just too many and I was already in a wretched state, I was badly beaten and left for dead. Also, embarrassingly, I was drenched in their urine."

"My dear man, that sounds quite — what is the word I am looking for...? Hilarious. So, you've not sought revenge since you set the pub on fire?" Little Dog laughed.

"Well, Little Dog, once I had burnt the pub down, I did not know where I could go next to pursue these individuals, as I had destroyed their spot for congregation. Also, back then, as chemical hedonism was my top priority, I did not fancy putting huge efforts into aimlessly searching the area for them and it was not long until I had simply forgotten about them. It was only more recently, a day before I started the bumblebee campaign, that by chance, I came across the old pub, standing there as if nothing had happened to it at all. Unfortunately, I didn't have the time to investigate as I had far more pressing matters to attend to." Rather than waiting for the supernatural being to respond, I quickly spun around on my chair to face the computer and typed the pub's name into a few search engines.

"Well, according to the local news and social media, it's still a place filled with such far-right dregs. I think we have a winner, Little Dog!" I said with surprising enthusiasm.

I did feel a bit odd afterwards, as I assumed the process of planning mass murder would have at least given me some ethical misgivings, but I felt none at all. In response, Little Dog barked in excitement and wagged its tail.

"There wouldn't be much use in walking on down straightaway, it's much too early. I imagine mid-evening would be the time to make our move, Little Dog. Until then, I am going to do something I've not been able to do for quite a while. I haven't read a book in such a long time and we are, of course, in a library. I know you've had to put up with me getting food and dabbling in a prostitute or two, but I assure you that you will see some very interesting violence later."

"Don't worry, my good fellow. I'll pop back when you're ready. See you soon and please do enjoy the reading," Little Dog replied with a vicious grin.

Chapter 18

The way time goes by when you're omnipotent is different from the way a human feels time. Depending on one's frame of mind, in certain circumstances, one second can feel as long as a billion years. For Little Dog, due to its level of excitement, it felt that it was stuck in one of these moments. Waiting, for an omnipotent being isn't a difficult task, it was just that the deity had given itself the characteristic of impatience, as it thought Earthly reality would be far more entertaining with that personality flaw.

It had tried billions of combinations of character traits in its lifetime, so it knew which ones kept it the most entertained for longest. The omnipotent canine only had to make it so that it no longer felt boredom, but it knew, as soon as that happened it would be a slippery slope down into the eventual pits of Nirvana. Being one with all of creation and simply "being" did have its perks, as there was a sense of contentment that coursed through every fabric of space and time with the one who was in Nirvana; but when you've done it once, there wasn't much point in doing it again as there was certainly nothing new and exciting about it.

Little Dog paced in a small circle in the sun, trying to think of ways to pass the time as it felt some distraction was needed. As much as Little Dog hated waiting, it knew that to outright force a life form into doing what it wanted quickly led to boredom. But there were times that required a nudge here and there to help the performance along. Even with billions — or perhaps trillions — of years of experience toying with life forms, Little

Dog still found it a difficult balancing act when it came to not trying to meddle too much or too little.

To end the sudden pang of tedium, the deity thought that perhaps it could look for an advanced civilization to destroy. Often such destruction created spectacular explosions that were filled with an incredible array of colours, crackles and smells. However, the downside with such life forms was that they had often reached such high levels of spirituality, with assistance from their technology, that they were never that bothered about being obliterated. There were rarely screams of terror or pleas for mercy; it was more a peaceful acceptance of their impending doom.

There was the option of destroying a backward civilization like the human race, of course. That would have been hilarious at first, due to the absolute terror it would have caused. The pleas, the prayers, the crying and subsequent infighting; it was the sort of comedy that the deity enjoyed, but it knew it would quickly fall into boredom again, as such total annihilation would be far too quick and easy.

Little Dog then tried to think of other civilizations or monsters it could extinguish, but it soon gave up, as it found it had far more of an urge to be the audience. It knew it wasn't going to find anything to watch that would be particularly interesting, but that wasn't an issue, since all it needed was something mindless and marginally entertaining, to distract the deity until Cain was ready.

To find out about the possible choices for such entertainment, Little Dog telepathically communicated with its intergalactic network of

RN7825 plants. The seeds of the RN7825s had been slightly modified by Little Dog so that they were linked to its own telepathy and then were scattered across the universe. The seeds would float through space until they came across an abundant vein of dark energy. When they did so, they melted into an adjacent dimensional layer so they could more easily latch onto the dark energy.

The plant itself grew out into our dimension whilst the roots remained on the different plane. It grew ten centimetres tall, with the head looking like a reflective bauble and the stem appearing to be made up of thousands of tiny sharp, purple crystal shards. When such plants grew, they created a permanent microscopic wormhole that could psychically interlink with other RN7825 plants and this ultimately built into a network through which they were all instantaneously connected. The most important thing about these plants was that they were able to sense minuscule reverberations within the flows of dark energy. From this, a grainy, low-resolution image of the complete galaxy was created by the plant, which originally helped the plant identify when to shoot seeds off into space. This live streaming of the galaxy was what Little Dog tapped into and was one of the tools it used to help find fun things to do. Little Dog did have the option of splitting itself into trillions of copies of itself and then having a root around but existing as more than one of itself felt quite wrong for the deity.

After tuning into this network, Little Dog came across various different ideas of what it could watch to pass the time. After a fantastically quick and complex thought process, it decided on a bloodthirsty, insect-like alien species called the

Braxins. This species' queen, fortunately, survived its planet's destruction and was hibernating deep in a meteor that was the last remnant of her homeworld. The queen's luck went near to the point of the impossible, as fortune had allowed the meteorite to head on a collision course with a planet filled with an assortment of humanoid snacks. Of course, if the meteorite hadn't been nudged a few metres by a black Scottish terrier's paw, it would have harmlessly floated in space until the queen eventually starved to death a few months later.

Just as Little Dog was about to fold the fabrics of space and teleport, it remembered that there was someone left on Earth that had far more potential to entertain than the Braxins. The deity's tail started to wag and a mischievous grin arose.

"Ah yes, the doctor!" the deity said to itself.

Within a split second, Little Dog had disappeared and reappeared in the small but very well-groomed garden of a small modern detached house in Leeds. The deity thought Cain would probably find the meticulous symmetry too cold and calculating. Under the rare shine of an English sun, Little Dog merrily paced towards the house. As the deity was about to step within the view of the attached surveillance systems and alarms, they all powered down.

Little Dog reached the back door and it happily greeted the deity by opening itself up wide. The kitchen that it skipped into was well stocked with equipment, ordered like army regiments and fastidiously clean. The deity then reached a fashionably decorated living room where the walls were made up of open brick and white painted wood panels. Bright, abstract paintings decorated the walls and a brown leather Chesterfield sofa was the centrepiece of the room. The doctor sat on a medicine ball at a nearby dining table, typing away on a laptop.

Just as the doctor looked up and saw Little Dog, the front door was booted through. It was perfect timing for the deity. The doctor jolted up and within a second reached behind a large bookcase, pulled out a French duelling sword and put himself in an offensive stance. As ready for a fight as the doctor was, he certainly would have stood no chance against the five machine guns that were held by the five men dressed in combat gear. The men seemed to completely ignore the doctor as they scanned the room. After a couple of quick hand gestures, the intruders spread out and disappeared to search throughout the house.

Little Dog lazily strolled to the sofa and jumped onto it. The deity sat there and, with some bemusement, watched the confused doctor put his sword down. By the time the five men returned to the room after searching the house, the doctor's face was calm and collected.

"Fiorella instructed you people to monitor me after that incident at the court with my patient," he remarked.

"Yes, Doctor Knörr, there is no use hiding that now. The surveillance systems and alarms we set up all powered off, so it seemed that you were set to be the next witness of the patient to be eliminated. However, there are no signs of any threat. It is most unlikely that such technology would have all ceased functioning ... can I ask if you have noticed anything unusual, perhaps, or whether it was yourself who tampered with the devices?" one of the five grim-faced men questioned without a hint of emotion in his voice.

"Please, call me Mads. Well, first of all, I am not a traitor, so I would not toy with your obviously placed devices ..." Mads stopped and glared at the henchman who asked the questions for a few seconds, before speaking again.

"The only thing I have noticed out of the ordinary is that lost Scottish terrier over there on my sofa. Somehow it has wandered into my house. I do not know how, as all of my doors were locked."

Immediately the five henchmen raised their weapons and pointed them at the deity. Little Dog inquisitively tilted its head as one of the men was motioned to investigate. As the henchman approached, Little Dog lazily fell onto its front.

"Mr dear boys, I do worry that your meat looks much too lean and tough. You all get far too much exercise — but then again, perhaps it will have given you all a rich musky flavour," Little Dog teased.

All five guns were raised and all five fingers pulled at triggers that did not work.

"We can't be disturbing the neighbours, it would be terribly rude," Little Dog joked.

The men were so well trained that they didn't even flinch at the oddity of the situation. All pulled out their pistols and squeezed the trigger, but as they did not work either, they then pulled out their knives. Just as the closest one was ready to pounce, a tentacle with a vicious wolf-like snout morphed out of the deity's back and rapidly grew in size. It then shot out and chomped the closest henchman in half. Before the legs could fall down, it chomped again and swallowed them whole. A look of panic could be seen from all but Mads, who had a look of morbid curiosity on his face.

Four more tentacles with fanged, wolf-like snouts grew out of Little Dog and all immediately went about feasting on the remaining henchmen. Within seconds it was all over and not a drop of blood was left.

"I must say, I was quite right, their delectable flavour certainly made up for the toughness of the meat."

All the tentacles licked their lips and snouts before they morphed back into the deity, which was still lying on its front on the sofa.

"Take a seat, my good doctor, take a seat," Little Dog encouraged and nodded at the space next to it on the sofa.

The doctor cautiously approached and gingerly sat down at the other end.

"Marvellous, you have passed the first test. If you had chosen to run, I'd have eaten you as well. A coward does not deserve to be involved in my fun."

Mads raised an eyebrow in response.

"Who and what are you?" he enquired in a deadpan manner.

"Right to the point and somewhat rude, I must say. Anyhow, I am Little Dog, not my real name but what people seem to be calling me these days. A pleasure to meet you."

Both gave each other a quick nod.

"Well, to be brief, as I do not wish to waste our time, I am what you humans would call a *god* and I am here to make you a deal. It is, of course, one that you can refuse, but I imagine that you will see the perks quite irresistible."

The doctor did not respond, as his brain was hard at work trying to analyse what was going on.

"A sceptical mind is a healthy mind, so I will not hold it against you if you do not so easily take me at my word. As for you, your mind has just witnessed a small canine eat five highly trained killers and then claim that it is a god. For a human, a great deal of mental gymnastics is required to process something that novel. But as I find my patience lacking today, I will do this, as it may more easily convince you. Look to your left."

Mads turned his head to see that his laptop was floating just beside him. Although his face remained inscrutable, he quickly grabbed at the laptop and looked at what was shown. Little Dog was patient and allowed him all the time he needed to fully analyse the information. The doctor let out a heavy sigh after he had interpreted what was shown.

"All those years of work ... and it is completed in a mere few seconds. My purpose and all that sacrifice made meaningless," the doctor muttered.

"My good doctor, your research is nothing compared to what I can offer ... I suppose someone like you will have to see it to believe it. Come, look into my eyes."

Mads did as he was told and it was just a second later that his face, in quick succession, became a mask of total surprise, happiness and then absolute sadness.

"I had to dumb it down quite significantly for you so that you could comprehend some of the majesty. Also, that was only a small taster; the wonderment of the whole universe can be made known to you — that is, for a price."

"What do you want from me?" Mads was just able to hoarse out with a manic glint in his eyes.

"Well, it's rather simple, really, I want you to entertain me, my good doctor." Little Dog chuckled, with an ear-to-ear grin on its face.

Chapter 19

Little Dog and I both stood watching the pub's entrance, a good distance away. A picture of a simple chess-like castle that was coloured in with the cross of St George was the pub's emblem. The name of the pub was George's Fort. The closest signs of civilisation were three giant, ominous blocks of flats that stood a kilometre away and huddled together like suspicious teenagers. There was nothing else around the pub but a few of the patrons' cars and a couple of flashing streetlamps.

The pub's walls were once a creamy white, but parts had become so mottled by dirt that they resembled a cowhide pattern. Broken glass littered the floor all around the place like a riverbank of colourful pebbles. The downstairs windows were boarded up with metal screens, something that gave no indication that the pub was open for business. It was the loud muffled shouts, roars of laughter and the occasional outside smoker, that were the clues to this Salford pub being open for business.

I put my rucksack down against a nearby lamppost and walked all around the pub to see if there were any better ways in than the front entrance. At the back, immensely tall, jagged fences and a locked metal gate — both with that extra touch of barbed wire on top — blocked the way. Although the pub seemed identical to how it was before, it had certainly become more armoured.

There were a number of choices with regard to how I was going to make my entrance. Of course, the most sensible method was to go back home and collect some tools so that I could easily break in from the back, but as sensible as that sounded, I simply didn't have the patience. Also, I had the urge to be dramatic and such theatrics were now possible as I didn't have to worry about evidence. I walked back around and spotted a couple of thirty-something male skinheads who had come out to smoke in front of the entrance.

The tall one, who was so tall that he towered over my rather average height, was sporting a muscular physique but also a chubby baby face and a large potbelly. The other was a short, skinny man with a sharp face. Both were dressed in smart, short-sleeved shirts and jeans. Their arms and necks were decorated with various tattoos, some of which had nationalist iconography. They shared the one lighter and took turns lighting up their cigarettes before they talked. It didn't take long until they both noticed Little Dog and me standing close by, watching them.

"Oi. Fuck off, we haven't got any change," the shorter one snapped.

They carried on with their conversation, which appeared to be about an experience at a brothel. The story sounded quite tedious and it was clearly aimed at inflating their own egos. I carried on staring at them as I let my rage fill me up, drip by drip.

"Oi! Didn't I tell you to fuck off, you fucking smelly Paki cunt. Take your curry-stinking arse and fuck off with your stupid fucking dog," the shorter one shouted.

"I don't think he's a Paki Tim. Looks a Chink to me," the taller one said with a chuckle.

The shorter one turned back to his friend and gave him a scowl before turning back to me.

"All right then. You Chink-Paki-Nigger foreign cunt, take your fucking lunch that you're walking and piss off. Otherwise, I'm going to come over there and stomp your fucking face into the pavement!" the shorter one screamed to the point where his face went blood-red.

I felt the final drip fall into my tank and a little smile crept onto my face as there was no turning back. I calmly walked over to the two men with my face to the floor and my right hand behind my back, holding a heavy steel bar. Little Dog followed and then stopped when it was a few metres away from the two men. I stopped when I was about a metre from them both.

"Are you a cunting retard or something? YOU SPEAKA INGRISH!? That's it …" Before the shorter one could carry on, I raised my head to look him in the eyes.

In response he spat in my face and just as he raised his fist, I whipped out the steel bar from behind my back and swung it right into the side of his temple. Blood spattered all over me and his compatriot as his skull crumpled. Just as the shorter one was falling to the ground, I quickly moved my arm back and swung overhead with enough force to leave a deep indentation in the top of the taller one's cranium. Blood spattered all over me again as he slumped to the ground. I stood there frozen for a couple of seconds and then took a huge gulp of the cold night air. I slowly breathed out, sighing with pleasure.

"Very cathartic, that, Little Dog."

"Ho-ho! I can certainly see why, Cain. Out of frivolous curiosity, do you recognise these two at all? Are they faces you remember from that night before?"

"Unfortunately, I couldn't say so. To be honest, after all that, I don't particularly care. Aren't you going to eat the bodies?"

"Afraid not. They don't look particularly appetising; also, I am not fond of my food being that boozy or that dead, my good chap! Personal preference, but I feel both ruins the flavour. But don't worry, I don't have to eat everything to rid the place of the evidence."

I shrugged before I went and moved both bodies to line up adjacently and horizontally just outside the pub's front entrance. I stood next to the door for a few seconds and took another long breath of the crisp night air. The muffled noise of laughter and yelling could be heard through the large crimson door. For an odd reason, I thought about the blood not showing up on the crimson paint and started to think about which colour paints would best show the stains. I was interrupted by Little Dog.

"Having second thoughts, Cain?"

"Oh, sorry. No — no. I was just lost in a silly train of thought. It's quite odd what the mind can bring up."

I pulled the door open and casually strolled through. The pub itself would be quite indistinguishable from many others if it hadn't been for the odd decoration. There was a St George's flag with the SS skull in opposite corners of it. There was also a Third Reich eagle statue with, instead of a swastika, a St George's flag attached at the bottom.

At first, the clientele and staff, who must have numbered twelve in total, barely recognised my presence, but then pair by pair their angry eyes fell upon me. The lights weren't the brightest, so my blood-covered face probably looked merely dirty to them.

Around a metre away from me sat a heavily bearded giant of a man and a middle-aged woman who appeared to have so much fake tan on that I was unsure if she wasn't actually a minstrel. Suddenly I remembered her face as she was the one who had urinated on me after I was left for dead. Without hesitation, I grabbed the back of the woman's hair and smashed her head right into her pint glass. All that could be heard was the crack of the glass and her body hitting the floor. I quickly turned tail, with Little Dog merrily following behind and waited a couple of metres away on the other side of the entrance.

Angry shouts and screams cut through the cold night before the door swung open and the giant man burst through. He saw me, roared with rage and charged. As predicted, he did not see his two dead compatriots on the ground just in front of him and tripped over them, causing him to careen face-first into the pavement. I simply side-stepped the falling giant, waited until his head hit the ground and stomped my heel with all my might into the nape of his neck. An almighty crack could be heard and the gurgling noises of his death throes quickly followed.

Little Dog jumped and yelped with approval at the brutality. Another patron came rushing out and spotted the bodies on the floor. He jumped over them but found his momentum coming right into the path of my steel bar, which cracked him right on the corner of his forehead. His lifeless body carried on forward and hit the floor whilst skidding a couple of feet. The next man out was far more apprehensive. I walked towards him and was about to rain down a few swings of the steel bar, but he quickly turned on his heel and ran back inside. The door swung shut and I opted not to follow, as they would have either barricaded themselves in or would all be waiting to pounce on me as soon as I opened that front door. Of course, all was not lost.

I piled all the bodies up against the door and then went to an old sedan that was parked up. I smashed the driver's side window, got in and hot-wired the car. As the thing was quite an old beast, it did take a bit of a run-up before it picked up enough speed to break through the pub's back fence. It certainly wasn't the smoothest of rides and, unfortunately for the owner, the car was definitely a write-off. A quick shake of the head was all that was needed to get me over the crash and within no time I had collected my rucksack and pulled out of it three rag-stuffed glass bottles filled with the only cocktail that I have ever enjoyed.

The back windows had not been boarded up with metal screens, as perhaps they felt it was unnecessary, with the intimidating fence that they had. I lit all the bottles and threw them through different windows. It was only seconds later that the shouts and screams came forth.

"Fuck! Try the back! TRY THE BACK!" I was able to make out.

I gave a few shrugs and moved my head from left to right to give my muscles a little warm-up to ensure that my body was ready for what was to come. The smoke started to really pour out through the windows, when suddenly the back door crashed open and out came the patrons one by one, until there were six. They were all coughing, spluttering and some were vomiting. I went to what was left of the fence and leaned against it as they recuperated. Little Dog followed and sat nearby. Eventually, one of the men looked up and saw me: it was the fellow who had run back inside before. He quickly jumped back to be closer to his friends.

"It's him! It's fucking him!" he tried to scream but could only hoarse the words out.

Still coughing and spluttering, the rest of the patrons got up and jumped against the other side of the courtyard. All the angry and scared faces stared at me whilst I glared back at them. I then furrowed my brow as I focused my attention on two of the patrons.

"Little Dog, I should give my memory more credit than I do. I recognise those two, from the night they left me for dead."

I pointed at the only two middle-aged men of the lot. They both looked at each other in confusion. Their faces explained that I wasn't even a memory to them.

"I won't lie. It hurts the ego a bit that you don't even remember nearly killing me. It's rather surprising but I feel a bit awkward now."

I turned to look down at Little Dog and shrugged. I waited until they all seemed a bit less out of breath and then made my first steps forward. They all looked at me and then at each other. Suddenly they came charging at me all at once.

The closest swung wildly at me with his right hand. I struck him square on his knuckles with the steel bar before the fist was even close to reaching me. I followed that with an almighty boot to his testicles. As the fellow was falling to the ground, a compatriot of his popped up next to him. I swung the steel bar right into his jaw before he could attack me and he collapsed on top of his friend. Just as I was about to move into a better position, I felt a rugby tackle from the side and went flying into the air and onto the ground. The wind was taken right out of me and straight after the attacker got off me, a flurry of kicks came from all directions as the remaining lot tried to get their share in.

I let go of the steel bar, grabbed one of the flailing legs and ripped right into the side of the calf with my teeth. Blood filled my mouth and I heard screams as the leg's owner fell to the ground. I quickly used the opening and scrambled away from the barrage. I jumped onto my feet and turned around, to see a steel bar heading towards the side of my head. My left arm shot up, blocked his swing at his wrist and then grabbed the back of his head, pulling it straight into my forehead hard a couple of times. I stood back and launched him back into his compatriots with a vicious push-kick. As the body went flying back, I picked up the steel bar that my latest attacker had dropped.

I edged backwards and soon came to the man whose testicles I had crushed, trying to get his friend's limp body off him. I clubbed the struggling man over the head and he was no more. The man whose leg I had ripped into hobbled over to his three remaining friends. We all stared at each other for a few seconds, waiting to see who was going to make the first move. Not one to ever want to be *too* polite, I charged at the man whose leg I had bitten, as he was the closest. I jumped high into the air and brought down the steel bar onto him ferociously with both hands. He tried to block it, but the steel bar broke through his wrist and went straight into his forehead. The man collapsed on the ground and his blood-spattered onto all those around him. I left the steel bar lodged in the skull, ran at the next closest foe and launched a right elbow that smashed into his chin. The knocked-out man careened into the wreckage of the car and cracked his skull on some metal that jutted out.

The two left were the two faces that I recognised. One of the men took flight and ran. Before the other could make the same decision, I rushed at him and rugby-tackled him to the ground. It wasn't much of a struggle to get him into a rear-naked chokehold. A few seconds later I squeezed hard enough to break his neck. I jumped to my feet and sprinted straight after the last one that was trying to get away. I felt that perhaps he regretted not exercising more, as it only took me ten seconds to catch up. I quickly tripped the wheezing, rotund mass, and he fell to the ground face first. He was quite quick in trying to get up, but I kicked his arms out from underneath him and he fell back down.

"Please — don't! I'm a father …"

"That doesn't negate the fact that you tried to kill me."

"Fuck off, you darkie cun —" Before he could finish, I reached over and twisted his neck like a chicken's.

Just as his body went limp, I noticed a black tentacle grab one of his legs and with a quick snap, it flung the body into the night sky.

"When astronauts land on Mars in around fifty years, they're going to end up with quite the headache trying to figure out why there are human bodies there!" Little Dog chuckled.

I turned around and saw Little Dog sitting nearby with an enormous smile on its face and numerous gigantic tentacles writhing out of its back. The tentacles shot back towards the pub and straight after, bodies started rocketing up into the night sky. When one of the bodies was launched, I heard a scream emerge from it.

"Whoops! My apologies, my good chap, but it appears he was still alive," Little Dog said, laughing, whilst another tentacle launched itself after the body.

A couple of seconds later the tentacle came back holding the gibbering man in the air for inspection.

"I know I shouldn't, but I can't but help feel that I might enjoy it," Little Dog said with some apprehension, before he popped the man into his rapidly growing mouth.

A few chews later and Little Dog huffed.

"I knew he would be far too boozy. Absolutely ruined the flavour!" it sulked.

Chapter 20

It was quite the fun little show for Little Dog. The way humans crumpled or shot out their liquids at the slightest of touches was the most delightful part for the deity. Little Dog certainly preferred the blood being red as well, as it added far more to the atmosphere than any other colour would. Red was bright enough to create a distinction and heighten the emotions, but it was not too bright as to become a distraction. Little Dog had watched violence where the species' liquids were blindingly luminous green and this simply made the brutality look silly. Human blood, on the other hand, perfectly complemented the savagery, so much so that the deity could not but help feel giddy with excitement whenever it spattered.

If the Little Dog did have one criticism of the entertainment it had subscribed to, it was that Cain could do with conflicts that were more challenging. For now, Little Dog did not mind that the fights were somewhat one-sided. It was still somewhat novel entertainment, but it knew the human would have to evolve, otherwise he would soon become far too predictable. Fortunately, Little Dog was quite confident that this was going to happen, whether it was to happen organically or with a few tweaks here and there.

Rather than wait, now that Cain had gone back to his home to sleep, the deity decided to go for a walk around Manchester in the morning hours. The deity didn't fancy sleeping just yet and wanted to wind down with a few more bits of distraction. As Little Dog trotted through the streets of Manchester, it realised it had not actually had a personal look around the city. It did, of course, know every nook and cranny of the place, but it felt that knowing was quite different to experiencing.

As Little Dog walked through Manchester it didn't spot anything particularly exciting or spectacular in comparison to other human cities. In fact, it looked rather similar to every other one, as they all seemed to resemble oversized termite mounds with flashy lights stuck on them. The deity briefly wondered why humans were so full of themselves and had such huge egos when their creations were so simple and uninspiring. A quick deduction and it decided that their confidence came from an overabundance of stupidity, as only such levels of ignorance could hide the fact of how incredibly backwards they were. Little Dog felt that this was to be expected, as humans were just apes who suffered from an extreme form of alopecia.

As Little Dog trotted through an empty park, a young, hooded, scrawny and aggressive looking male walked towards it with three even angrier looking pit bull terriers. The young male spotted Little Dog and looked to see if there was anyone else around. A terrible grin crept onto the young man's face, as there was no one to be seen. The young man unhooked his dogs' leashes and shouted at the animals.

"Get! NOW!"

The three dogs raced without hesitation straight towards Little Dog, all with eyes filled with murderous rage and ready to try to tear the deity asunder. Little Dog didn't run away, of course, but simply carried on trotting ahead. When the three pit bull terriers were within leaping distance, Little Dog turned to face them and lazily raised an eyebrow. All three pit bulls immediately skidded to a stop: just the one look into Little Dog's eyes was all that was needed to convince them to reconsider their ambitions in life.

"OI! What the fuck are you lot doing? I said GET!" the young man shouted.

Little Dog didn't fancy eating dog, as it wasn't a fan of the taste, nor did it like the look of the scrawny, unappetising man, so instead of turning them all into a snack, the deity gave a cheery little bark to the three pit bulls. The three dogs started to whine and looked at each other — they then looked back at their owner. The deity gave another happy little bark. A second later, the three dogs turned and charged at the young man.

"What the fuck are you lot doing? I'm going to fucking lay into you all when we get back. NO! what the fuck …?" he said as the three dogs leapt at him.

Little Dog pottered over and watched with an inquisitive tilt to its head as the young man was torn to pieces. When the screams had become no more, Little Dog left as there wasn't much fun to be had in watching someone else eat their dinner.

Little Dog still felt there was more mischief to be had, so it carried on strolling into Manchester. As the being walked by a busy road, it thought about perhaps causing a multi-car accident — but that didn't arouse any feelings of enthusiasm. It was the morning rush hour and although that would have certainly added to the entertainment, Little Dog wanted something a bit more interesting.

As the deity trotted deeper into the city, the occasional bystander ogled it and exclaimed how cute it was. A couple of people tried to stroke the canine but found that their hand simply went through it. That led to shocked gasps and in one lady it brought on a psychotic episode. Although Little Dog did chuckle a little at her nervous breakdown, it was not entertaining enough for the being to stop and watch the fallout. When Little Dog turned onto another road it felt and heard a large rumble as a large, colourful tram drove by. Fortune had struck: the tram had brought the deity an idea of what it could do.

The idea tied in with a Russian novel from Cain's book collection, the entirety of which the supernatural being had read, as it wanted to have a bit more of an understanding of the human modus operandi. It felt that a lot of what was written was quite tedious, but there was one ubiquitous character that it took a slight interest in and that was the Devil. The fellow sounded somewhat interesting and could potentially be someone Little Dog could have a bit of fun with. But then again, the Devil fellow seemed quite obsessed with humans, perhaps to the point of tedium.

There was one particular incarnation of the Devil from a Russian author that gave Little Dog the spectacular idea of what it could do with the trams that rumbled by. The deity plonked itself near a busy pedestrian crossing that bisected the road and tram tracks. It then watched all the people that walked by. It only took a minute until Little Dog saw a loving old couple holding each other's hands a good fifty metres away and viciously grinned to itself. Little Dog then spotted a food-shopper who was about to go over the tram crossing and telekinetically caused her plastic bag to rip. Out fell glass jars of pasta sauces and a glass bottle of olive oil, all of which smashed on the floor. The shopper was quite the respectable sort, as she immediately picked up most of the smashed glass and rubbish to put into the bin. Once she thought it was clear and all thrown away, the lady made haste to get away from the cause of her embarrassment. Conveniently for Little Dog, she missed two metal jar lids, which were face down and also very well lubricated by the oil.

The old couple ever so slowly — almost to the point that Little Dog felt the urge to force them to hurry up — approached the crossing. It wasn't that Little Dog had any dislike of the old couple, it was just that it felt that playing with such a bastion of true love would provide the most joy. Just as the couple nearly reached the crossing, the red pedestrian light went on. Naturally, the approaching tram did not slow down, but it did pick up speed. The reason for this acceleration was that the tram driver thought she was running late to finish her shift, straight after which she was due to have a more-than-just-friendly drink with a work colleague of hers.

Unbeknown to the tram driver, the tram's clock had a temporary glitch that caused it to show a time that was ten minutes fast. As the tram thundered towards the crossing, the old couple both trod on the oil-covered jam jar lids and slipped forwards onto the tracks, just as the vehicle approached. The tram driver slammed on her brakes as the old couple fell forward, but it was too late. Both their heads rolled off as the tram's wheels went over their necks. Blood spurted all over and some of the nearby bystanders fainted at the sight. Screams and shouts could be heard as people rushed over to see if they could help. Little Dog roared with laughter at the sight: the fainting bystanders made a perfect accompaniment to the ordeal. To get a better view, it teleported onto the top of the tram and looked straight down at the mayhem. Both the heads were grey, as all the blood had leaked out onto the pavement and both were fixed with a look of surprise.

Not that the deity hugely cared, but after a quick think it rationalised that it had actually done the couple a favour. Both of them had died instantaneously and both had died at pretty much the same time. There was no "one dying first and the other being forced to live without the other" malarkey. Little Dog then considered that perhaps it was getting soft, performing such a charitable act. Another bystander fainted and that set the canine off laughing again. A fair few of the bystanders, namely the ones with their mobile phones out recording the carnage, looked around in confusion about why there was someone chuckling away. To get a more encompassing view, Little Dog teleported onto the top of a nearby building to look down.

"Nice to finally meet you ... (unintelligible screech and static noise)," a posh and flamboyant voice said. Little Dog turned around to see a very smart-looking Arabic man with long and slick combed-back grey mottled hair, a long but perfectly trimmed goatee, perfectly sharp eyebrows, and furiously bright red eyes. The man wore a deep burgundy suit with a black shirt, unbuttoned at the top, underneath.

"Perhaps it's best to use Little Dog, as the readership is human and they aren't the most intelligent of sorts," the deity responded.

"What?" The man flashed it a brief look of confusion.

Little Dog responded with a sneer of contempt.

"Oh, so you're being written about, as well? I see. For the sake of the readers, I will use Little Dog then," the man said raising an eyebrow.

The deity's sneer quickly disappeared.

"I see you're stealing ideas, Little Dog. If I may add, rather clumsily, as well."

"Improving on ideas is more like it. So, why are you here pestering me, child? Are you here to join the show?"

"Well, you are visiting my world and you are my guest. So, I am here to greet you, albeit rather reluctantly. Unfortunately, I am not here to entertain, so I hope you do not think me a terrible host. Also, I must add, please don't take into account some of the many dreadful assumptions about my hospitality that you may have read about, as they all fall into the realm of the absurd. Humans can be melodramatic, to the point where they are being quite silly." The man let out a heavy sigh before speaking again.

"I am afraid the reason I am here is to bring to your attention the fact that you are being incredibly clumsy and ruining my own little project that I have going here."

He moved his hand out and spun around to indicate all that was around him. Little Dog stayed silent and stared at the human-looking being.

"I suppose I need to explain a little further. An example is that the tram driver, in a few weeks, was going to have to make a decision on whether to become an adulteress or not. Of course, I would have been there to prod her slightly in one direction or the other, to get the most vibrant and beautiful effects. But now, with your clumsy intervention, she will probably stick it out with her buffoon of a husband and live a dull, uneventful life cowering in the dark due to the PTSD she will have developed. That is only one of many interesting chains of events that you have heavy-handedly demolished with your methods. If you are truly seeking entertainment, then let me show you the importance of the finer details of the human connection and the glorious nuances that these bring," the man animatedly said as his red eyes shone more brightly.

Little Dog rolled its eyes in response.

"By Jove, how boring. Is that what you do for entertainment, child? Whisper in an Earthling's ear to break up their relationships? How on Earth have you managed to do this for so long? It must be as tedious as it sounds," Little Dog mocked.

"Please don't be so flippant and closed-minded. There is much more to it than the vacuous violent entertainment you so enjoy. Slowly manipulating a man or woman is an art form that requires the utmost skill. Do trust me when I say the results are the most spectacular and the creation of such emotional energy when viewed up close is an absolute beauty. The build-up of pain and strife in contrast to the happiness that they have felt is quite simply ... *Art*. You must see that pain has to be slowly built up with finesse, and not so clumsily —"

Little Dog loudly yawned to interrupt the man.

"How incredibly dull. Surely you are not so blind that you can't tell that I am not the type who enjoys such pretentious forms of recreation! I hardly think these barely evolved amoebas are that special, although I will admit that I admire their propensity towards violence. If you had existed as long as I have, I think you'd stop with such silly endeavours ..."

"Please do not belittle me so, Little Dog. Perhaps we got off on the wrong foot. I apologise for that. I have heard of you before, so when I found that you had arrived here on Earth I was perhaps naively hoping for the best. Perhaps in my younger days, your arrival would have brought excitement as I would have been equally keen to partake in such savagery, but now it just isn't as enjoyable as it once was. I must give you credit for having sustained your interest in brutality for so many aeons."

The man then gave a sincere and polite smile. Little Dog's tongue lolled out of its mouth and then dived in on its nether regions for a few long seconds before it spoke.

"You might find this odd, child, but the less powerful something is, the less I find that being's petulance a slight against myself. You, of course, are not the weakest of sorts, so unless you desire the complete destruction of your little blue project after I am through with my toy, I'd suggest you show your elders more respect and not interrupt when I am speaking. If you know of me, then you certainly know what I can do ..."

Little Dog paused for dramatic effect.

"To be honest, child, I still may decide to consume this world after all, as these humans are so delicious," Little Dog chortled.

The Arabic man's jaw clenched and his eyes howled for bloody murder; then, in a split second, he returned to his sincere and smiling self.

"Again, my apologies. I should try to be a more hospitable host. This conversation has been, how shall we say, interesting. I am glad we met, but unfortunately, I must go. If you need anything, anything at all, please do tell me. I will be more than happy to help," the man said with an affable charm and a bow.

"Much better child, much better," Little Dog mocked.

The canine had an almighty urge to consume the being. But it knew it wouldn't be a straightforward task and that the galaxy — or far more — would certainly be destroyed in the process. Little Dog would ultimately be victorious, but it didn't want any serious distraction from Cain and it didn't want to kill his new toy in the process. Also, it felt that this being it had just met certainly had the potential to add to the entertainment.

The man looked at Little Dog and for an infinitely small second, his face turned to one of absolute hate but just as quickly turned back to his cordial self.

"Adieu, Little Dog."

The man then vanished into a puff of smoke. Little Dog shrugged and turned around to watch the carnage below, but to its dismay, it saw that the bodies and the heads had been covered up by blankets. The emergency services were about to move the bodies, but then a terrifyingly strong gust of wind that came out of nowhere, blew the blankets away and rolled the heads into the crowd. A few more bystanders fainted at the sight and Little Dog roared with laughter.

It was only a few seconds later that the deity yawned and realised it had its fill. It felt it was a good time to go to sleep, so Little Dog teleported onto the sun and curled up for a snooze. Just before nodding off, it smiled at the memory of the day's events and felt glad that it had just made an exceptionally powerful enemy.

Chapter 21

It wasn't the most pleasant of dreams and I certainly couldn't figure out the symbolic meaning behind it, especially as I was never one who was competent at understanding symbolic representations. This is because, to me, symbolism is simply invented meaning attached to statistically random behaviours or occurrences and as I don't find life particularly meaningful, I have never bothered with such attempts of understanding. Even though that is the case, the dream I had was such a peculiarity that I could not but help rack my brain to deduce the potential interpretation. I do think perhaps it was all the exercise and endorphins that had been released that gave it such an intensely vivid feel. However, that did not explain the incredible unease I felt about the dream.

My memory of the dream started with me in the middle of a small, sunny and immensely soft, flat grassland that was surrounded by gigantic meadow flowers. The flowers were made up of a myriad different psychedelic tie-dye colours that swirled together and all these giant plants, every so often, uprooted themselves and moved to plant themselves in a different spot. Out of curiosity, I walked towards the flowers. As I got closer, I was able to make out that, from some of these plants, sticky nectar flowed with such abundance that it slowly dripped down onto the ground below. I took advantage of this and went over to put my hand into a sticky glob of the stuff that had pooled. The nectar coated the whole of my hand like a bubble and I gobbled the sweet substance up. It was such a delight that I found myself craving more. I walked around picking up the stuff handful by handful and waffling it down like a hungry gannet. Then, for some odd reason, I had the feeling that I was being watched, so I looked up and saw all the flowers above giving me a disapproving look. I could not help but wonder why they were giving me such daggers, so, sheepishly, I looked around. That was when I spotted that I was wearing a black jumper with yellow stripes. What I was supposed to be doing then clicked.

I trundled through the mud, which for some unknown reason became incredibly sticky; each step took quite some effort, as the wet dirt tried to suck me in. I finally reached the stem of a flower, but it had somehow become ten times the size it was before. It was enormous and the only way up for me was via the hairs that covered the stem. They were just large enough for my hands and they looked as if they could be used as a ladder. I started my journey and after a short while it felt as if I had made wonderful progress, but when I looked up, I saw I still had miles left to go. As I was duty-bound, I continued to climb. After what felt like hours, I looked up again to check my progress and it seemed there was *still* miles left to go. This same process of climbing for hours and looking up occurred a couple more times with the same result: no end in sight. In frustration, I looked down to see if I was moving up at all and all I saw was a giant green stem that went into a deep abyss down below. There was definitely no going back. I tried going faster, thinking that this would be the solution, but it was not the brightest of moves as when I grabbed one of the hairs, I used too much force and caused it to break. I put too much weight on the hair in my other hand to regain balance and that caused it to break, as well. It felt like an eternity as I tried to regain my balance and grabbed at another hair when none were within my reach. I fell right back into the abyss.

As I fell, I felt humiliation and embarrassment due to my failure to be a bee. Such thoughts were the only things that went through my head until I collided with the muddy ground. When I hit, an almighty splash of mud exploded all over. Fortunately, the sticky mud had softened the blow and I was relatively unscathed from the fall. I quickly got up and was ready to give it another go when I noticed an ominous black and chrome elevator sticking out of the ground with its door open. Out stepped a short, round, bald man dressed in a tuxedo. His face had the wobbliest of jowls and he wore a monocle.

"Come, come, young man. He doesn't have all day," the fat man said in a posh English accent.

He then looked me up and down.

"We can't have you looking such a mess when you see him. He most definitely would not allow it."

He waddled into the elevator and came back out with a folded tuxedo outfit. Without any further discussion or introduction, he threw the clothes right at me. The black tux suit and shirt suddenly came alive and immediately began their assault. By the time I had an inkling of what was going on, the tux had already ripped my old clothes off. I resorted to wildly swinging at the blasted thing, but it easily dodged. Whilst this was happening, the shirt kept grabbing scoop after scoop of clean water that had puddled on a dead leaf and threw it at me to clean the mud off. Obviously, I was not impressed and roared in anger. Just as I was about to leap onto the tuxedo, the shirt leapt into my arms and then forced itself onto me until I was wearing it. I then felt the trousers crawl up both my legs. The trousers then became my focus and I tried pulling them down, but they would not budge. Next, the bow tie flung itself at my neck, and when I tried to block it, the tuxedo jacket grabbed my arms from behind and pulled me to the floor. The shirt, still being quite alive, flipped me over and pinned my arms down to the ground so the jacket could casually put itself on me whilst the tie made itself look presentable. Just when I thought it was all over, I felt my feet being tickled and that caused me — reluctantly — to giggle. I was able to turn myself over and looked down to see that a pair of socks and Oxford shoes had squeezed themselves onto my feet. Once the complete tuxedo outfit was on me, it let me get up. I tried to rip the blighter off, but the suit just wasn't having any of it and stubbornly stayed put.

"I am afraid, young man, it's pointless doing that. Anyhow, you look so much more respectable and like a true gentleman. If you did not and I had let you see him looking like a dreadful mess, then I would never have heard the end of it. He is very particular, you see," the old, rotund man insisted as he turned around to waddle back into the elevator.

"Come, come."

As confused as I was, I was curious about who wanted to see me, so I followed. Inside, the black elevator was ostentatiously decorated with a marble floor and gold panelled walls that were overlaid with smaller mahogany panels. On one side of the elevator, there was a mirror, which created the infinity-of-mirrors effect. What made the effect unique was that each reflection of me was doing something different. There were only four buttons on the elevator, two buttons to close and open it and two buttons that had an arrow pointing up and an arrow pointing down. On top of the elevator doors, there was an odometer that simply read *up* or *down* on either side.

"This décor is too much for my liking, but as I said before, he is quite particular," the old man sighed when he noticed me looking around.

He then pressed the down button and it only felt like a second went by before there was a loud *ding* that announced our arrival. The door opened and the old man stepped out.

"Come, come, we don't want to make him wait any longer."

We stepped out into a long, wide corridor. There was a long red velvet runner on black and white chequered flooring that led to two large mahogany doors. The corridor was lit by a warm orange light, but the source of this could not be seen and the light didn't seem to reach the walls. The walls simply appeared as if they went into a deep, dark abyss. Gingerly, I followed the old man to the double doors, which he then opened to present a large office.

Inside the office, the chequered flooring continued and on the farthest wall, there was a large half-circle of a window, with what appeared to be swirling molten magma pressed against it. A large empty mahogany desk and a leather office chair stood near the window. Somehow, on the walls of the eternal black abyss hung framed pictures, all of which were colourful paintings of naked men with large, erect appendages and who constantly moved to change their pose. There were two marble statues in the far corners, both of which had female forms and their own large, erect appendages. The statues regularly changed their positions as well, all of which could be described as lustful. Before I could make head or tail of what I felt about such art, the office chair swung around to reveal a slender and very smart-looking Arabic man with a goatee and slicked back, long, mottled grey hair, dressed in a burgundy suit, slouched and pressed back into the chair with his legs crossed.

"Thank you, my darling Winnie, for bringing me this most interesting man. I imagine you dressed him up, as I certainly didn't expect someone so marvellously cute and dapper," he said in a camp manner.

The slick-looking man then signalled Winnie to come towards him with his finger. Winnie sighed, waddled across and then bent over. The Arabic man sat up and squeezed both the old man's facial cheeks.

"Isn't he the cutest thing you have ever seen? As soon as I saw him, I knew I'd have to have him. At first, he refused to wear his little tux and he was always so quick to throw a little tantrum. It was, 'How dare you, don't you know who I am? blah blah' and 'You will feel the imperial might of the British Empire, blah blah', then he'd huff and stomp around like the little cutie he is. He soon learned to step into line and now he's my most loyal and adorable little servant," the slick-looking man gushed with animated body language.

He then gave a firm spank on Winnie's bottom and shooed him away with his hand. The old man sighed and waddled out of the office.

"Nice to meet you. I have heard so much about you, darling. You are quite the talk of the town — well, on this little blue planet you are." In response, I stayed silent.

"Quite the chatterbox, I see. Any idea who I am?" I shook my head in response.

"Most don't. They have this incredibly silly and extravagant image of me. It's usually filled with wrath, fire, pitchforks and torture. They also all seem to have this awful assumption that I am quite inept in the interior design department. All those images of my home are simply dreadful. Honestly, people don't realise that if you spend aeons living somewhere, you'd have to at least make it tasteful ..." He then paused for a few seconds.

"If you haven't guessed, darling, I am the fellow that many of you call Satan. Although I'm certainly not like the raging monster that those religious types think of me as. Winnie thinks I should do a PR campaign, so they get to know the real me, but you know what, I am not bothered ... well, not enough to do that. Don't get me wrong, I do care about you silly little things, as you are what keeps me on this planet, but to be so vain that I'd go out of my way so that you apes thought of me in a more positive light would be quite a depressing state of affairs," Satan explained and ended with a wry chuckle.

Again, I stayed silent.

"Oh, dear me. Darling, all this silence has me worried that you'll be as grumpy and tantrum filled as Winnie when he first arrived. Perhaps this will put you at ease: if you hadn't gathered, this place really isn't like what those dreadful religious bores say. I don't just let anyone into my home, you know, so perhaps you can feel a bit more appreciative of being invited here. I will tell you what, darling, if it helps, I'll let you ask me anything that is on your mind and I'll answer you as truthfully as I can. Although, let's leave the 'Why am I here?' until last, just so you get comfortable first."

"Am I dreaming?" I asked.

"Someone tells you that they are the Devil himself and you ask such an inane question? I suppose I shouldn't be so hard on an ape like you, it is quite a unique experience for someone of your cognitive powers. Depends on what you define as dreaming, darling, but I can assure you that you certainly are here with the one and only."

I raised an eyebrow, looked around again and saw that all the paintings and statues were watching me. I thought that I might as well play along; after Little Dog, being sceptical had become far more difficult.

"Fine. If you exist, does that mean Jesus, Heaven and a monotheistic God exist?"

"Well, as far as Jesus goes, I can tell you that he certainly doesn't, as that was just some theatrics of mine. Heaven: surely you know that's just wishful thinking? The last part of the question is quite a bit harder to explain. Again, what is a god and what is *the* God? I suppose that's a yes and no."

"What do you mean Jesus was theatrics?"

"Ho-ho! Darling, now you're getting the hang of it. Oh, it was such a marvellous idea of mine. Well, I wanted to create a rather simple religion to follow, one forged of the most compassionate of human attributes. I wanted values that held each human in the highest esteem and that valued love above all else. Of course, there was much more to it, as the beauty of this creation came through what inevitably followed. To do all this, I had to do what I was born for and that was to create theatre. I was the director, the producer and the protagonist." Satan then spun around on his office chair.

"Yes, darling, you might have already noticed that I played Jesus himself. I must confess that I enjoyed the role so much that what you see in front of you, albeit with far less style, is the human costume that I used," Satan said before moving his head from side to side to show off his profile.

"Forgive me, but you don't seem the pious type so why would you create such a religion?"

"Yes, yes, of course, darling, I am certainly not that! Let me explain. As simple as my rules and aspirations were, it was obvious that humans could never live up to them and they would inevitably corrupt the message and add more of their own fictions into that tedious book of theirs. Anyhow, due to its simplicity and how it was promoted, all these poor, depressed folk — and there were oh so many back then — took to it like the most tasty of vices. Once I had planted the seeds, all I needed to do was watch as something that started off so pure and small grew into a leviathan that was shamelessly corrupted by a human taint. What followed was simply marvellous, my darling. The guilt, the shame, the pain, the rage — and those who were the most devout, becoming the most heinous. The beauty of this raw emotion conflicting with a religion built on feelings of love and compassion, brought on such breath-taking performances. Not only that, but it still continues to this day!" Satan cried excitedly.

"I don't understand how you found such beauty in it. To me, it is but human idiocy acting to idiocy."

"Ah. You are looking at it from one quite reasonable perspective; I, another. Of course, there is insurmountable stupidity within your species, there is certainly no denying that, but you neglect the fact that the energy of human emotion is such a sight to behold. To have something so pure of love become corrupted and then for it to bring about so much pain ... the juxtaposition brought from this is what makes the passions appear like an exploding firework within the night sky. This light shining in darkness is given layer upon layer of colour with each twist and internal conflict of the human spirit."

My face must have looked quite unimpressed, as Satan took a pause in his speech and then raised an eyebrow.

"It is like when you were molested by that vicar. The fact that you were so desperate for salvation from your pitiful existence and that it was a devout man who should have been filled with empathy who was the one that utterly destroyed your hope, made the act so much more tragic. That was but one layer that added to the raw beauty of your experience. What added more to this was that this devout and heinous man's internal conflict built for months before that act. He begged God for the fortitude of strength against such desires and yet, ultimately, he succumbed and he would continue to succumb to such desires hundreds of more times with many others. Then there was the disgust and guilt he felt straight after each transgression. Such feelings then corrupted his behaviour at home with his own family and this then twisted and disfigured their own beings. This explosion of pain would then infect others and the art would continue in millions of different shades of raw emotional energy that naturally followed. It is such majesty that one can only quiver in awe."

I responded by exploding with rage and tried to charge at the alleged deity, but he simply wagged his finger at me.

"Darling, I am afraid I don't have the patience for that," Satan scolded.

I found that every sinew of muscle in my body tried to propel me forward, but the tuxedo and shoes had me firmly locked in place. I struggled and grunted but found every effort led to nothing.

"Where was I. Yes, to stop me from yammering on even more, especially as I do love the sound of my own voice, I'll simply say that religion is one of the most wonderful brushes with creating the most beautiful of effects. Now, shall we get to the point of why I have brought you here?"

By then I had given up trying to break through the tuxedo to see if I could kill Satan and had reverted to playing along.

"Fine, fine, I will bite. Why am I here?"

"Well, it's due to your canine friend, darling. The issue is, Little Dog is quite well known for being the petulant sort. I'd destroy the blighter if I could, but to put it bluntly, I don't have the strength or the patience. In a roundabout way, the cretin has said that this little planet will be destroyed if it doesn't get its fill of entertainment. I don't want him to rubbish my pet project, of course, as I am having an absolute ball here and it's at an era that I am finding simply marvellous."

Satan then let out a long, deep sigh. I was in disbelief, as it appeared that another supernatural being was wanting me for their own means. Perhaps some would find some sort of flattery in this, but I just found it a complete nuisance and hoped upon hope that it was only a dream, yet it seemed too real to be one.

"This is where you come in, darling. As silly as it sounds, you are the one that is potentially keeping the old dog from destroying your species' little blue home. This is why I felt I had to introduce myself to you."

Satan then slowly spun himself around in his office chair and stopped to face me again.

"Please don't take offence, darling, you're certainly not my cup of tea. Too much machismo and aggression. Also, what you wear really isn't to my taste. Of course, it is all in the eye of the beholder, but honestly, at the very least try a bit of colour …"

I sighed and rolled my eyes in response, that being the worst that I could do to Satan.

"Ho-ho! I must admit, though, you do certainly have a good amount of chutzpah. I can see why someone like Little Dog would like you. Anyway, I just wanted to introduce myself to you, to see what's so special about you and to say that I will be watching you very closely, as we can't have Little Dog throwing one of its tantrums that it's so very famous for and obliterating the world in the process. Just so you know, if you don't do so well and my beloved project is destroyed, I will be looking for someone to take my anger out on," Satan said with a wink and a smile.

Satan then swivelled around in his chair to face the swirling magma. Before I had a chance to respond, I felt a hand softly touch my shoulder.

"Come on, young man. Time we got you back to where you need to be," Winnie said gently.

The tuxedo had released its grip and that brought on the brief wish to give it another go and try to jump Satan. It was only a split second later that I decided against it, as clearly it would not have succeeded. I followed the servant back to the elevator, downbeat and downtrodden. As if on cue, Winnie tried to comfort me.

"I wouldn't worry so much. Don't get me wrong, he can have his tantrums, but wrath and torture isn't really the Master's thing and if he does go down that route, then he'll quickly grow bored of you. So, if it does go all wrong, I'm sure you'll eventually be okay."

"Are you looking forward to when he is bored with you?" I asked when we reached the elevator.

"HA! Of course not. It would be such a shame. Once upon a time, I was the leader of the greatest empire the world had ever seen, but now I am one of the closest servants to a god! I've gone up the ladder so much, my dear boy, I certainly don't want it to end," he declared, just as he pressed the 'up' button on the elevator.

Straight after, I awoke in my bed.

Chapter 22

"Ma'am, the FSB have confirmed that they will not interfere with the retaliation. They are grateful for the incriminating data on the Chechen leadership and the info around the locations of six turncoat ex-KGB operatives. They are also appreciative that the stripped assets of the Volgograd Bratva mob will go to them," one of Fiorella's minions said in a monotone voice.

"Good. We need to promote this correctly, so get Marketing to send across their ideas to me immediately. All major syndicates and organisations need to be aware that this is what happens when the contracts we enforce are broken. We need to try to recover as much as we can of the market share lost following what the Russians did. Marketing will need to promote the act in such a way that even the Cartels become squeamish when they hear about it," Fiorella commanded.

She frowned and leaned back in her office chair whilst playing with her hair.

"For the Afghans … Once they have been re-established, loan out a platoon to ensure that their production is up and running to full capacity until they have fully restored their manpower. Also, provide fifty thousand US dollars for each man of theirs that was murdered. Throw in a couple of assassinations of their enemies as a token of good faith … And make it clear, in a tactful way, that if they speak badly of our service, they will end up the same way as the Volgograd Russians will."

Fiorella spun around in her chair and rasped like a horse before coming to a stop. In her younger, despotic days, she sought to maintain a rigorous professional image at all times, as she felt that otherwise, her own men would see weakness. This was until she reached such levels of control and power that she could be far more honest in her mannerisms without fear or criticism.

"A quick lesson for you, my *chica bonita*. The hard part is never the killing. To find a way to kill even those with significant power is not a hugely difficult feat. The issue is making sure that there is no retaliation, or no retaliation that will seriously hurt you. To make sure of that, I need diplomacy and for that to be successful, I need to create certainty." Fiorella paused and watched her minion's emotionless face for a few seconds before speaking again.

"This diplomacy started so long ago that it was the KGB I was dealing with back then. Of course, faces have changed and so have attitudes, but because of the work I have put in with and against them, my reputation with the Russians has remained the same. This means that even a new face over there will know where they stand with me. I have created such a stone-clad certainty in what I will do and how I will respond that they put more trust in me than in any syndicates in their own country. Because of this, they can predict the costs with someone like me and can put themselves in a favourable position. But they also know that they have to make a deal with me, as otherwise blood will flow and their impotence to stop it will be shown to the whole world."

"Understood, ma'am," the henchmen responded in the same monotone voice.

Fiorella sighed. She should have known she wouldn't get much conversation out of the woman.

"Any further updates on Dr Mads Knörr's disappearance and the men watching him?"

"My apologies, ma'am, but there are none. Operations have reported no significant evidence that could link to an organisation or perpetrator. They are continuing their investigation."

"Thank you. You may go."

Fiorella puffed and frowned.

The lady saluted. As she left, Fiorella stared at her buttocks, but the sight didn't create any feelings of lust. There was nothing wrong with the woman that had just left, she was one of the most adept in the art of gratification, but for some peculiar reason, the megalomaniac just didn't feel in the mood.

Fiorella's lack of libido was perhaps because she had worked non-stop for the past twenty-four hours, or perhaps it was due to her anxiety arising from this new hidden threat. She had spent many work hours obsessing over who this enemy of hers is, but ultimately, it had led nowhere as there was minimal evidence for her to analyse.

Fiorella took a break from her work, opened a drawer, took out a foil wrapper and popped out a couple of pills. These drugs went down with a cold, left-over black coffee. The medication she took boosted her immune system to a level where it easily eradicated all cancers and any harmful pathogens and also dramatically slowed the ageing process. Another set of foil-wrapped pills came out and Fiorella took a couple. These fooled the body into thinking it had vigorously exercised. Such chemical enhancements meant that, even with such an unhealthy lifestyle of chain-smoking, poor sleep patterns, regularly being sedentary on an office chair for near twenty hours a day and being rarely out in the daylight, Fiorella was at the peak of physical fitness and looked twenty years younger than her actual age. However, even with such chemically aided rejuvenation, her concentration flagged, as random thought jumped to random thought.

There was still so much of her empire to micromanage and check up on, but it did not matter, as her mind was in revolt. Fortunately, the AI carried on undeterred, never needing to stop for any breaks, analysing every bit of information that flowed into her empire and flagging up whether her HR and Operations were needed to investigate, or if, more importantly, Fiorella was needed to investigate. Not one detail was left unanalysed by the AI and its algorithms.

If it hadn't been for the AI, it would have been an impossibility for Fiorella to efficiently run her empire. It was just too big for human competence alone and not only that, the size of her empire was ever-increasing. This meant more and more work was being delegated to the AI. Many others would have been phobic about such choices for internal management, but Fiorella was more than happy to embrace such technological innovation. This was partly because she trusted the AI far more than she ever trusted any human being. It was this technological tyranny over her organisation that allowed her to quickly weed out the disloyal, through analysis of the most minor of changes in their behaviour patterns, work task completion rate, financial records, internet and social media activity, physiology, and movements. It also allowed her to spot the incompetent. However, due to the lack of labour supply within the black market, incompetence was often nipped in the bud with only a severe beating, mild torture and then extensive retraining.

Fiorella spun around in her office chair again. Unfortunately, when one is as powerful, as feared and as hated as Fiorella, there are severe limitations in terms of what you can do to pass the time. Part of the reason why she worked so hard was that there wasn't much else to do. There was the option to go out for a walk, but if she did that, then at least six of her bodyguards would need to accompany her as assassination attempts weren't an uncommon occurrence for her.

Fiorella spun around in her office chair again and she felt her wants and thoughts slowly starting to emerge and link. She knew that the urge to go out somewhere was growing and that she would not be able to fight it. She had been stuck inside her office for the past month and she knew that for her own psychological well-being, she would need to venture out. Also, she knew that frustrated leaders made silly decisions, which was the last thing she wanted when she was so close to the finalisation of APEX. But where to go and what to do? She thought perhaps somewhere in London but didn't want to tempt providence to send another assassination attempt her way, as she was too well known by underground forces in the city.

Fiorella spun around in her chair again as she thought of what to do, when suddenly a flash of childhood memory burst through. It was so vivid that it was as if she had been transported forty years into the past and she was spinning on an office chair in Lima, waiting for a customer to arrive at the flat. Aside from the obvious shortcomings of providing care, her pimp and her madame didn't focus any energies on creating a child-friendly home for Fiorella or the other child prostitutes. There were no toys and no decorations that would have conveyed that any children lived in the apartment. So, all that was left for her to enjoy was her imagination, the wood-panelled television that struggled to pick up channels, and the office chair that she spent hours upon hours a day simply spinning on. Well, that was on the slow days.

Fiorella cast her mind back to those times and tried to think when she specifically decided to kill her pimp and madame. She tried but couldn't remember, it was almost as if the decision had simply *happened*. She did recall that they definitely hadn't expected it of her and never would have, as she was the most agreeable in the group. She did everything that was asked for the four years she was captive and was often pronounced the model prostitute that the other children should emulate.

The megalomaniac fondly recalled that when she did come to that murderous decision, she set about studying her captor's every nuance. She did this to the point that she memorised their habits and could predict with near-perfect accuracy where they were and what they would be doing just by looking at the time. She was even able to pinpoint the times when they were in their deepest sleep.

The day that the act was committed was a normal working day like any other and she put on the same cordial mask that she always donned for such days. It was when the last punter left that Fiorella felt deep down that tonight was the night, as she felt she had finally built up the necessary courage.

The pimp and his partner went to bed without a drop of alcohol and that was what Fiorella wanted, as she didn't wish their terror to be softened one bit. The twelve-year-old Fiorella picked the lock of her room door and sneaked into her captor's room at a time when they were in the deepest slumber. On the bedside table lay two weapons. She had a choice: use her pimp's six-shooter or his hunting knife. She opted for the hunting knife, as she wanted the personal touch.

Fiorella went for the pimp first, as he was the most likely to be able to physically overpower her. She didn't go for a fatal blow straight away, as she wanted him to wake up and realise that he was going to die. After three deep breaths, Fiorella plunged the hunting knife deep into the pimp's abdomen and pulled it out. He let out a groan and she saw the abject terror on his face and just as he put a hand up to defend himself, she stabbed him in his ribs. A gurgling cry leapt out of his mouth. Straight after that, she pulled the knife out and rammed it into his throat. Blood shot everywhere and then the madame awoke, screaming.

The madame quickly reached over her dead partner to grab his gun from the bedside cabinet. She cocked the gun and pulled the trigger, but nothing happened, as the bullets had been emptied by Fiorella just before. Fiorella gave a sincere and kind smile that looked terrifyingly out of place on her blood-covered face.

She remembered that she had taken her time with the madame and savoured every moment.

The memory faded and a little smile had crept onto Fiorella's face, back in the office. It was a memory she had not thought of for what must have been years. She had always felt that was the point where the first domino piece fell that started her empire, as that was her first true taste of power. Because she was so perversely proud of that moment, she kept the name that had been given her by her pimp.

Fiorella realised that she was falling into feelings of nostalgia and quickly shook herself out of it. She spun around in her chair again and that was when the idea of what she could actually do struck. Her cash-cow chemical company, Oso, one of her many legal enterprises, had opened a new office in Manchester a short while ago, but they had only recently fully completed the interior decoration. She was a big influence on such decorations and thought a personal look to the office was needed so she could admire it first-hand. Also, she had never been to Manchester — perhaps there were some sights to behold and enjoy. The added bonus was that a surprise visit to somewhere she had never been before meant there was less chance of an assassination attempt.

Fiorella clapped her hands in excitement and went to the bedroom attached to her office, where her gigantic built-in wardrobe, filled to the brim with designer bespoke clothes and shoes, resided. For someone who rarely went out in public, Fiorella did have an awful lot of choice when it came to fashion, and this meant she now came across a problem that she hadn't faced for a while and that was: *what should she wear?*

Chapter 23

I didn't wake up in the happiest of moods. What made me feel worse was that I had difficulty brushing aside such a silly dream because Little Dog had made a profound dent in my ability to reason. In an attempt to forget about such imaginings, I went and lay down on my sofa and picked a random novel from the floor. As soon as I started, I realised that it was a Russian novel about the Devil visiting Moscow. I quickly threw the book away in a fit of anger, as I certainly didn't have the urges to absorb myself in any story involving Satan. I quickly lost the urge to read after that, so I slowly slunk to the floor and lay still. Every few minutes, I sighed heavily or groaned. Eventually, the sulking stopped and, lethargically, I pulled myself up, sat in the lotus position, and started meditating.

I opened my eyes when I felt that my mind had become as sharp as a samurai's *katana*. With my mind grounded and confident, I was able to see where my path led me that day. The stomach immediately piped in from down below, saying that that amount of violence was going to require a hearty breakfast. It was quite right and there wasn't a thought in sight that disagreed.

I am a zealot in my belief that breakfast is the most important meal of the day. Unsurprisingly, when I do go without morning nourishment, I am far more likely to be caught up in fits of rage and tearful tantrums. As I had recently been imprisoned, I hadn't had time to restock my provisions, so there was a dilemma around what I was going to eat. I looked in my larder and my cooler boxes, but all I could find was a small, potential meal. I wanted to rip into far more than a small, potential meal: I had the urge for juicy, salty, fatty, chunks of meat and with that in mind, the decision to have a classic full English came through.

I got dressed, checked the money in my pocket and quickly had a cup of tea to prep me for my little mission before I was off onto the streets of Manchester. On the way out, the thought that I had killed a fair few people the night before appeared in my mind. I did think that perhaps I would feel a modicum of guilt, but I didn't feel a thing. In my eyes, they had brought it upon themselves all those years ago when they left me for dead. I will admit that there was also many a face there that hadn't been involved. But they were of the same hateful ilk and that was a good enough tie-in for me. Rather than remorse, I went down another avenue and felt emanations of pride in what I had accomplished.

I could not help but feel that I had improved the quality of life in Manchester by just a smidgen. A big smile took hold of my face as I realised that I had taken my first meaningful steps down the path of benevolent vigilantism. What further added to my chipper outlook was that there was far more to come that day.

I walked and whistled along with the morning bird's lusty songs. Soon the noises of nature were replaced by the honks and vibrations of traffic as I went deeper into the city; but even so, my merry whistle stayed. A horde of the morning rush hour came at me from the opposite side of the pavement, but I didn't move out of the way. Grumbles and mutters came my way as I barged straight through the groups of people who so clearly thought the pavement belonged to them. One particularly pretty and dainty lady screamed as she fell over after thinking I'd move for her. Even with such misguided aggression directed at me, I kept my composure and carried on whistling my jolly tune.

Eventually, I reached a butcher's shop on the edge of Salford that had held strong against the increasingly battering waves of gentrification. The butcher was a polite enough man and never showed any fear of me, something that I found somewhat pleasant. He had the attitude that "business is business" with whoever is polite and will pay, no matter one's appearance. He was also always upbeat in communicating with me — I suspect having various meat cleavers and knives behind the counter helped give him confidence.

"Look what the cat dragged in! How do, mate?" the butcher boomed with a friendly smile.

His charisma was so pervasive and infectious that I could not help but respond.

"Hi," I said, just before I squinted and bared all of my teeth in an attempt to smile.

Fortunately, the shop was empty and that meant immediate service. I breathed in the beautiful aroma of raw meat and spices that filled the air. I grabbed a tray of fifteen free-range eggs and put them on the counter.

"A whole ring of Cumberland sausage, eighteen rashers of that free-range beech-smoked bacon and a roll of Bury black pudding ... please," I ordered.

My mouth salivated as the butcher wrapped the produce in beautiful brown paper, like little presents. I paid up and we politely thanked each other before I left. Rather than saunter back home, I opted for a quick sprint. I was travelling at such a velocity that any pedestrians unfortunate enough to remain in my way were smashed over like bowling pins. Within ten minutes I was back underground in my kitchen with a giant grin on my face. The food was prepared with the utmost of speed and efficiency.

On top of what I bought, from my larder I added tomatoes, portobello mushrooms, crusty sourdough bread and the ingredients for homemade baked beans. The hobs were switched on and soon the most heavenly of meaty aromas lazily spread themselves across my kitchen. The sizzling that the bacon and sausages made was the most sensual of music to my ears. Every few seconds my stomach growled for the food and every few minutes I had to (almost violently) stop one of my hands from taking a morsel to nibble on before the whole meal was cooked.

Eventually what lay in front of me were two large plates of identical full English breakfasts. I cooked all the meat I had bought, grilled slices of the sourdough bread, added tomatoes and mushrooms from my larder and went with ten fried eggs. There was, of course, the requisite pot of loose-leaf English Breakfast tea brewing right next to the lot. A crack of black pepper, a little sprinkle of salt and then thirty minutes later I was sitting back on my sofa, the top button of my trousers undone, belly stuck out and burping away in near ecstasy. I was about ready to fall asleep when I heard Little Dog speak.

"Glad to see you're up and about! I didn't wake you before, as you clearly needed the rest and I want you to be on top form." Little Dog sniffed the air.

"My good chap! You lose so much flavour when you cook your meat. Also, where is the fun in eating an inanimate object when half the pleasure is in ripping into a creature that is still alive? I understand that the science is that you humans derive more calorific energy through cooking and it protects you from a myriad of pathogens, but honestly you really are missing out. Also, the smell of cooked meat is so peculiar that it is downright disturbing."

I opened my left eye to see Little Dog standing on the other side of the sofa. The canine sat on its behind and gave me an inquisitive look.

"I suppose at least you haven't evolved to the point where you're just feeding off little blue pills like the Tropziums. A most strange lot they are. Unfortunately, my curiosity got the better of me and I thought, why not give it a go? I tried one of their little blue pills and it was so foul that I had to eat the poor bugger who gave it to me to get rid of the taste. Well, I tell a little white lie: I had to eat a whole *city* of the daft things to be rid of the taste. Now let me tell you, Tropziums are not the nicest tasting things, so you can imagine how bad those little blue pills must have been for me to resort to such measures …"

I was much too content and lethargic to pay attention to Little Dog's inane chatter. Perhaps it was a sign that I was growing comfortable with the critter, but it didn't take long for me to realise that perhaps I shouldn't be. My eyelids grew heavier and heavier as Little Dog waffled on about why Tropziums were so unpalatable and what other species there were that tasted just as bad. I was just about to completely nod off when I heard the licking of lips and felt heavy breathing coming from all directions. My immediate thought was to open my eyes, even though there was another part of me that implored me not to. When I opened them, I took a short, sharp breath of shock, as I was completely surrounded by a host of vicious snouted mouths of various sizes, all bearing sharp jagged teeth. All the mouths breathed heavily and the occasional black forked tongue sprang out of one to lick its lips. I was clearly at a disadvantage, but for some reason my instinct told me to not wither in fright, but to say something quite unexpected.

"Stop being an arse," I snapped.

The mouths all shot back into Little Dog, whom I then saw had a mocking pout on its little face.

"My dear chap, you were the rude one there. Really you should learn some manners yourself, not I!" Little Dog mocked.

The creature then chuckled to itself.

"You did quite well there. I thought that perhaps I would have got at least a little peep from you. For most, it's usually screaming and blubbering when I tease someone." A surprising curiosity then took hold of me.

"I hate to sound rude, but do you ever do anything nice for anyone, Little Dog?"

"Isn't removing the evidence for you an act of kindness, my good fellow?"

"You could say it is, Little Dog, but there is certainly something in it for you as well. I should rephrase that: do you act altruistically in any way?"

"Arguably, most of the bloody time, my dear chap. Isn't allowing others to become food or entertainment for a god a form of the most ultimate altruism? Obviously, the life form might not see it that way, but with a slight change of perspective, they would see how so much divine importance has been bestowed on them. Their purpose has been brought up to the upper echelons of meaning itself, far beyond the petty dilemmas that they face day in, day out. Who cares about serving society or family when you can directly serve a god — albeit potentially as a snack, but a snack in the most divine sense!" the supernatural being laughed.

Little Dog appeared for the briefest of seconds deep in thought. It then, with a merry trot and a wagging tail, came over to me. With no obvious inclination, it jumped on top of me and all I could do was let out a sigh, as I thought I was either going to be eaten, or it had some other nasty trick up its sleeve. I was completely wrong: Little Dog opted to give my face a few licks all over with a very long, black forked tongue instead. A sticky, luminous, purple saliva lecherously clung to my face and became entangled in my beard.

I groaned and gently swiped at the canine to move it off me. Surprisingly, I was able to and it felt like merely a small dog that I had just shoved. Little Dog merrily yelped and jumped off me.

"Is that the sort of altruism that you are looking for, my good chap? In my younger days, we might have gotten a bit of immaculate conception going on with that amount of affection. Although, many of the life forms that I have copulated with didn't quite feel that it was immaculate for them, as to them it was just a small canine that appeared to perform the act. Still, I gave them gods as children, what more could they ask for?"

"So, you have children?" I could not but help say in bewilderment.

"When you have lived as long as I have, it's rather difficult not to leave a spawn or two of yours here and there. Haven't a clue what they're up to. I could quite easily find out, but honestly, I couldn't care less. It isn't like they're going to have much trouble defending themselves like a child of your species. The very second they opened their eyes they had access to an abundance of power and knowledge."

Little Dog yawned and fell back onto the ground with its paws curled up. The canine then rubbed its back from left to right on the ground, with its tongue lolling out.

"I am enjoying the interrogation, Cain; it's not every day I get to tell a being my story. But enough about me, how about yourself? Do you ever act altruistically?" Little Dog enquired after it stopped scratching its back.

"Of course, I do. I have evolved into a surprisingly righteous man. If I wasn't, I doubt I would be able to sleep so easily."

"Although, I have no issue with it, many humans would see your violence as clear evidence that you are not as altruistic as you think you are. I only ask to understand your perspective and see how it differs to that of many of your species."

"As you said, Little Dog, it is about perspective. Altruism, in a way, is about the sacrifice of the self for the benefit of the many. I do agree that my actions aren't the epitome of altruism, as I do find a great deal of joy in such violence. But if we looked at what the benefits are, we would see that such bloodshed is a necessary act of kindness. Those I murdered in the courtroom were a corrupt cancer within the legal system; eliminating them would allow a fairer system to be put in place. Those who I will end and have ended for the bees, well, aside from attempting to save a particular species, so many other plants and animals would rejoice, too, as many an ecosystem relies on them. Of course, I do not feel I even need to explain that at the pub."

I paused and looked at Little Dog for a brief few seconds before I spoke again.

"I could spend all day rationalising my actions, but I am sure that would bore you. However, I will add one encompassing justification and will explain with an example. On our planet, in many nature reserves, when the deer population increases to unsustainable levels, a forceful act of altruism is needed to reduce their numbers. This is so that the deer do not destroy the ecosystem irreparably, which of course would harm them and other animals. I am sure you can see where I am going with this. Humans are clearly at the same unsustainable level and have no predators to keep their numbers in check, so, acts of murder are the same way quite the altruistic service."

"Ho-ho! Cain, you are not as naive as I thought you might be. I do quite like your ability to rationalise — yes, yes, it's rather delightful. Your species may see such views rather differently, but they are a sort who are quite caught up in their own delusions of grandeur. Honestly, of all the civilisations I have come across, this is one of the most egotistical. Which is, of course, quite marvellous for me, as such insecurity equates to greater bloodshed. Anyhow, I do feel we have been chattering away for far too long. Perhaps it is best to make preparations for wherever we are going to go next. I do hope that this campaign of yours will be an improvement on the pub."

"It will be, Little Dog. It might be a bit of a long one, though, which is why I've eaten a large breakfast. I will certainly need the energy. Okay, I am going to get ready. Please do make yourself at home whilst you wait," I insisted.

Chapter 24

The young man leapt off the bus and then sprinted through the streets of Manchester. Every morning was near enough the same, a mad dash to work so that he wasn't late enough for a disciplinary. Every morning it was a battle as his body fought for every extra second of sleep it could get. It was routine that the snooze button on his phone was continually pressed until he was running late. Each time, he'd shout a swear word, leap out of bed and tell himself that he was going to change his ways. He'd then spend the morning worrying that his employers would eventually notice his repetitive tardiness and give him his marching orders. Yet no matter what he told himself or what he felt, every morning remained the same, as his body simply refused to obey him.

On the day of the attack, the young man arrived at his work seven minutes late. He flew through the front door and skidded to a halt. To make it less blatant, when inside he slowed to a casual walking pace. As streams of sweat dripped off his face, he tucked in his uniform shirt over his little pot-belly, brushed his long scraggly brown fringe off his pale face and walked to the reception desk.

"How do, Mark,"

"All right, John," replied the young man. He stepped around the reception desk and flung his backpack underneath the table.

"Where's Sarah?" asked Mark.

"Afraid she's off sick, mate, so you've got reception duty as well. You better spruce up some more for it, you look as sweaty as a Catholic priest in a playground," his colleague chuckled.

"Fuck sake. Swear that's like her tenth sickie. She's only able to get away with it because Pete is so desperate to fuck her. You notice he always heads to the toilets straight after talking to her. Probably to wank one off, the dirty old git."

Yet Pete wasn't the only one who wanted to enjoy Sarah's company. Many a night Mark spent imagining that it was Sarah in the pornography that he was watching and that he was the stud doing the thrusting.

"He ain't the only one. I'd hit it so hard that — "

"Fuck off John, you'd cum in your pants before she'd even touch you … just need to ask Jen," Mark laughed.

He then looked up and saw an elderly employee giving him a disapproving look as she walked by. The last stream of employees was flowing in. John waited until there were fewer people going by and then made a poor attempt of a whisper.

"I told you, Jen is fucking lying. She's just upset that I didn't want to take it any further after the Christmas party."

"I prefer her story, mate, sounds far more believable. Two pumps and you're done."

The younger security guard stood up, pretended to thrust the air twice and then gave a perverted groan as he pretended to ejaculate over John.

"HA! Bell-end. You see, leave them unsatisfied and they come back for more. Also, two pumps are better than none. You reverted to being a virgin yet?" John teased.

"HA! Dickhead," replied Mark.

A flash of intense disappointment slipped through the laddish mask he had on. It wasn't just due to his sexual frustration: he felt his life becoming increasingly more vacuous as he worked this dead-end job. Becoming a security guard wasn't the career path Mark had wanted to head into after university, but there wasn't much choice for someone as unambitious as him. He was hoping he'd just walk into a well-paid job, but quickly found out that wasn't the case. The low pass grade on his sociology degree might have set him up with a decent enough job thirty years ago, but not any longer. Mark didn't regret his choices at university, as he had copious amounts of fun during those three years of partying, from what he could remember of it. However, aside from the ability to drink large amounts of alcohol and getting a couple of STDs, there didn't seem to be much else that he had left with.

His work colleague noticed the change in his mood and quickly changed the topic.

"What are you up to this weekend? You've got it off, right? Not sure what I'm doing yet, but I've found someone who sells a really nice gram of coke for seventy. It'd make your whole face numb good. If you're up for buying a few grams, then I could probably get it down to sixty-five."

Both security guards looked around, something that would probably have been more effective if done before the drug talk. Fortunately, there was no one in sight.

"Yeah, I got the weekend off, so yeah, fuck it, I'll put some money in. We can hit the Northern Quarter as well, if you fancy it, mate," Mark said excitedly.

"Sweet as, mate."

Just then an adolescent girl walked by in a tight white shirt that was unbuttoned to the crease of her cleavage. Small parts of a white lacy bra that clung to her large breasts poked out on view. This was coupled with a tight black miniskirt clinging to a round, pert bottom and red high heels that emphasised the titillating shape of her legs. Both men looked at her face last and both realised they were caught out ogling. The girl rolled her eyes as the men quickly turned their heads to pretend to look at the CCTV monitors. When she walked past, they turned back around and stared at her firm bottom.

"Fuck me. Is that one of the new apprentices they got?" John asked.

"Yeah, I'm pretty sure it is. Fuck, amazing body but her face says she could be jailbait. How old do you have to be to be an apprentice?" Mark asked.

"If there's grass on the pitch, mate."

"Yeah, tell that to the judge just before you get made a sex offender. Fuck that, if she isn't seventeen. I think she's got to be at least seventeen … Man, I'm fucking blue balls at the moment. It has been months since I've fucked … I swear she needs to be the one to break this famine."

"You're not getting laid because you're too desperate, mate. Girls smell it a mile away. Also, you're too picky. As you're single, you might as well fuck around as much as possible, that is until you meet the right girl. Otherwise, you'll regret it when you're old and can't get your tiny dick up no more," the old security guard said, attempting to sound sage.

The young security guard grimaced and fell back into his chair. Both then swung around and started to surf the internet to twiddle the time away until the shift ended.

Out of boredom, the younger security guard looked at the internal recruitment intranet page at Oso. There were a few jobs going, the top one being Sales Director, with an annual salary packet of £800,000 before bonuses. That was money that he knew he'd never have but it still didn't stop him from fantasising about what he'd do with it. Mark thought the first thing would be to move out into a nice flat in the town centre and then hire a fair few escorts — all at the same time, of course. There would be many a cocaine-fuelled party to follow. A new car would be a requirement. In Mark's case, he'd need to learn to drive, but that was a negligible fact in his daydream. He didn't know much about cars, he just fantasised about one that looked expensive that he had seen on television the previous day.

The fantasy quickly became more erotic and Mark imagined pulling up to his place of work. As soon as the car came to a stop, he saw the apprentice come out, this time in an even shorter skirt and more buttons were undone on her shirt. As fantasy is fantasy, he nonchalantly beckoned her to come over after opening the passenger door and she didn't hesitate. As soon as she got in, she had her hand on his thigh and was moving it upwards. Within seconds she had his penis out and was about to start giving him fellatio. At this point, the young man thought it best to continue his daydream in the toilet cubicle.

"Just going to take a piss, mate."

John grunted in response, as he was engrossed in making bets on the weekend's football games. The younger man looked around to see that the coast was clear, stood up, hunched slightly forward to ineffectively hide the bulge in his trousers and scurried off to the bathroom. The auto light in the toilet switched on as he stepped in. A quick look and Mark breathed a sigh of relief, as no one was in any of the cubicles. He had tried before with others in the cubicles and found that he simply couldn't reach the point of climax when men were close to him and vacating their bowels.

Within a couple of minutes, it was job done and he was washing his hands. He had a look in the mirror and pulled a few poses that hid his pasty white chubby cheeks. At certain angles, some would say that he was quite an attractive chiselled young guy. Of course, this meant all of his social media pictures were of him, in said angles and with added photo application distortions added through an application's effects. In his social media profiles, he thought he did look like quite the stud; it was just unfortunate that many women didn't feel the same when they actually met up with him in real life.

The security guard sighed: gone were the sexual urges and lonely desperation took command instead. He prayed to himself that he was going to get lucky tonight. As he didn't have the looks, he had to rely on confidence and charisma to seduce women; unfortunately, he did not have these either. To compensate for his inadequacies, he used alcohol and cocaine. This chemical cocktail still left him completely devoid of charm, but it did give him an abundance of unpleasant boldness. Most ladies still opted to avoid him, but at times a desperate, inebriated and very lonely woman would begrudgingly accept him as a just-about-good-enough vehicle for sex.

Mark gave a quick wink to himself in the mirror before leaving the toilet. When he returned, he saw that John was still sitting at the desk and still looking at betting odds.

"I've got Oldham to win on the end of this multiplier. Everything else is sure-fire. If they do, it's three hundred quid extra to wax for me," John said without looking up.

"Fair do's … Mate, I just had a wank thinking about that new apprentice. God, I really want to fuck her," Mark whispered.

"Knew you went off to do that. Dirty bastard. You know she's fourteen? You sick fuck."

"What? Fuck off, how do you know?" Mark said whilst taking his seat.

"I searched her name on the internet while you were in there wanking off. Her social media is saying her age is over that, but a status update says she just celebrated her fourteenth. You're a fucking paedo. Going to have to report you, mate!" John laughed out.

"Fuck off. She definitely doesn't look it. For fuck sake …"

John kept chuckling to himself, so much so that it dawned on the younger security guard that his friend was lying.

"You bell-end. How old is she really?"

"Eighteen, mate, eighteen. You fucked off too early. You need to see the dirty, dirty pictures I found! Not naked, like, but practically. Definitely good for a deposit at the wank bank! Come, look."

"Fucking hell! Jesus, she's pure filth! Mate, is that her mother who's given her the like? Weird shit, that. John, mate, I think I'm going to have to go for another wank," Mark joked.

Just then John looked up and realised there was some actual work that needed doing.

"Mate, there's a fucking tramp and his dog in here. For fuck sake. You can sort it," the older security guard exclaimed.

"Why me?" Mark retorted.

"Because I found you the pictures you'll be using to wank over for the next couple of months!"

"True, true." Mark got up from the reception desk and headed across to the homeless man.

The tall security guard looked down and saw he was with a cute, black Scottish terrier.

"Sorry, mate, you can't come in here to beg. Also, we don't give drinks or anything like that. So, if you could please move on," Mark politely informed the man.

The homeless man didn't appear to hear him and simply looked around the reception instead. Then he looked at his dog, who appeared quite happy with its tail wagging. The little dog then went behind the homeless man and nudged him in the back of the leg. Then Mark swore he heard the critter speak, as the homeless man's lips didn't move and there wasn't anyone else around.

"Come on, Cain. Think of the bees! It's them or these people. They are all cogs in the same machine that continuously defiles and destroys your beloved creatures. There are no innocents here."

Mark quickly rationalised that this must be a ventriloquist's trick and was how the homeless man made money for whatever drugs or booze he took. He saw the vagabond close his eyes and take a couple of deep breaths. Then the homeless man's lips started to tremble and tears started to trickle down the side of his face.

"Yes, yes. The bees, I keep forgetting about the poor little things," the man said in between choked sobs that crept out.

Mark thought he had better get rid of the — clearly mad — vagrant quickly, as the last thing he wanted was the police being called, because that meant paperwork.

"Sorry, mate. Cool tricks and all, but you still have to leave," Mark said, just before he grabbed the vagabond's arm.

As soon as he touched the arm, the homeless man's face became stone and his eyes shot wide open. The look he gave Mark communicated that something very bad was about to happen. Panic took hold of Mark. He stepped back and pulled out his metal baton.

"Fuck," Mark groaned as the vagabond reached behind his back underneath his trench coat.

The man pulled out what appeared to be two golden knuckle-dusters with two vicious-looking knives attached. Mark swung his weapon down at the vagabond's head and it struck him right on his temple, but it didn't even cause the homeless man to flinch as he kept a hateful stare pinned on him. Without even seeing the movement, Mark felt cold metal scrape along the front of his throat and a split second later, he felt the same on the other side.

There was a sudden drop in ambient volume and this kept on decreasing until Mark's world was completely silent as he fell. The security guard kept trying as hard as he could to focus on the wildly swirling colours around him, but the more he tried, the darker it became and suddenly the darkness completely surrounded his world and squeezed until there was nothing more …

What must have been just a few seconds later, clicking of fingers by Mark's right ear could be heard.

"Come on, young man. No dilly-dallying. He doesn't like that sort of thing," a gruff, but quintessentially English voice said.

The young man groaned and then suddenly shot up as the memory of his throat getting cut flew through his mind. He looked around wildly, felt his neck, found there was no wound there and then saw that he was sitting in the middle of a void in which only a black and chrome elevator stood out from its black surroundings. Next to him was a fat old butler who looked remarkably like Winston Churchill.

"F-f-fuck … Am I dead?" the young man asked as he felt his neck again to check that there was still no wound.

"Of course you are, young man — well, in the traditional sense, that is," the elderly man said, before frowning. "Also, none of that language, please, otherwise I'll leave you here to be absorbed by the void," he snapped.

"S-s-sorry," Mark replied and looked around frantically again.

"To save time I'll explain it quickly. It's quite simple, really. You either choose to join the eternal darkness that is around you, something that I hear eventually becomes quite relaxing, or you come with me and work for our Lord and Saviour."

Mark looked around at the eternal darkness and decided on the other option.

"I'll work for our Lord and Saviour. Does that mean I am going to heaven?"

"HO-HO! I forgot how naive we humans are. Chop-chop. You need to get up, young man," the butler sang with a smile.

He stood aside so that Mark was able to enter the elevator.

"Now, you'll be on a five-hundred-year probationary period. Also, during that time you'll only be entitled to a day's rest every hundred years. After your probationary period, that will move up to a day's rest every fifty years and each millennia after that, we'll throw in another day's rest until you have earned a full month off. Your remuneration is the fact that you won't become absorbed into the eternal darkness. Oh, your role may change to whatever his present whim is, so please bear that in mind."

The butler squinted and looked into Mark's eyes until the younger man averted his gaze.

"You might think that sounds like a terrible deal, but time really does fly down here and on your days off you can do absolutely whatever your heart desires. We'll start you off on just sweeping and mopping the floors, and then we'll go from there. Oh and one more thing, this will be your uniform."

With a single finger, the butler pulled out a pair of tiny black latex hot pants and a bow tie. At that point, Mark realised that he definitely wasn't going to heaven.

Chapter 25

My one-man invasion did not have the best of starts and was not the good-versus-evil battle that I had hoped for. When I killed the first security guard, his comrade did appear as if he was going to get the flames of battle going; I remember that he sauntered towards me with his chest stuck out and that there wasn't a single nervous twitch or shake from this cool soul who then swung out his extendible metal baton and set himself in a fighting stance. At that point my heart thundered, blood rushed to every muscle that was needed, my mind sharpened to the point where it could cut a gnat in two and just as I felt completely ready for combat, the cheeky blighter threw his baton at me and ran, having changed his mind about the whole ordeal. I shouted after him and gave him words of encouragement to come back — but he ignored my pleas.

Surprisingly, a childish tantrum came out of nowhere and took me over after he took flight. I picked up one of my knives by the end and threw it in frustration at the fleeing security guard. It was by sheer luck (as the weapon certainly wasn't meant for throwing) that I was able to stick him right in the back of his neck. He fell to the ground gurgling in his death throes. I saw that Little Dog did not look particularly impressed, so I shrugged my shoulders at the supernatural being.

This initial hurdle didn't sour my mood as, ever the optimist, I thought that these drones of malevolence would be sure to put up some sort of fight, as they would see that I was but one and they were many. I pulled my knife out of the dead guard and before I went upstairs, I looked back at the entrance and then at Little Dog. As if on cue, the supernatural being spoke.

"Do not worry, Cain. None of your human law enforcement people will become involved in this."

As I walked up the stairs, I built myself up to the point where I was in a berserker trance. I burst through the doors and onto a floor filled with cubicles and office workers. I then roared with an almighty, bloodthirsty rage. It did not take long for me to simmer down, though, as their response was mainly a barrage of cries and wails. Given that there was only one of me, I hoped that with so many of them they might have tried to fight me, but I was wrong.

I spent fifteen minutes encouraging the workers to act more appropriately to the situation at hand, by chasing them around the office and giving a few slaps here and there, but this was mostly to no avail. I thought perhaps I should just massacre them all, but even though I knew it was right to do so, I simply found that I couldn't, as they were far too pathetic and cowardly. There was a brief reprieve from this frustrating situation when a worker tried swinging an office chair at my head, but I easily ducked and followed up with a knife in his ribs. I hoped that this was the cue for others to follow in his footsteps and I was going to be put onto the back foot. Disappointment quickly followed when this did not happen.

It was another ten minutes of me attempting to inspire these people before a computer monitor was flung my way. It wasn't difficult for me to backhand it out of the way and I gave a growl in the direction of the offender, but he had already turned on his heel and run. Reality soon started to dawn and little discomforts took hold as my adrenaline dissipated with the onset of my disappointment. My back started to nag with a dull ache, as I found that I had to keep on bending down to drag people out from under their desks.

It was a few more minutes before I caught up to the thrower of the computer monitor, who had opted now to use a fork as a weapon. He swung down at me with the piece of cutlery and I blocked it with the blade of one of my knives. A quick stab into his neck with my other hand brought him to a quick end. Again, that brought a little excitement, but it quickly died out, as there appeared to be no further threat of violence.

I had finally reached the other end of the office, where there was a huddle of all the workers who were left from that floor. It appeared that Little Dog had somehow locked the doors, as they repeatedly and unsuccessfully tried forcing the fire escapes open.

"I've locked the doors so that they don't all end up on the top floor, as I felt the entertainment needed to be spread out more evenly. However, at this moment, I'm not sure I should use the word *entertainment*," Little Dog huffed.

I simply nodded my head and walked toward the frightened masses. I naively thought that this was when they would all rush at me and I was going to have to tune into every sense to survive the mob onslaught.

There was one portly, elderly man who tried to tackle me headfirst. I kept my composure like a matador, side-stepped to let him go by and swished my hand up to slice his throat as he passed. There was also a young male who tried to swing a punch at me. I say *try,* as his form was quite terrible and that meant I didn't feel much when his fist hit my face. I stepped forward and simply stabbed a few times at his abdomen, until he was no more. Following that, there was only crying, whimpers, screams and begging. Not the most pleasant on the ears.

It became obvious that all these white-collar workers were simply not going to play the role I wanted them to, which I probably knew would happen, deep down inside me. I palpably felt that I didn't want to be the abattoir slaughter-man and I was not capable of being one, but it appeared that was the job that had been thrust upon me.

During this fiasco, an unexpected feeling started to grow inside me. It came about because there was a terror in the workers' faces that I found familiar. Perhaps it was the repeated exposure to this dread that awakened childhood memories of my futile attempts to run away from my father as he hunted me down in his home. I turned my eyes down to look at my hands holding the weapons and then at the frightened Oso employees. I tried telling myself they were all Adolf Eichmanns, who'd caused immeasurable pain and suffering behind their desks, but the words felt empty. I then started to feel a heaviness in my chest, as feelings of guilt grew. I wanted to fight the good fight, but it didn't feel like I was doing that. Soon I started to think about whether the whole campaign was perhaps a bad idea, but such thoughts were interrupted by Little Dog's loud yawn.

"I won't lie, Cain, but I am finding this incredibly boring. Also, I can't help but see that you are not finding any joy in it either."

Little Dog sighed and then yawned again.

"I have to agree, Little Dog. Unfortunately, I am finding that to slaughter all of them in such a manner simply isn't my cup of tea and I hate to be presumptuous, but I feel that even if I did, your tedium would continue. None of them seems to be willing to put up much of a fight."

"I suppose, my dear chap, we might as well make some use of them."

Suddenly a school of tentacles shot out from Little Dog and grabbed all the people that were huddled up together. The screams and wails leapt in volume to a point where my eardrums became quite discomfited. One by one the tentacles shot back, all holding a screaming, and crying survivor. Little Dog's head then grew to a gigantic size and it opened its mouth. Each tentacle, in perfect and speedy sequence, threw a person into its open jaws. The mouth closed and the head shrank back to its normal size just before Little Dog crunched down on its still-screaming food. However, the deity did not appear to enjoy its favourite snack.

The tentacles then shot back out and brought all the dead back to Little Dog and hung them in the air as they waited for further orders. Straight after, a bright, colourful, orange portal, a couple of metres high, opened up near the canine.

"As I really don't fancy eating such rancid, rotting food. If you haven't already guessed, it's a portal to the sun, and it only allows one-way traffic, which is why you're not cooked to a crisp, my good chap."

Each tentacle threw the corpses into the portal rapidly and then they shot back to the office. Mouths opened wide at the ends of the tentacles and then somehow sucked all the remaining blood off the floor. Then the same process of returning to the portal, but this time they all spat out the red liquid into it.

"I don't know how your species does it, the taste of rancid meat is simply revolting. Perhaps even more so for me, as I have become so spoilt from dining on so many of your kind while alive … Anyhow, I digress. It appears there are around a hundred workers left and more of the same will simply not do. I had quite high hopes for this planet, but it seems there is nothing to be done and that this world is only good for one thing …"

I saw a few signs of rage appear on Little Dog's face and I knew that an idea from me was needed before the deity's anger took hold.

"I am sure you'll gather, Little Dog, that I am in agreement with you. It appears I am not as righteous as I'd like to think I am and a lot of my joy comes from the fight. To do without it is a travesty when it comes to your entertainment, as well as mine. Also, I feel that I have learnt that I don't seem to have the fortitude to end those that are not trying to harm me or have not harmed me in some way, even if ending them would be as righteous as righteous can be. I know you aren't supposed to intervene and it may constitute as breaking your rules, but there is surely something that you can do to remedy the situation and make it more interesting for us both?" I stammered.

Little Dog raised an eyebrow and then gave a happy yap.

"I suppose, my dear chap, that if I made it more difficult for you, it wouldn't break our agreement or the rules I've set out. I feel that I made out that my relative level of intervention would always be in relation to not make it easier for you; so, making it more difficult is contractually proper. Also, such rules are in place to ensure my entertainment, so making it difficult will certainly be the right thing to do. So yes, at your request, I will help improve the situation, Cain."

Just as I had processed what Little Dog had said, he spoke again.

"My idea is that I give everyone who has survived hand-combat weapons and sell them the importance of a good fight. Those that still choose to run — well, we both know what will happen to them."

Little Dog greedily licked its lips.

"I will agree to that, Little Dog."

"There, I've left the remaining lot an assortment of weapons, but there is still one more task to complete ..."

Little Dog gave a brief cough to clear his throat.

"Greetings, ladies and gentlemen. As you can see, you have been provided with a weapon. It might be a bit of a shock to you, as it's quite the change from spreadsheets and emails. I've not given you these weapons to fight amongst each other, but to defend yourself from a gentleman of the most heinous nature ..." Little Dog gave me a quick wink "... who will be looking to slaughter you all. If you look on your computer monitors right now, you'll see what he has already done to your work colleagues, all of whom put up an abysmal fight. I wouldn't bother trying anything with telephones or the internet, as I have stopped them all from working. Also, all exits have been locked. There is only one way to stop this and that is to kill this new-found enemy of yours. Oh, one last thing and most important of all: please do put up a good fight!" Little Dog bellowed from every corner of the building.

A delighted smile had erupted on Little Dog's face and its tail started to wag again. I swung my arms around a bit to give myself a few dynamic stretches, as I had stiffened up from the previous tedium. It was quite a surreal experience and ever since meeting Little Dog, the prospect of insanity had died down, but the prospect of my existence being a dream had started to play up. Whilst stretching, I started to wonder whether there was anything tangible about reality, especially one that seemed so mad.

"You seem quite deep in thought there, my dear chap. I am assuming this is what you wanted?" Little Dog asked, interrupting my rumination.

"Yes, it is," I grumbled.

I wiped my knives on the cushioned seat of an office chair. Little Dog raised its eyebrow and suddenly the same orange portal appeared below the chair and straight after it fell through, the portal disappeared. This time I raised an eyebrow. I headed to the stairwell with Little Dog merrily trotting behind and my heart started to drum an exciting beat. As soon as I reached the next floor, I took a couple of seconds to gather in a few deep breaths just behind the doors. I felt a momentary hesitation, as it was going to be a first for me to fight so many who had weapons. After one more deep breath, a pin-point focus took over and I stepped through the doors.

A strip of office lighting that hummed and shone brightly showed a near identical-looking office to the one on the floor below. The door swung shut behind me and made a subtle sweeping noise on the floor from the brush insulation stuck to the bottom of it. At first, the office appeared empty, but as soon as I heard a small thud of the door behind me, I saw a flash of movement from within the maze of cubicles that lay ahead of me.

I looked around at the walls as I edged through the short corridor that led into the office itself. Either side of the walls hung many a calming photograph of nature. I slowly moved on, sideways, one weapon in front at an arm's length and the other close to my body.

"NOW!" a gruff shout was heard.

Suddenly a group of six men and women, armed with various weapons, jumped up from behind the cubicles and charged at me. At the front of the charge was a large, fat man swinging a flail and behind him were others with a katana, a battleaxe, a mace, a pair of sais and a bo staff.

Fortunately for me, the cubicles meant that it would be difficult for them to swarm at me from all directions, as there was only a clear path behind and in front of me. They were smart enough to split up and approach me from both directions. The large man who led the charge from one side tried to connect his flail with my head. I ducked and stabbed his arm with my forward knife. This caused the trajectory of the flail to alter and swing right around and smack right into the back of his own skull. He crumpled and fell to the floor. I turned around in time to see a woman with a bo trying to jab me in the head. I tilted my head from side to side to dodge the blows and quickly moved forward step by step. I got close enough and launched a vicious right hook at the side of her temple with the knuckle duster part of my weapon. She was sent flying into the side of a cubicle and crumpled in a heap on the floor.

I ducked down just as a battleaxe swung and became lodged in the wall where my head had just been. The attacker tried to loosen it, but before he could, one of my knives went straight up through his chin and into his skull. I then felt cold metal scrape in and out of the back of my arm. I roared in anticipated pain that I didn't actually feel, due to the adrenaline. I spun around whilst stepping back to see a diminutive lady trying to skewer me with a katana. I was able to get back into my fighting stance just as she tried again. I moved my front blade down to pull the approaching point of the sword away to my left and then leapt forward. A quick stab into the side of her neck ended her and just as I did that, I felt a further cold metal stab me in turn, this time in my left upper back. I turned around to see a smart-looking man with a trim moustache recoiling with a sai in his hand and another man standing next to him, holding a mace like a baseball bat. I glanced at my back to see a sai sticking out of it. They must have seen on my face that I was not amused.

I flicked my knives to get the blood off and put them back in their sheaths on my back. One of the young men initially looked quite puzzled about my perceived disarmament, but clearly felt it was an opportunity, as he charged. Just as he rushed at me, I gave him a vicious front push kick that sent him backwards onto his rear end a good few metres away. I then grabbed the handle of the battleaxe that was still stuck in the wall, wrenched it free and spun around swinging it right into the side of the man with the mace, who stood there waiting for me to make my move. The axe sent the man flying into the wall and pinned him there. He let out a gurgling breath and dropped his mace. Before the mace hit the ground, I caught it by the handle, leapt forward and swung the mace like a tennis shot with topspin, as the other man was trying to get up. This caught him directly in his face and sent his smashed head flying backwards.

"Ruddy good show, that, Cain. I particularly enjoyed your use of the battleaxe, it was damn near a piece of art. Should never have doubted you. It was only a few moments ago that I was starting to think I had made the wrong choice with you."

I didn't respond and thought that although I was feeling quite exhilarated, there was something missing to top the sensation off.

"It is a shame that only six out of thirty on this floor have opted to fight you, as that was quite the show. The rest seem to be cowering away all over the floor. Please leave them to me, as they clearly aren't fit for the stage," Little Dog sighed.

Tentacles shot out from all over the supernatural being's body and raced to all corners of the office. Like before, one by one the tentacles snapped back with screaming survivors. The canine's head then grew to a horrific proportion and it greedily shovelled all the people into its mouth as if it was eating a handful of popcorn.

"Bloody hell, Cain, that is absolutely divine. You really should try some. I can spit some out for you, if you'd like? They'll still be alive, although obviously quite disfigured. So much nicer than this rancid *cooked* meat that your kind enjoy so much," the canine enthused whilst chewing away.

"As open-minded as I am, it just doesn't tickle my fancy, Little Dog. I'm quite happy being accustomed to cooked — and even at times — raw, meat. Anyhow, food isn't the craving that I have now; we must have a quick look for the break room, as I have a mighty big urge to quench my thirst with a cup of tea after all that exertion."

"It is no worries, my dear chap. Now, let's go find you a well-deserved cuppa. You still have a few floors to go through before you reach the top," Little Dog replied with a smile.

It was only a minute before I found the break room, which I must admit was very well stocked. There were even a clear glass teapot, a strainer and a jar filled with a glorious smelling, loose-leaf English Breakfast tea. There was also — very handily — a first-aid box in a cupboard. I decided to have my cup of tea before I tended to my wounds. A couple of minutes later, the enticing nectar was freely swimming and brewing in the pot. I looked down at the canine, which was licking its nether regions, but I also noticed that little portals were appearing and disappearing all over the office, sucking in the weapons that were leftover from the fight. There was also one lone tentacle coming out of Little Dog's back that was getting rid of the blood and bodies with extreme haste.

"You can have a brew as well if you want, Little Dog."

"No thank you, Cain. The stuff isn't my cup of tea," Little Dog chortled, without looking up.

I grimaced at the terrible joke. Once I finished the pot, we moved to the next floor, and that was when my stomach gave a little whine and rumble of hunger.

Chapter 26

Mads felt the front of his chest and then the back of his head, an unintentional habit that had come about since he met Little Dog. There was no sign of scarring or injury at all and as fascinating as this was, it was also deeply disturbing for the doctor. He had spent his adult life researching human biology and how to medically help it. Many would say he was a genius in his field and the frontrunner in the development of biotechnology. Well, that was before he suddenly disappeared from the scientific research community. Instead of basking in the limelight, he opted to enter the black market to further progress his knowledge and understanding, as it was the only realm that would allow his desired leaps and bounds in research, due to the lack of ethics. Within this underground, he had revolutionised biotech, and his advancements were far beyond anything on the mainstream market. Yet, even with his unique intellect, he simply could not fathom how Little Dog did what it did.

Although there was no physical scarring or pain afterwards, Little Dog had certainly left its mark on the doctor. He touched the back of his hand — again no pain — and not a sign of any wound. The memory of that interaction forced its way back into his mind.

The deity knew that with someone as scientific as Mads, some effort was needed to convince him to abandon his life's work and escape Fiorella's grasp. So rather than debate the issue, it simply took Mads to the event at which the universe was born. Then Little Dog allowed the doctor to interpret this event in a few more dimensions than he was used to. This was, of course, indescribable —quite literally. Nonetheless, such beauty and horror, coupled with the fact he didn't think he would be allowed to live if he said no, was enough to convince Mads to play the deity's game.

Mads thought back to what he had seen: the intense colours and cosmic explosions were awe-inspiringly beautiful, but this was nothing compared to what he felt. Even though he couldn't quite remember it, as his brain couldn't retain such complex sensory experiences, he felt that he had had a divine communion with the very essence of the universe. It left him so much at peace and filled with understanding of all that had ever existed and would exist. From that moment he knew he could never live the life that he once had. He was also allowed to feel that there was so much more that Little Dog could show.

"How do you want me to entertain you?" Mads whispered.

"I am not sure if you have gathered, but I am something who thoroughly enjoys watching the more violent sides of life. It's a hobby of mine and it certainly helps alleviate the tedium that comes with being immortal."

Little Dog gave a cough to clear its throat.

"Currently I have a plaything, a human, like yourself, who keeps me entertained by fighting other people. You have briefly met him before. Anyhow, to the point: I feel he needs a little more competition, as he is perhaps too competent compared to his fellow humans and if he so easily wins all the time, it will bore me."

The deity briefly stared at Mads to gauge his emotionless reaction.

"This is where you come in, as I feel you will pose more of a challenge to him. It's a simple task for you: kill him for me and you can take his place. Once you have, I will feed you all the secrets of the universe and not only that, but I will make sure you have the permanent capability to understand them all. Fair deal, no?"

Mads simply nodded his head.

"Splendid! Absolutely marvellous that you are in agreement," the deity gushed.

"Who is this play-thing and how do I find him?" the doctor said and swallowed deeply.

"Well, my good doctor, as I have just said, you have met him before. In fact, he was one of your patients. He has a silly little obsession and that is what will lead you to him. I am confident that you can figure out what that is through your past interactions with him."

Little Dog gave a small yawn.

"Oh yes, my good doctor, there is a slight issue around your implants. I can quite easily remove them so that Fiorella will no longer have any hold over you. Of course, I can do it quite painlessly, but where would the fun be in that?!" the deity had chuckled before it methodically and sadistically ripped out Mads's sensors.

During the purposely heavy-handed surgery, the doctor was convinced that he was going to die, especially as one of the implants had been forcibly pulled out of his cracked-open skull and brain by one of Little Dog's tentacles. However, by some unknown force, Mads was kept very much alive and conscious throughout the whole ordeal. Then, when all the implants were removed, he was miraculously healed by Little Dog.

The doctor had always seen pain as a message that he could react to at will, but this was at such a level that it hit him like torrential rapids that had broken through a dam. There was no self-control that could prevent or diminish the all-encompassing agony. The body should have fainted due to the overloading of its circuitry, but Little Dog didn't allow this, as it felt that the least the doctor could do was repay him back with a little fun.

"Oh, before I scamper off, I'd like to say one more thing. Be sure to put on a good show for me," Little Dog chuckled just before he vanished.

It was all quite surprising for Mads and minimal deliberation about what to do took place in his mind as soon as Little Dog disappeared. He knew that even if he was willing to risk the wrath of this beast and go back to Fiorella, she would probably not believe any explanation he provided and given his removed implants, she would consider him a traitor and that meant the most painful of fates. It was clear that there was only one path he could take if he wanted to stay alive; and because of Little Dog also dangling the prospect of his learning the secrets of the universe, Mads was enthusiastic to go follow it. Within minutes he had packed his belongings, emergency cash savings, fake identification and was out into the streets of Leeds.

The doctor went to a park that was a couple of hours away and sat on a bench so that he could think. It did not take long for him to whittle down the chances of who Little Dog's plaything was. He did have a list of competent violent types in his head, but there was only one that made sense and that was the patient of his who had survived being shot fifty-one times. It also didn't take long for Mads to figure out what this patient's obsession was. Even though it had been only a brief interaction, there was no difficulty in remembering word for word all that the man had said, in particular when he was talking in his sleep. Often the patient had cried out apologies to bumblebees in his sleep. At first, Mads had thought it was just the silly dream-talk of a mad man, but after what Little Dog said, he assumed that this must be the psychopath's obsession.

Later that night, lying down in a hotel bed, Mads thought about every potential thread between bumblebees and the patient. He naturally fell to thinking about pesticides, disease and agriculture, as these were the primary threats to insects. Each link, as implausible as it might have been, was followed until it led to nowhere. It was not much later that he followed a thread to Oso, as they had become market leaders with regard to such potentially damaging pesticides. The doctor then suspected that perhaps the company was going to be targeted by the man. What added to this possibility was the missing Sales Director, who potentially had already been kidnapped or murdered by the deity's plaything and also, Oso recently moving into an office in Manchester.

After analysing everything he knew about the man, he decided that an attack on Oso's Manchester office was the most likely thing to occur. It was, in a way, quite fantastical and a lot of such reasoning relied on a gut feeling, but after what he had experienced with Little Dog, such a deduction seemed plausible. Although there was some apprehension due to Fiorella's link to Oso, he still decided to travel to Manchester to stake out the Oso office.

It was the following day, then, that Mads, with his fake ID, managed to acquire a zero-hours contract and become employed in Oso's outsourced cleaning company for the Manchester office. A disguise wasn't necessary, as facial recognition security technology was not used in Fiorella's legal companies and no one from Oso knew Mads, as he had not worked there before.

On his first day he mopped the floors, cleaned the toilets, emptied the bins and wiped the desks. Even though it was his first day, his boss harangued and harassed him to hurry up, as he was being far too slow and meticulous. It was the following day that his manager decided to fire him and when Cain arrived with Little Dog.

Mads was making sure his cleaning trolley in the caretaker's cupboard was stocked, when he heard Little Dog's disturbing voice permeate the building. As soon as the deity finished speaking, a large Bastard Sword materialised next to his cleaning trolley. One look at it and Mads knew the weapon would not do. He quickly rooted around the cleaning cupboard, taking everything out and then finally came across a long object wrapped in a dirty blanket. He unwrapped it and out came his French duelling sword, something that he had kept from his fencing days. He turned around and came across his manager, who was trembling in fear.

"Did you see that on the monitors?! What's going on? There are weapons everywhere ... I can't fight. I simply can't. Are you —"

Before he could finish, a quick flick of the wrist by Mads had opened his manager's throat up.

It was an opportunity that he was not going to waste and he gave a wry smile as the body fell to the ground. It appeared that he would have to wait a while, as he imagined that his old patient had a few more floors to go before getting to his. Mads, therefore, went on the search for the staff break room, so he could relax with a cup of coffee.

The doctor calmly strolled by many a blubbering employee and many an employee trying to work the telephones or computers to communicate with the police. He also saw a few employees gather in little groups to plot what they needed to do, but these he also ignored. Finally, he reached the break room. Fortunately, it was empty, as Mads did not want to deal with any of the panic-stricken employees. He slowly — and with the utmost precision — made a cup of coffee. The doctor found a newspaper and sat back on one of the chairs and read. He continued his reading even when he could hear shouts and screams on the floor that he was on. Eventually, he heard the clash of weapons just outside the staff break area, so he slowly folded the newspaper and put it down.

Little Dog skipped into the room and casually gave Mads a cheeky wink. A blood-covered man, holding a knuckle-duster knife weapon and what seemed to be the same weapon with the knife broken off, followed the deity a few seconds later. Although he now had long hair, a beard and was covered in other people's fluids, Mads definitely recognised him.

"YOU!" Cain roared.

Just as he did so, Mads leapt up into a fencing position and stabbed at a shoulder, but Cain was able to parry it with his knife. The vagabond moved back again to avoid a quick diagonal swipe downwards, but this was not enough and the bridge of his nose was slightly cut into. A step forward and rapid thrust from Mads was deflected away by Cain's knife whilst he stepped backwards again. The next diagonal swipe caught a lock of his hair and cut it clean off.

"My hair!" Cain moaned.

That split second of distraction allowed Mads an opening and a swift stab of his sword went into the vagabond's left shoulder. Mads pulled the sword out in time to stop his nemesis from grabbing the weapon with his free arm. Both came to a standstill and both took in gulps of air whilst they stared at each other hatefully. The vagabond broke the stare to look at the wound on his shoulder and shrugged. He then felt his chopped hair and a look of rage erupted on his face. This time it was the doctor who shrugged. Mads then quickly went on the attack again.

Thrust, thrust, parry, swipe, parry, thrust, swipe and all the while the vagabond had to keep moving back, and defending himself from the blows. Cain then stumbled as his leg caught the hand of a dead body and this allowed Mads another opening. A quick stab into the right bicep was the result. Before he could respond appropriately, another swipe from Mads's sword came down and left a gash on the vagabond's cheek. Cain tripped over another body and another speedy stab went into the upper left part of his chest. Instead of stepping back, Mads thrust the sword in further as he came forward. The doctor easily blocked Cain's punch and then swiped the vagabond's feet off the ground. Mads leapt back, pulled the sword out and pointed it a hand's length from Cain's throat. He was pinned against the office window with bodies either side of him and had nowhere to back away to. Mads waited there for a few seconds and then quickly stabbed through the opposite shoulder. Before the vagabond could grab the sword, Mads pulled it out and moved it back close to his throat again.

The doctor was about to finish the vagabond, who could only glare back, when he noticed a foul smell coming from a dead body that was next to them. Mads crinkled his nose in disgust and that allowed enough time for curiosity to bubble up from within and like all good scientists, he could not fight it.

"There has been so much of the fantastic that has gone on, almost to the point that I question whether this is reality anymore, or if I have simply gone insane. A part of me wants you to live as it yearns to talk about it all with you, and there is no one else to do it with."

Mads let out a long sigh.

"Unfortunately, this can't be done as your life is a barrier to my finding out the secrets of the universe. But I feel there is just enough time for one question before I kill you. I must ask, as it puzzles me so, why are you so obsessed with bumblebees, to the point where you have committed so much violence? Why risk your life over something so … how shall we say … *insignificant*?" Mads enquired.

Cain scowled back at the doctor and his first instinct was to spit at him, but he realised that it was a futile gesture.

"I suppose it would be nice if someone knew, as I am about to die, but … I feel that this really isn't the time and place for a therapy session," Cain replied with a wry grin.

Suddenly a flash of bright, orange light erupted at the edge of the doctor's vision. He quickly turned right to see, ten metres away, a confused and pot-bellied young man in latex hot pants and bow tie, holding a mop and standing next to what appeared to be a swirling portal.

"How does the fat, bald shite expect me to help with a bloody mop when you have a sword!" the young man cried.

One menacing look from Mads was enough to cause the scantily clad man to leap back into the portal, which closed straightaway. When the doctor turned back around, he saw Cain with his hand down a dead man's trousers. Before he could make out what he was doing — and before the thought that he should end him immediately appeared — the hand flew out and a brown sludge came his way.

Mads was able to dodge most of the sludge, but as there was so much of it some of it still hit him in the face. The foul substance covered his eyes and went into his mouth. A split second later the smell of human excrement roared through his mind. Pure feelings of disgust tugged at every neuron in his body. The taste of it intruded, too and added to the explosion of revulsion. The doctor pathetically screamed and retched at the same time. He tried wiping the excrement from his eyes, but before clearing it all, Cain had already got up, ran away a few metres and then ran back to drop-kick him with such ferocity that the doctor went smashing through the office window. A few metres out of the office and gravity took hold of the retching Mads and pulled him right down from the fifth floor into a luxury convertible below.

"HA-HA! A bloody marvellous idea, Cain! The good doctor's face was simply priceless. I'll have to allow Satan's little intervention, as not only did that pathetic young man tickle me, but it would have been simply awful if you had lost and I'd had to deal with that insufferable bore. I'd probably just not have bothered with the good doctor and eaten the whole planet instead," Little Dog gushed as he skipped around the vagabond, who lay on the floor, exhausted.

Little Dog, clearly still wanting more from his entertainer, poked at Cain's side with his snout to encourage him to move.

"Yes, yes, I know, Little Dog. Please let me have a minute, though. Then I'll need a cup of tea and I'll need to wash my hand, as it bloody stinks to high heaven," Cain said hoarsely, whilst still lying down.

The deity raised its eyebrow, then shrugged its shoulders.

"I suppose I do sometimes forget that you are only human. You know what, my good chap, you relax. For such riveting fun, I'll make you the cup of tea," Little Dog said just before skipping away.

Chapter 27

I sat outside the Chief of Operations' office, propped against a wall. Whoever was left inside were the last employees of Oso's Manchester arm. The hope went through my mind that such a gaping wound to the organisation would leave it so that it could not defend itself, as other predators in the same pond would hopefully go for it.

I sucked in air gluttonously, as I was nearly drained of all energy. Even with my level of stamina, getting through thirty heavily armed office workers *and* the doctor, whilst being stabbed and hit, was exhausting work. Fortunately, Little Dog's appetite remained ever ravenous and when the critter consumed those that cowered and hid, it gave me a much-needed breather.

As I sat and waited outside the closed office, I saw Little Dog come trotting back, with a white mug floating next to it.

"Thank you, Little Dog."

The mug floated towards me and I grabbed the handle. It was, of course, another cup of tea. It was perhaps my eighth cuppa since I had started, but even after so many, the nectar still provided a rejuvenating effect.

"You make a surprisingly good cup of tea, for one that doesn't drink the stuff, that is."

"Well, I am omnipotent, so you'd hope that it was good."

Little Dog gave me a cheeky wink. I blew and sipped at the drink. Each sip complemented the soak of endorphins that pumped throughout my brain. As I sat there, blood slowly trickled onto the floor from my hands and elbows. There was only so much that my haphazard attempts at bandaging with first-aid kits and bits of ripped clothes could do to stem the flow.

Knuckle-dusters still remained on my hands, but the knives attached to them had long since broken off. I could have changed my weapons for those that the employees had dropped, but I felt quite attached to my own broken tools. I, on the odd occasion, used a different weapon out of necessity, but I didn't continue with their use, as they didn't have that personal connection.

"You have been doing quite the riveting job in this affair. Mightily entertaining stuff. But I was wondering, Cain, what are your plans once you have disposed of the last of these culprits? Is it onward, Germany bound, for the headquarters?" Little Dog enquired.

"In all honesty, I am not completely sure. It'll depend on the consequences of all this. If this is enough to destroy the company, then it will be back to the drawing board in terms of what else I should do."

"Apologies if this is sticking my oar in, but you do realise, my dear fellow, that destroying this company is nowhere near enough. The gap in the market is there and the invisible hand of capitalism will simply seek to fill it."

"Yes, I do agree; what will happen is quite obvious. I do know that if the firm does not survive, it still has plenty of coveted patents to make it quite the desirable catch for a takeover. I am afraid that, for me, it is an awful lot to think about, so I will probably need to spend a couple of months or so planning my next move and seeing what the fallout is. The campaign is, unfortunately, quite the long haul. Do not worry, it'll only be a brief reprieve."

Little Dog didn't say anything but gave a quick huff of annoyance.

I didn't think anything of it and carried on sipping away.

When I finished my cup of tea, I put my mug down and pushed myself up against the wall to force myself onto my feet. I moved into position, took a deep breath and then gave a ferocious front kick straight into the middle of the double, black-painted office doors. The doors flew wide open and I saw two very well-dressed men armed with a katana each. They both stood still, with anxious eyes wide open, like children frightened by someone dressed up as a monster.

One of them was a middle-aged, rotund man with a receding hairline. He appeared to be the Chief of Operations, as once he had gathered himself, he gave a scowl to the younger, slimmer and taller one to cajole him into attacking me. The younger man inched forward with the sword in front of him.

"You honestly don't know who you are coming up against. It doesn't matter who you work for, they can't protect you from her. She will come for you all and she will come for everything you love. Then she will make you all suffer in the most terrible of ways," the older man hissed.

I ignored such empty threats and calmly headed towards the younger man. He lunged to stab at me with his katana, but I side-stepped and twisted at the same time so all he got was air. I then twisted back the other way as he pulled back and let loose a right hook that caught him directly on the chin. The lackey hit the ground hard. I picked up the katana that he dropped and stabbed it straight through him and into the floor.

Surprisingly, the older man found some bottle and charged at me with both hands on the katana, ready to swing down. I was far quicker to the mark, though and before he was able to get the sword down, I had a fist lodged right in his abdomen. Air shot out of his mouth and he slumped to the floor. Instead of finishing him off, I picked up the coughing, spluttering director by the front of his suit and pressed him against the office wall, as his legs were too wobbly to stand. An informal interrogation was then held, with my face a couple of centimetres away from his.

"Do you know why I am here?" I asked with no hint of emotion.

The Chief of Operations was only able to shake his head in response.

"It's because you are killing the bumblebees!"

I heard a little snigger behind me from Little Dog.

"What are you on about? A-a-are you fucking insane?!" he cried.

I pulled my head back and gave him a vicious head-butt. Blood streamed down his broken nose and onto his pristine suit and shirt.

"I am afraid you're not in a position to talk to me like that, or even ask questions."

As soon as I had scolded him, I remembered his empty threat.

"Who is this woman you were talking about? There isn't a woman who is the CEO, Chairman of the Board, or even *on* the board. So please do tell."

The Chief of Operations gulped and stayed silent, as it was quite clear that he wished he hadn't said what he had just said.

"Don't worry. I have my methods of convincing those who do not wish to talk to become far more vocal."

One broken shin later and the man had given me his whole history and as much as he knew about the organisation. He explained that Oso was one of many cash-cow organisations that fed a great deal of their hidden profits through smoke-and-mirror accountancy into a mother organisation, which was nameless. He told me that this mother organisation's less than legitimate side was something he used to work for, but then to ensure better control of Oso, as it was an ever-growing cash cow, he was moved across to it. He also spoke about his leader, a mysterious woman who was rarely seen, but absolutely feared due to her ability to know every move her own people made, to weed out treachery and punish it, to dispatch these traitors gruesomely, and to defeat her enemies. This leader was also respected because she rewarded her people wildly and on merit. The Chief of Operations was about to carry on spilling further details about this leader when a look of sheer terror came across his face and he broke down in tears.

"You really don't know who you are up against! She will know what I have done, she always finds out. Why did I tell you! Oh god, what have I done!" he cried out.

Hysteria had taken over. I sighed, as I didn't have the patience to bother trying to coax anything else out of him. I dropped the wailing Chief onto the floor and looked over at Little Dog.

"He's all yours."

"Thank you, Cain. He does look particularly appetising. Look how ripe his jowls are," the critter replied with a colossus grin.

The critter's head rapidly grew to be a metre in diameter and it then prodded the wailing man with its nose, as he had not noticed the beast.

"Excuse me. Excuse me. That's better. She really isn't the one you should be worried about right now."

Little Dog chuckled to itself when it saw the absolute terror in the Chief of Operations' eyes. The supernatural being quickly wolfed the screaming man down. The head shrank back and a few chews later, Little Dog was talking again.

"He was all style and no substance! Quite a disappointing flavour. Oh well, you can't expect them all to be so tasty."

I gave a little grunt, as I still could not help but feel that one day it might be me.

"I was about to ask what now, my good chap, but it appears that we have new guests at our party."

"How so? I thought you were preventing people from entering the building?"

Little Dog gave an innocent shrug and stayed silent. I frowned at the critter and thought that it had let in a few extra people because it wanted a few more snacks. Unfortunately, I wasn't ready for a fight, as I was now feeling rather peckish, since my stomach had decided that the violence was all over and felt it an appropriate time to hijack control. My brain didn't put up much of a fight, as it needed food for energy. So rather than investigate straightaway, I had a root around the Chief of Operations' office.

There was a small black fridge in the corner. Inside, I found a few slices of Serrano ham, leftover Manchego cheese, a few thick slices of chorizo, a small wheel of goat's cheese, sparkling water and a couple of crackers. Admittedly, I had hoped for more extravagance, although after eating the entire contents of the fridge, I must say that I was not disappointed about the quality, merely the quantity.

The stomach growled with a sulky frustration as it craved more delights. Naively, my brain thought it had convinced my stomach that as soon as these new guests were dispatched then I could go and root through every break-room fridge to my heart's content. I didn't know my stomach had disagreed, but now I found that I had walked into the top-floor break room and not the stairway. I gave a loud sigh but told myself: definitely no more than one fridge.

Again, I didn't find enough to completely satiate me. There was more than enough food; it was just finding food that reached my standards. I did find a large Tupperware container filled with a just-about satisfactory pad Thai. Even after it was microwave heated, it still retained some decent flavours. Whoever had made it had used chicken thigh instead of breast, something I was thankful for. I never could understand people's fascination with chicken breast when its neighbour was infinitely juicier and more delicious. I wolfed that down and found a homemade pecan pie with double cream that someone must have brought in for the office. It was a wonderfully decadent and sticky treat. Clearly the pastry was homemade and not any pre-made swill. This was all accompanied by another cup of tea.

Once I had finished, I scolded my stomach about the deception and was more forceful about completing the task at hand before any more food was sought. My stomach stayed in a sulky silence as I went to go and rid us of these new threats.

Of course, in hindsight, I regret how casually I approached the situation because I assumed that it was either more employees of Oso, or another company's employees here for a meeting. With Little Dog following, I sauntered downwards whilst whistling a jolly tune. I opened the first-floor office door and after a short jaunt into the office itself, I came across a group of four particularly mean-looking men holding pistols and a mean-looking (but colourfully dressed), tanned woman, all of whom were standing in the cubicles and looking around. They all turned and looked at me. The group of men then looked at the woman, whose face was cold and emotionless. I stood still and tried to assess the situation and quickly deduced that the odds were not in my favour. As soon as the woman nodded, a rain of bullets came my way.

I turned on my heel and ran away, as I had no means of defending myself against four guns. I was able to make it to the stairway under the hail of fire and shot up the stairs in no time. The adrenaline filled my body again and because of this, I didn't feel the extra holes in me. As I ran up, I shouted at Little Dog, who was sprinting up alongside me.

"Why the bloody hell did you give them guns?!"

"Well, before you get into a huff about it, I didn't," was the abrupt answer.

My mind raced to find a solution as I ran up another floor. It was clear that I was in no fit state to attack four men armed with guns who were clearly trained in the ways of killing with such weaponry. I had also spent most of my energy on the previous battles and that meant there was only one option: escape.

I finally reached the fourth floor and saw a cracked, giant windowpane. A mace was sent flying into the window after an employee had tried to swing it at my head and let it go by accident. Without stopping to take a break, I ran to it, picked up a nearby office desk and hurled it through the window. As I started to feel weakness creep up on me, I had a quick look around my body and saw that I was leaking blood liberally. I turned to see if Little Dog had followed and if the critter was perhaps going to eat me, out of anger.

"Ho-ho! Don't mind me, my dear chap. You can't win them all. Where would be the fun in that?"

I didn't bother with a retort, as there wasn't enough time. A quick glance outside showed that there was some luck still running in my favour, as one of Manchester's canals was possibly just about within jumping distance, although perhaps that was an overly optimistic analysis. I quickly ran back, sprinted forward and leapt as hard as I could. Just as I hurled myself over the edge, I heard gunshots and felt a couple more thuds go into my back; but again, I didn't feel any pain.

I landed in the canal with a gigantic splash. I had taken a gulp of air just before I hit the surface and immediately swam underwater, away from the building, until I damn near passed out. When I came up for air, luckily, I had reached a road bridge up above and I was clear out of sight. Of course, I still wasn't free yet, so I pulled myself out of the water and ran. Fortune seemed to have taken a bloody good liking to me, as a heavy Manchester rain began to pour. It was what I needed to wash away my dripping blood, so I wasn't so easy to track. I went back route upon back route, over fences, through abandoned buildings, through alleyways and over railway tracks. I thought that if they hadn't caught up with me after twenty minutes, I had definitely lost them.

It felt like enough time at this point and as there were no signs of the armed men and their leader, I let myself fall to the ground and slumped against a wall in an alleyway, between two boarded-up buildings. There was also no sign of Little Dog. I gathered my thoughts and noticed I was taking in quick, heavy breaths. I saw the blood flowing out of me and onto the stone-paved ground. Even the most optimistic person would have believed that I was going to bleed out very soon. I could only think of one possible way to get out of this situation — and that was nigh on impossible — but I had no choice. I focused my mind on slowing my breathing, with the aim of slowing down my heartbeat. My plan was to slow down my circulatory system in the hope that somehow, I would be found and saved by someone before I slowly bled to death. Just as I felt that I had got my breath to the level I wanted it at, I blacked out.

Chapter 28

To kill or not to kill? was the thought going through Fiorella's mind. In the grip of an ice-cold rage, she considered killing at least one of her bodyguards. She knew it wouldn't be the best for henchmen morale though and such issues had become far more of a priority over the years. She had learned the importance of staff well-being a fair few years ago, at the cost of a large knife wound to her abdomen. The megalomaniac lightly touched the scar through her dress as she contemplated her dilemma. Instead, she decided on saving the rage to take out on whoever this unknown enemy was when they were found.

"Ma'am, please, we need to go," one of her bodyguards urged.

Fiorella raised an eyebrow in response but complied and speedily walked out of the building to her blacked-out SUV. Two other bodyguards had gone to search for the dishevelled-looking man who had fled.

As the megalomaniac walked back to her car, she noticed a luxury convertible with its roof caved in and a few blood splatters on its white paint... but there was nothing else around to suggest what had happened. As soon as Fiorella was safely in her vehicle with her bodyguards driving her away from the scene, she logged on to her IT system via a tablet linked to a secure wi-fi link within the car. She then went into deep thought about what she had just observed.

With regard to the vagabond, she thought at first that he had just wandered into the office and taken advantage of its being empty; but the way he was able to withstand multiple gunshot wounds, get away in such haste whilst wounded and still be able to make such a long jump from the fourth storey into the canal meant he must have been far more than a simple vagabond. This assumption was further confirmed when the CCTV footage was checked.

A quick check of Oso's cameras showed that there was absolutely no footage from the rest of the building of anything important. It simply showed her employees coming to work, doing nothing out of the ordinary and the recording becoming blank for a few hours from 10:32 a.m. The CCTV footage then came back on as soon as the vagabond had jumped out of the window. This man was far more interesting than he looked, Fiorella thought.

Self-preservation immediately snapped her back and focused her on the immediate task at hand, namely: damage limitation and putting her empire's defences up. A few taps on the screen later and she had deleted the CCTV footage of herself and her bodyguards. Fiorella checked her AI to identify whether there were any anomalies anywhere in her empire prior to the incident, but none was brought up and all systems appeared to be in good working order. Nonetheless, after a few passcodes, retinal identification, voice recognition and fingerprint identification, she was able to put her empire on a Code Orange. This meant her entire command structure was automatically notified that a threatening event had occurred and required extreme vigilance during whatever work they carried out. Code Red required all-out war and although a large-scale kidnapping was significant, it certainly was not at that level.

As the megalomaniac was ever the cautious one, she sent a quick email request to her IT and AI departments:

Hi,

*This needs to be prioritised with the utmost urgency. Our systems need to be checked and rechecked for any potential hacks or flaws. This is a complete system's check, but not only that, our AI and all its algorithms will need to be fully inspected as well. I am aware of the magnitude of this and I am aware that a check for both was only completed a couple of months ago, but this needs to be done **NOW**! Get all necessary staff members to start this by tonight.*

Fiorella

Fiorella rarely ever used bold, underlined, or words in all capitals at the same time in her emails, so she knew they would understand that there would be serious repercussions should they not immediately enact her orders. She sent another email straight after, this one to all her directors on the black-market side of her empire.

Hi,

For those who are in the country, we are having an emergency meeting at 9:00 p.m. tonight at the London office. This is a meeting that all UK-based directors must attend, as it is of the utmost importance. There will be another meeting the

following day. It will be at the London office again
but at 4:00 p.m. I expect all international directors
(as well as UK directors) to attend the follow-up
meeting, too. No ifs and no buts. Any costings to
ensure attendance has been approved.

All will be explained in person.
Thank you and see you all soon.

Fiorella

Fiorella realised that it had been a long while
since she was fighting anyone so competent.
Unfortunately, as of yet, she didn't know who her
opponent was, but she was confident that she
would find out. As she mulled over who the
potential enemy was, a radio call came in from her
other two bodyguards, who reported that they had
been unsuccessful in finding the vagabond.

"Instruct them to return to base," she said with
a grimace.

There was not much else to do other than
complete further preliminary investigations.
Fiorella loaded up the data that had been collected
from her AI systems on the Chief of Operations.

As the Chief of Operations was previously
involved in the less-than-legal aspects of her
empire, he was "willingly" technologically linked
to her systems through implanted sensors. These
sensors measured his heartbeat, brain activity,
blood pressure, GPS location and blood-related
health markers, all of which were regularly
analysed by her AI. This data link had been cut off,

however, at the same time that the CCTV was switched off.

If the Chief of Operations had simply been executed and his body dumped, there would still be a connection from his implants, unless they were all destroyed, she thought. And the only way for the implants to be destroyed at the same time would be through a powerful explosion, but there was no sign of this in the Oso offices. It was identical to what happened to Doctor Mads Knörr and the five men that watched him. Fiorella deduced that this meant there must have been a device used that blocked all electronic communications and radio waves, something that harnessed something like an electromagnetic pulse.

The area she looked into next was the Chief of Operations' phone records, messages, e-mails, his physical location history, social media and recordings of all of his calls. This was a lot of material to sift through, so she used her AI to compile a report on all information gathered prior to the day of the incident whilst she looked into his activity on the day. The AI found no unscrupulous activity to report and rated him as low risk. This was as expected, because if he was a higher risk, he would have been previously flagged up by the AI. Fiorella's own search produced the same uninteresting results.

On the day prior to 10:32 a.m., the Chief of Operations messaged friends with lewd innuendos, arranged work meetings, discussed costings with other employees, arranged a rendezvous with two transgender escorts that he regularly used and ignored phone calls from his wife. As with his sensors, no data was sent back to the servers as

soon as the time reached 10:32 a.m..
Communications completely ceased after that point
and there was no further connection.

Thought upon thought whirred through
Fiorella's head, none of which gave her any
comfort. She felt that the likely conclusion was that
the hundred and forty employees present that day
— it would have been more if it wasn't for a
conference that took some of the staff away —
were all kidnapped and since advanced technology
was used, it must have meant the organisation that
did it was extremely well developed. Fiorella still
needed to wait for the police to complete a
thorough scan of the office but based on her own
checks, as well as her men's check, there did not
appear to be any observable traces of blood in the
building to suggest murder. Fiorella grimaced at
the thought of subsequent media and police
involvement. Another worry was that there would
potentially be MI5 involvement due to the scale of
the kidnapping and the professionalism involved.
Even though she had enough of her own within the
organisation, there was still a risk that luck would
go against her and Oso's connections to her empire
would be spotted by those not on her payroll.

Such potential ties back to her empire threw
her into deep contemplation about Oso itself. There
were only a few employees left in Oso who knew
of her ties to the company. These were the CEO,
the Chairmen of the Board, a small number of
major shareholders and a couple of directors.
Another email flew to her Operations Department:

Hi,

I need complete but absolutely covert monitoring of our higher-grade employees in Oso. There will be further orders tomorrow evening.

Thank you.

Fiorella

The main conundrum around Oso for Fiorella was whether to completely clean up all ties to her empire and liquidise the assets of the firm so it could be absorbed back into her empire. The competence of her IT and accountancy firms with her AI meant that any money moved would be near untraceable. But even so, there was still a possibility that she could neglect the most minute thread that might tie her empire to Oso. Also, this would bring mainstream attention to the fact that someone as powerful as her existed and there was also the fact that her many enemies might see this as an opportunity to implicate and hurt her.

She mulled over the option of framing a known enemy for the kidnapping and the subsequent "theft" of Oso's assets. There were, as she called them, the "Mumbo Jumbos", of whom she would have been quite happy to implicate and expose. The desire was there, but as much as she disliked them and thought them silly types who had a ludicrous penchant for dressing up in absurd costumes and exhibiting frat-boy like behaviour, she knew that they would figure out it was her and then there would be all-out war again. She craved for such a fight, as there remained the small fact that they wouldn't let her join because she was a woman — one small incident of gender discrimination led to a five-year war in which thousands were brutally murdered and neither side won.

The more she thought about war with the "Mumbo Jumbos", the more tempting it became. She started to convince herself that it was probably them who organised this attack on Oso, even though her surveillance and spy network had not reported anything untoward from them. Just as her bloodlust nearly reached its crescendo, common sense took drastic action to burst such fantasies. It reminded her of her ultimate plan and that she needed to stay focused on this. Also, if she did, it would significantly hurt her adversaries as well as moving her closer to her grandiose ambitions.

Such sensibilities led her to feel that the likelihood was that she'd keep Oso up and running. It would potentially cost her hundreds of millions to make sure nothing came back to her and to make sure the company remained a profitable cash cow in her control. She had already started to plan so that, when the dust settled, a phoney takeover from one of her other companies would happen, so that the missing staff could be more quickly replaced and restructuring would be far easier; that was if the staff weren't found and Fiorella had a strong hunch that they would not be.

Fiorella shrugged and let herself slide back into her seat. It was just another challenge to surmount and she felt she had come up against far worse, especially in her drug baroness days. The megalomaniac put her tablet away, as there wasn't anything further that could be done and let idle thoughts go wherever they wanted to go. They, of course, went back to the incident and lightly probed the oddity of it all.

Firstly, the very act of kidnapping that many people: although certainly not uncommon elsewhere, in the UK it was quite unheard of. Not only that, but aside from her Chief of Operations, the actual worth of those that had been kidnapped was not high. Her systems said it was only people in sales, administration, marketing, cleaning and PR staff who were taken. They certainly were not as valued as those from the R&D side of the firm. So, the question was, why bother with such a professional job to take employees who would not hold any valuable corporate secrets? Fiorella didn't even try to answer this, as she knew she couldn't.

Next, she fell to thinking of the man who looked like a vagabond. She had already linked him as her organisation's previous kidnapping target. The similarities of his escape from the court and the present incident were uncanny. The question for Fiorella was: who was this man? She felt that his look was a disguise and that when the police analysed the DNA from the blood from his bullet wounds, she would find it a match with the man who escaped from the court. Anyhow, she was glad, at the very least, that she had her own visual confirmation of a face from this shadowy organisation.

Fiorella was just about to close her eyes and go to sleep when a thought about the little dog that the scruffy man had with him came into view. She hazarded that the critter was his, as it had followed him. The odd thing about the animal was that it was brought along in the first place; it would not have made sense to bring such an animal to a professional, large-scale kidnapping unless there was some purpose to it. As bizarre as it sounded, Fiorella started to feel that the animal was perhaps a genetically or mechanically modified creature that somehow created an EMP type field to block all electronics from working. It would make some sense, as the CCTV immediately switched back on when the scruffy-looking man jumped out of the window, probably whilst holding the canine.

One of her bodyguards interrupted her train of thought before it went any further.

"Ma'am, we have word that the operation against the Volgograd Bratva has started. It is estimated that all targets will be taken out within six hours."

"Finally, some good news. Please get someone to consult the Afghans, once we are successful, on whether they wish us to broker a deal with them and the Georgians, as they will need new buyers and transporters."

As soon as she finished speaking, she felt an urge to volunteer her own organisation to move the heroin into Europe, as she still missed the thrill of her drug cartel days. Fiorella sighed, as she knew that as much as she enjoyed it, she just couldn't take such a step backwards, as she had grown far too much. The fun simply did not warrant the risk of direct involvement.

"Thank you," she said, before pressing a button which raised a blacked-out window between herself and her two bodyguards on the other side. Surprisingly, Fiorella stopped her ruminations about the day's events and absent-mindedly stared out of the window as they drove through Greater

Manchester. Like London, she did not find anything particularly fascinating about the place. There were too many buildings that hadn't been aesthetically designed for a higher purpose. Their sole purpose was to satisfy those who only bathed in the swill of capitalism. She was no socialist, and she was also a believer that a great deal of human prosperity was brought by such profit orientation. But to her, it was obvious that such a mode of development had run its course and that evolution was required for progress.

Her chain of thought soon jangled with worry about human extinction. This was not uncommon for the megalomaniac, as it had become an obsession and was a major reason for her recent ambitions. She felt that one only had to look into the night sky to realise the myriad of ways that absolute destruction could befall the Earth. Then there were the numerous other possibilities of Armageddon here on this planet. Fiorella felt certain that something cataclysmic would happen; it was just unfortunate that there was no certainty as to when. The universal law of entropy would ensure that such doom was an inescapable fact — this death was spelt out from that very first Big Bang. That is what science told Fiorella and as terrible as it sounded to others, she simply saw human extinction as a challenge to overcome. However, she was realistic and like a medieval cathedral builder, she knew she would not live to see such dreams completed, but simply wanted to put the foundations in place so that such grandiosity could one day succeed.

The megalomaniac's thoughts briefly fluttered to the completion of her ambitions, but she pulled herself away. She was a believer that if she regularly fantasised about her dreams, then it made them less likely to come true. Instead, she closed her eyes and let the chaos in her mind die down as sleep slowly took hold of her.

Chapter 29

The Russian man absent-mindedly stared out of the bullet-proof car window as the Volgograd cityscape went by. He lightly stroked a long, thin scar that clung around the front of his neck. Since that fateful day when the syndicate made that terrible decision, every day for the past month, the scar had produced a persistent burning sensation. He had argued against such actions, but he was outvoted. His compatriots thought it was much too good an opportunity not to take and they were not convinced by the stories and reputation of Fiorella. Rodion smirked to himself about how such a monster had such a pretty name.

The top of the Mamayev Kurgan came into view from afar and that momentarily distracted the Russian man from his anxieties. It wasn't that the statue conjured up emotions of pride and awe, but rather that it simply indicated that it wouldn't be much longer until Rodion and his troop arrived for the celebration, this being the birthday of the Volgograd Bratva. The Russian felt it unwise to go forward with an event and argued it was best to remain on high alert. Instead, because their contacts in the FSB had assured them that there was no sign of activity from Fiorella and that they would not allow such action on Russian soil, the celebration had been given the go-ahead. Even though most of the leadership believed that Fiorella's reputation was built on clever marketing, Rodion was at least able to convince his comrades to put heavy security in place for the party. The cautious Russian had also brought along an extra seven men to add to the mob's safety.

The convoy pulled up at an extravagant, marble building that had looming, sentinel-like pillars just in front of the hulking mahogany entrance door. There was many a grim-faced man in black suits outside on guard. They were all heavily armed with sub-machine guns. Usually, such a sight would cause the intervention of the authorities, but with the amount of control the mob had over the city, there were going to be no questions asked about this public display of strength. The happy, smiling families of the upper echelons of the syndicate going into the building seemed oddly juxtaposed against such a backdrop. It was expected, of course, that families should attend, along with all of the Bratva bosses, but as Rodion could not shake the feeling that revenge from Fiorella was coming, he had convinced his wife to remain at home with their child.

As the car approached the entrance to the hall, the mob boss looked at his reflection in the tinted glass that separated him from his driver. A rotund, grey, heavily stubbled and tired-looking man, dressed in a smart grey suit, looked back at him. He was of an age wherein any other job he would be on the verge of retirement. He sighed in dour acceptance of the sight and then sullenly thought to himself that he did not know how much longer he could continue working this hard for the syndicate.

Before he could become any more morose, the car came to a stop and the door was opened by one of the guards. Rodion stepped out and saw a square-jawed man with a short blond crew cut, dressed in a smart, all-black ensemble. This formal attire did not match the sub-machine gun that was under his arm.

"Sir," the guard said gruffly to Rodion.

"My men will stand on guard outside here as well," Rodion informed him.

"That isn't necessary —"

"It may not be necessary, but it will be happening," Rodion asserted whilst giving a couple of soft slaps to the side of the guard's face.

Without letting the guard reply, Rodion headed towards the hulking entrance door. As he approached, one of the two guards in front swung open the door and Rodion gave them a nod of acknowledgement. The syndicate boss stepped into an ornate reception area where a monstrous chandelier that resembled a spider hung over the scene on a strand of its web. There were many other guards inside, scattered about and patrolling various spots. Rodion spotted the family of a fellow Volgograd boss and waved at the happy faces that headed into the main hall. He turned around as he felt a tap on his shoulder and saw a smartly dressed and voluptuous blond woman, wearing bright red lipstick.

"Sir, your jacket?" she asked softly but authoritatively.

"No — no. I am fine with it on, my love," Rodion replied with a wry smile.

He turned back around, took a deep breath and then walked to the main entrance. A guard opened the door and loud, thumping pop music met him. Families and other assortments of relatives could be seen having fun on the dance floor and stage. His compatriots and other bosses from the Bratva leadership sat on the other side of the hall, where there were numerous tables and chairs with dinnerware laid out on top. Rodion headed towards the men and on the way dodged a few children that almost ran into him while playing. He came to a table filled with younger faces than his. The syndicate's leadership had all become younger whilst Rodion had grown older, it seemed. It was not because of anything untoward, but rather the fact that most of the superiors had died of old age and the only replacements happened to be those who were a couple of generations junior, in their thirties or forties.

As Rodion greeted all those around the table, he had to focus on keeping his anger from rising up. He was not fond of the personage who had taken over, as he felt they had too much to prove, which was probably why they had voted to take over the Afghan production line. When Rodion had tried to convince them, he had tried all manner of arguments, from giving a history lesson, to tales of his own experiences fighting over there. They all simply ignored him, as the noise of their own greedy ambitions closed their ears.

"Rodion, where is Anna and little Liliya?" one of the bosses asked just as Rodion sat down next to him.

"Liliya has, unfortunately, come down with a fever. You know how Anna is, she is so protective of Liliya and would rather care for her than let the staff do it, so she is with her. How is your lot, Boris?" Rodion replied, without putting much conviction into his lie.

He turned his head to look at Boris and saw a near chiselled, blond-haired man with slicked-back hair, in a fashionable suit.

"As per usual, Maya is drinking herself into oblivion and the two little ones are running wild with their cousins —"

"Where is Viktor?" Rodion interrupted.

"Ha! That fool is in the hospital with his family right now. Do not worry, it's only food poisoning."

"Then who is in charge of security? Were all the staff here vetted by Viktor before he was admitted?" Rodion said with some alarm.

"It's Yury. I am sure everyone has been vetted, Rodion. You worry too much about this Fiorella. It is all tall stories and even if they weren't, the FSB is on our side so she cannot touch us. Lighten up, relax, drink some vodka."

Boris poured him a drink and a lecherous smile crept onto his face.

"When the women and children leave, we will have some fun. I have a real show lined up. I can tell you I have personally vetted every girl myself," Boris laughed out and gave Rodion a smack on his back.

The night continued with the expected gross level of opulence and the most expensive alcohol flowed into every glass each time they were emptied. It was only Rodion who nursed the same half-full glass of vodka throughout the night. He had also barely touched his food and did his best to avoid all forms of conversation. He thought that he had probably offended many of his compatriots with his behaviour, but he had reached the point of not caring, for it seemed to him the syndicate was at war and needed to act like it. He was about to leave when the stage lit up and the music died down. Spotlights came on and the music changed to a more rhythmic, R&B pop song. Out walked eight provocative-looking women, all dressed in garter belts, corsets, stockings and stiletto heels. Rodion's curiosity was momentarily sparked and he thought he'd wait another minute or two before leaving.

The eight women were more than adept at their work, and acted out perfectly choreographed, sensual dance moves. There were a few blown kisses and as time went on, more and more of their clothing came off. Just as the eight women bared all to the audience, Rodion decided it was time to leave, but then he remembered that he needed to remind Boris that the date of the next shipment of heroin needed to be confirmed in the next two days. The syndicate director looked around at his comrades, all of whom were focused on the show, but Boris could not be seen anywhere. Rodion was too tired and bored with the party to think anything of it, so he headed to one of the fire exits without letting anyone know. When he tried the door, it didn't budge; it was clearly locked from the outside. The Russian swore under his breath and walked to the main exit of the hall. Just as he tried that door, the show finished and the ladies vacated the stage. Again, this door was locked and this time, Rodion realised something was awry.

As he went to try the last remaining door, automatic gunfire came from behind the stage and from outside of the hall. Rodion instinctively pulled out his gun and as he headed towards his compatriots, numerous cans of CS gas were thrown out from behind the stage. A thick fog quickly appeared in the centre of the hall. The syndicate boss backed away, opting to cling to the edges of the room to avoid as much of the gas as possible.

The music had completely died down and was now replaced by the noise of shouting, retching, coughing and gunfire from outside the room. Rodion decided to see if there was an exit through which he could help get his men out, but before he could make progress with the search, he spotted eight small figures with gas masks and assault rifles walking out from the back of the stage. The figures all rapidly fired, single-shot by single-shot. After one of them hit one of his compatriots, Rodion was able to make out that the eight weren't shooting to kill but rather to incapacitate.

The remaining mobsters tried to take aim but missed due to the CS gas causing them to wretch and splutter. Rodion was no different; he could barely see through the tears streaming from his eyes as he fired shots into the wall behind them. Before he could fire another bullet, he felt two heavy thuds go into both his shoulders. He dropped his gun and fell to the ground. The bullet wounds and the gas all became too much for his brain to cope with and he passed out.

The Russian boss came to after ice-cold water was poured on his head. He immediately shot up and tried to get up off the seat he was on, but found he was firmly tied down. Rodion turned around wildly and saw that his compatriots were tied to chairs as well. They were placed in two rows, facing outwards. Around them were the eight small raiders, without their gas masks now: they were the eight strippers. And now they were accompanied by ten just as heavily armed men.

"Well, the last one is awake. Let's get to business, we can't stay here too long," ordered the woman whose jet-black hair was tied up.

At the other end of the row, two of the women undid two of Rodion's fellow directors' trousers and pulled down their underpants. There was a look of confusion on all of the mob bosses' faces — that was, until the two women both pulled out menacing knives.

"Understandably, none of the men wanted to do this themselves," the dark-haired woman joked.

With the efficiency of a farmer handling livestock, the women removed the two men's genitals, stuffed them into their still-screaming mouths and then wrapped their mouths with duct tape.

"Please do remember as you pass into the next life, that this is what happens when you cross Fiorella. Your families will follow you into the underworld soon after," the dark-haired woman sneered.

They quickly and methodically mutilated all the captured mobsters, until they finally reached Rodion. The old Russian director was only able to swallow and gulp. The situation seemed too surreal, so much so that it almost didn't register. And now, the two mutilators cleaned their knives and put them away.

"You might not believe this Rodion, but Fiorella is a fair woman. She knows that you were the only one that respected the contract and the organisation. Unfortunately for you, you will still need to die, as you are a part of the Bratva. However, your family will be spared," the female platoon leader said with an odd kindness in her voice, whilst lightly stroking his face.

Rodion always knew that it was unlikely he would die a peaceful death, so this was not particularly shocking. In fact, at that moment he was quite grateful that he had lived to such an old age and that his family would live on. So, the mob boss simply accepted that death had finally caught up with him.

"Thank you," he replied softly.

The platoon leader stepped back and as she walked away, she barked her orders.

"Execute them all!"

Immediately two of the men pulled out pistols and moved down the line of tied-up directors, shooting each of them twice in the head. When they reached Rodion, he was reminiscing about the first time Lilliya started to walk, and then the memory stopped.

Chapter 30

When I came to, I immediately shot up off the floor ready to fight. My body had remembered the events quicker than my mind had and it took me a few seconds before I realised why I had leapt up in such a state of shock. Just as my brain was switching on the thought assembly-line, I noticed that I was in a near-empty and endless void. What stood out from the darkness was a large, black and chrome elevator. With only the abyss all around the contraption, it made it difficult to see how far away the thing actually was. That was when I remembered I had just previously passed out after being stabbed, beaten, bludgeoned and shot numerous times. Oddly, I didn't feel any pain and when I felt around my body, I found that I had no wounds. I quickly realised that I was not in Manchester anymore.

I remembered the black elevator and remembered it came from a dream that I was really hoping was only fantasy. The choice in front of me was an endless void of nothingness, or the elevator; I naturally chose the elevator. As I got closer to the machine, I expected the doors to open and Winston to step out. Instead, the machine just stood there looming over me. I huffed and pressed the down button on the outside. A little ding from a bell could be heard and the doors opened. Inside was exactly the same as it had been before, other than a giant piece of white cardboard stuck on with brown tape near the buttons. There were big red letters on the cardboard that read:

PRESS DOWN! He's waiting.

Winston,

X

I let out a deep sigh and turned to look outside the elevator. Nothing had changed, it was still an endless void that didn't tickle my fancy one bit. When I turned back, the writing had changed:

Come on. Chop-chop! Otherwise, he'll call me back from my annual leave to deal with you.

Winston,

X

I let out another deep sigh, as I knew that what awaited me was probably not going to be pleasant. I didn't exactly develop a fondness for Satan after my last visit. I pressed the down button and a second later the elevator dinged. The doors opened up to reveal the same long corridor with black and white tiles. There were no walls, just an endless void like before. There was, however, the young man in black latex hot pants who had distracted the doctor for me. He was near the elevator, mopping the floor. He didn't look particularly enthused with his job, as his shoulders hung down with the weight of dejection. I was able to hear that he was muttering but was unable to make out what he was saying until I stepped into the corridor.

"You missed a spot ... unacceptable quality of work ... you'll get sent back to the void ... bloody fat, balding shite ... hope you never come back ..."

The young man then stopped his mopping and, without even bothering to look up at me, walked to the elevator with his mop and bucket.

The scantily clad man carried on muttering to himself even as the elevator doors closed. I raised my eyebrows and then set off to the double mahogany doors. I grimaced as I knocked hard. A second later the doors creaked open on their own.

There wasn't much change in the décor in Satan's office or home. The only difference appeared to be that the nude paintings were life-sized. Also, the paintings were busy taking selfies on their smartphones. The statues appeared to be sitting down, bored, as they absent-mindedly looked at their fingernails, but as soon as they saw me, they all quickly — well, as quickly as marble and paint would let them — got up and began their erotic poses.

Before I had time to say anything, the office chair suddenly spun around to reveal an impeccably dressed Satan in a mustard-yellow fitted suit and an unbuttoned white shirt. As soon as he saw me his face exploded into alarm.

"Darling! How in Hell do you live with yourself wearing such a travesty!?" he exclaimed.

I raised an eyebrow in response, as being insulted by supposed deities had started to seem like it was becoming a theme for me.

"I really should have cancelled Winnie's annual leave. He would have made sure you were dressed for the occasion. Of course, it would have meant he'd stomp around and huff for a few weeks before he got over it, but at least I would not have had to endure your hideous crime against fashion in my own home. I know that out there anything goes, but this is not *out there*," the deity said with a slight wince.

Then with purposeful melodrama, he covered his eyes, turned away and used his free hand to click his fingers. I heard a slight rustle of fabrics and looked down to see a violet tuxedo set and shirt morphing out of the floor. When they had pulled themselves up, the clothes appeared to look around, even though there was nothing for them to look around with. I knew what was going to come next and this time around, I wasn't going to be violated without a fight.

Within a split-second I was down on the ground and wrestling with the clothes. During the tussle, the shirt somehow cleaned my hair and tied it back in a bun. The clothes had an impossible litheness about them and it was only thirty seconds later that I found myself wearing a perfectly fitted tuxedo ensemble. I tried ripping the suit off in a fit of rage, but it was not going anywhere. My feet felt different and I looked down to see that I was wearing a shiny pair of Oxford shoes. It must have been when I was rolling on the floor trying to fight the accursed clothes off that the shoes took my boots off and jumped onto my feet. It was clear that there was no point fighting, so I sighed and stood up.

"My, my, darling, you have such an, shall we say, interesting face! Such a shame to hide it behind all that hair. Anyway, I digress. Now we can talk, or perhaps it will be more that I talk and you listen."

Satan chuckled and gave me a wink. The deity spun around in his office chair to face the swirling magma that was pressed against the office window. Satan then spun back around to face me after a couple of seconds.

"Is the view to your liking?"

I shrugged with slumped shoulders and stayed silent.

"I do like the orange glow and the magma can be quite hypnotic, but I've had this décor for the past few hundred years. I am thinking about a complete change."

The Devil then clicked his fingers again and the magma turned into a clear, coral and fish-filled sea. The black and white chequered floor turned into light grey speckled marble, but the paintings, statues and the void remained.

"Oh darling, I do like it. I almost feel like a supervillain in his secret lair with such a design. I just need an evil plan to go with it. Perhaps one with lasers, as I've always enjoyed the noises they make and the lovely bright colours ..."

Satan then pretended his hands were pistols and made "pew pew" noises as he shot neon-green lasers out of them into both of the marble statues. Distorted screams could be heard as the statues disintegrated. Satan giggled and excitedly clapped his hands.

"Hmmmm, I really can't think at the moment what I can put there to replace them," he said and then shrugged.

The Devil clicked his fingers again and the statues reappeared. At first, they both had a look of absolute panic, but then quickly fell into complete relief. The Devil spun around on his office chair again and when he came back around, he looked straight into my eyes. For a split second his eyes lit up with a bright, furious red and within them, I saw a torrent of hellfire so monstrous that I felt it could swallow the entire galaxy. After becoming so desensitised by Little Dog, however, the look only managed to elicit a shrug of the shoulders from me. Satan's face quickly turned back to the mask it was before and he sighed deeply.

"I am quite sure you have noticed that Little Dog is an absolute cretin. Of course, the horrible beast knew I'd have to do something about you and now I find I am manipulated into its silly game. Here I am, interfering again so the petulant shit does not destroy the Earth. I hope it's listening to us right now, I really do …".

The Devil stopped and then slunk down into his chair. He mumbled under his breath and all I could make out was "It's my world …" and a few swear words. Satan then chuckled to himself and sat back up.

"Bloody family, they're a pain in the arse, aren't they?"

I raised my eyebrow and nodded in agreement. Satan crossed his legs and spun around in his office chair again, stopping when he came back to face me.

"Darling, if you didn't get it from my little tantrum just now, if you die this early in the game then it's a certainty that your new-found friend would eat or destroy everyone on this planet. That would ruin my pet project, which I've spent four billion years on. It might be nothing to that cretin, but it's certainly something to me. The only possible way for Little Dog to leave without eating every last Earthling is for you to thoroughly entertain the beast. Also, if you hadn't gathered, back on that little blue planet, you are, at this moment in time, on the verge of death, which makes the situation a tad precarious."

I shrugged in response; death didn't sound like a bad option considering what else was on offer.

"Darling, you're not a petulant teenager, so perhaps try speaking instead of just shrugging. Anyway, where was I? Ah yes, of course, I am not going to let a silly thing like death happen when so much is on the line, so you *will* live to fight another day, even though I'd prefer you not to. This will probably be the only time I intervene this much as it's quite obvious that if I continue to do so it will eventually ruin Little Dog's fun and the bastard will then ruin mine in return. As soon as I saw the vulgar beast it became clear as day that this was the way it was heading. I naively hoped otherwise. Anyway, we know the direction, the question is what to do to get you there?"

Satan jumped off his chair and approached me. As he got close, I clenched my fist and tried to swing at him, but the suit kept me rigidly in place. Satan walked around me, sticking his thumb up to judge the perspective and also viewed me in a frame made-up with his hands.

"It is something of a tightrope, this, darling. Of course, you must live, that is a given, but you are going to go up against an army of highly trained and heavily armed killers. The obvious conclusion is that I'll be needing to intervene again and without a doubt, Little Dog would quickly lose interest and we both know what it'll do if that is the case. So, what can we do to you, darling? We have to improve you somehow, but also it is obvious that if it's too much then the childish boor will become bored. Too little and you will die too soon and again, my precious Earth goes *poof.*"

I looked at Satan and for some reason, my very first memory of Little Dog suddenly popped into my head. I felt a pang of longing, as I missed how great those simple times were before I had met the deity. The memories then started to skip ahead as if they were being fast-forwarded and that was when I realised I wasn't simply being nostalgic. Suddenly my memories went back to the point where I was in the courtroom and Little Dog was about to show me its power and tell me its name.

"Unfortunately, darling — and there is no nice way of putting it — this will hurt quite a bit," Satan whispered in my ear.

"Bollocks," I replied with a sigh.

Chapter 31

As Little Dog lay on the sun, it let out a few moans of pleasure as the furious whip-cracks of solar flares lightly caressed its back. The deity daydreamed about the Oso office and the violence that had just ensued there. The blood, decapitations, torn limbs and screams of pain were all riveting stuff. Such joyful voyeurism, coupled with the abundance of fresh human snacks, meant it was a jolly good outing for the deity. Little Dog shivered with excitement at the thought of the human bones delicately crunching in its mouth, the meaty juices seeping out and the velvety fats caressing its taste buds. The deity suddenly had the urge to eat a couple of billion humans right then and there. Billions fewer people on Earth was hardly a big deal, after all, it probably wouldn't affect Cain's entertainment value … but then Little Dog remembered that it had promised itself to savour such scrumptious delights slowly, so that they did not become boring.

The deity rolled onto its back and looked up at the little blue planet. It had been a couple of days since Cain had jumped out of the office window. Little Dog hadn't followed as it was certain that Satan was going to intervene further. This would mean that Little Dog wouldn't have to be overly flexible when it came to its own rules about its own meddling. Also, the thought of getting another deity involved, albeit in a duplicitous manner, added to the fun. Little Dog found itself making guess after guess in relation to what Satan was going to do and felt its excitement rise.

Little Dog knew that Satan was probably having one of the tantrums that young gods are so well known for and the thought of this made the critter chuckle. The deity thought that this joy in winding up the young seemed to be a universal trait for all mortal and immortal life forms. There are, of course, potential consequences of such actions and in fact, the last time Little Dog toyed with a young god, a few galaxies were obliterated in the fracas that followed.

For a brief second the deity thought about snooping on the younger god, but then went against the idea, as it might ruin the suspense about upcoming events. Also, Little Dog could tell that, as young as Satan was, the god was certainly incredibly smart and cunning. This added to the drama of not quite knowing what to expect next.

As the game was afoot, the deity found that it could not simply go to sleep. Its impatience for the story to continue pulsated throughout its body. Time suddenly came to a near standstill as excitement sped across Little Dog's synapses beyond the speed of light.

"By Jove! Now the wait is going to be even longer," the critter lamented to itself. The thought of having to wait for relative aeons just for a few weeks to go by dampened the deity's spirits enough for its synapses to return to a more slothful state. It knew it would have to preoccupy itself somehow in that time, otherwise, it would end up in repeated stop-start states of excitement and boredom until Cain had healed.

A quick, purposeful whir of cognition gave it an idea.

"Certainly could spice the entertainment up," Little Dog said to itself.

Instead of teleporting, as it wanted to kill a bit more time, from its back the deity sprouted giant black bat-like wings. Such wings were only for aesthetic purposes, as there wasn't any air to enable them to push off in space, but nonetheless Little Dog liked the idea. The deity flapped its wings and shot off towards Earth.

It was twenty-four hours later when Little Dog landed in a graveyard in the middle of a cold, wet night. The journey was surprisingly pleasant and also broken by brief tormenting of a Grayzen tourist spaceship that was flying past Earth. Unsurprisingly, Little Dog ended up eating the lot of them and happily discovered that they were quite a decent species for cleansing the palette.

The critter looked at the wet, moss-covered gravestone it had landed next to. The wings morphed back into Little Dog's body as it read the epitaph:

Loved by all.

The deity chuckled to itself, as it was such a blatant lie. It knew that this man who lay six feet under was loved by *none*, but as the fear of him was so great that even in death his relatives still felt that they still had to lie to appease him.

In the far-right corner of the gravestone was a carved emblem of an anvil in a circle. Even through death, all Stonemasons still carried on their not-so-very-secret cult tribalism. Of course, like all not-so-secret secret societies, they all felt a superior link to — and knowledge of — the reality that lay around them and to Little Dog, that made them even more stupid than any other human being. Fortunately for the deity, the Stonemasons believed — perhaps half-heartedly — in an absurd prophecy. There was also the fact that the cult was linked to an even more powerful and silly organisation that dabbled in even more ludicrous notions. All these factors were going to be important ingredients that would add to this new performer's show.

Fortunately, this new plot development was contractually proper, as an agreement to make it more difficult for Cain had recently been made. At first, the deity thought that the new plot device was far too much of a cliché. Yet, Little Dog also felt it was the right way to move the performance forward to its liking.

It was the age-old fight between the old and the new, the aged and the young, or, in the most romantic sense, the parent and the child. It was a perennial trope that had been used throughout the universe since time began. Understandably for Little Dog, these battles did not bring about any emotional resonance, as the deity was its own father — and mother — and it cared not at all about its children. The only part about this dynamic that the deity cared about was that those involved in such conflicts seemed to try harder, as they invested far more emotion.

The deity sat down next to the grave and gave its nether regions a quick and thorough lick. Of course, there was no reason to, but for whatever reason, at that moment in time it felt like the right thing to do. Little Dog suddenly stopped and gave a wry chuckle before speaking.

"My boy, please stop being so melodramatic. It's only a coffin. Be a good sport and hurry on out," the deity teased.

The sound of light rain that pattered against the grass and the gravestones was the only response.

"You're really not going to add anything to the show by acting so pathetic. Honestly, boy, pull yourself together and get yourself out."

Again, the rain and its patter was the only response. Little Dog rolled its eyes and suddenly a tentacle grew out of its back and shot into the ground. It whipped back out holding a decayed but moving foot and shin.

"Oh, I must apologise about that. I forgot how delicate you humans can be, especially the ones who are quite past their use-by date," Little Dog chortled.

The tentacle dropped the skeleton leg and shot back into the ground. A split second later it grew in width and within a few scoops had flung away all the dirt above the coffin. The tentacle ripped the coffin lid off and threw it so hard into the sky that it eventually landed on an empty ice-cream van in Glasgow. The tentacle went into the coffin and grabbed the other leg, and before Little Dog could stop itself, the noise of cloth-tearing and bone-crunching cut through the night. It quickly put the second decayed leg next to the other one.

"It seems my excitement has made me a touch clumsy," Little Dog huffed.

It was third time lucky, as this time, the tentacle softly wrapped itself around the body of the writhing corpse and lifted it up for the deity's closer inspection. Up came a grey, dirty skeleton with tiny bits of drab, dirt-covered clothing clinging to it. While being closely inspected, the head and neck of the skeleton slowly swung from side to side and its mouth hung open as if it was trying to scream. The arms tried to move up, but each time they reached shoulder height they fell back down. All the while his legs wriggled on the ground.

"My, my, my, aren't you a terrible sight, boy. Quite clearly, you're going to need a bit of sprucing up; in this state at best you'll only muster up mild annoyance because of your smell and certainly won't be a challenge for him. Also, please do stop your incessant bleating about wanting to be dead. A fate far worse than that awaits you if you do not play along," the deity scolded.

The skeleton's head came to a stop and appeared to look at Little Dog with its empty black eyes. The corpse closed its mouth and appeared to wait.

"Now that's much better, my boy. I have the most marvellous idea of what needs to be done."

The skeleton stayed silent and continued to stare at the sneering critter. Another tentacle morphed out of Little Dog's back, picked up the moving legs and deftly reattached them to the body. The deity then coughed and hacked up some phlegm. After a few seconds of this, it spat out some luminous purple slime, right on the skeleton. Centimetre by centimetre, the thick slime crept all

317

over the skeleton and moved into all of its crevices. Little Dog then moved the glob-covered body and gently dropped it in the nearby grass.

"We can't have you turning too young and too powerful, can we," Little Dog mused.

One of the tentacles stabbed into the ground next to it and went straight into a water pipe that was a fair few metres below. After sucking up gallons of water, it came back up to the graveyard and sprayed clean what had become a naked and flesh-covered human. The naked, balding man groaned as he tried to get up from the ground and immediately fell back down.

"Why did you bring me back? It was so peaceful ... the silence ... please, take me back to the silence," the man was just about able to hoarse out.

"I am afraid it's too late for that, my boy. Also, you've been brought back for the most delightful of reasons. I am afraid that going back to such a peaceful slumber isn't really an option for you at the moment. By all means, try doing it yourself, but you'll find that it won't happen until I *want* it to happen," the deity chuckled.

The gaunt, clean-shaven, middle-aged face with tears streaming out of creased sapphire blue eyes was just about able to look up at the critter.

"Why? Why have you done this to me?" the man sobbed.

"Let's say I've given you a second chance, my dear boy. Even you can surely admit that your previous life was quite pointless and an annoyance to others. Now I've given you that most fortunate of gifts, a chance to try again and to live a life of purpose. Of course, not just any purpose, but a holy one. To put it simply, the meaning of your new life that I have so generously provided is to *entertain me*."

Little Dog then let a few seconds go by for the man to process what he had just said.

"You have probably noticed that I am not the most pious of sorts, so I am not asking you to act like a monk. I don't want you to love me, or even like me; I simply want you to be you. Well, that is, the you that sticks with his most violent of pasts, as I am quite a fan of the bloodier sides of life," Little Dog chuckled.

The man blankly stared at the deity as he struggled to process what was going on and what had just happened. The deity waited a couple of seconds in the expectation that there would be further questions, but soon realised that was not going to happen. It gave a sigh.

"It seems you are still in a bit of shock. Anyway, before I go, just so you know, you have coincidentally fulfilled that most silly of Stonemasons' prophecies that your lovely cult believes in."

Little Dog merrily trotted across to the softly sobbing man and looked him right in his eyes.

"Yes, my boy, once the cogs start moving in that head of yours, you'll see what path I want you to follow. Oh, one last thing: don't disappoint me with the entertainment, my dear boy."

The deity then teleported back onto the sun as soon as it had made its threat.

Although there was still going to be a fair bit of time left until Cain healed, Little Dog's mood had significantly improved, as it was quite happy with the pieces it had moved into place. It felt that it now deserved a well-earned snooze, but as soon as the deity closed its eyes, it found that sleep wasn't going to happen. Instead, thoughts about what else it could do to whittle away the time went through its head.

Chapter 32

I came to the noise of a crackling fire and a warmth that stroked my body. My mouth was terribly dry and it felt as if my tongue rubbed against it like chalk on pavement. At that moment, the only thing I knew was that I felt I was sandwiched between some thick blankets and my head was propped up on a pillow. I was so dazed and confused that I was barely able to remember who I was, let alone where I was and what had happened. I opened my eyes and all I was able to make out was several blurry fires that went around in a circle. The sight was too much for my head and my stomach, so I closed my eyes and went to move into a more comfortable position. As soon as I tried, the most violent of pain sadistically stabbed me all over with sharp needles. Because I was so weak, I was only able to respond with a gasp.

"You're actually awake. Thought you wouldn't make it. I wouldn't try to move, as you're riddled with all sorts of wounds. Here, have some water," a soothing female voice with a broad Lancashire accent comforted.

Although there was a sense of déjà vu, no alarm bells went off. I felt a cold cup touch my lips and greedily, I drank down the cool water. The pleasure was heavenly but before I could finish the cup, I passed out.

I was awoken by out-of-tune singing. At first, I thought a cat was slowly being murdered, but then realised it was whoever was caring for me. Again, I tried opening my eyes and again I saw multiple fires that went around in a circle. I had to close my eyes again, as the sight still brought nausea and intense dizziness. It was a near repeat of last time I had woken, because when I tried moving again, the pain ruthlessly kept me in place. The singing stopped and I heard light footsteps come towards me.

"You should stop trying to move. You'll rip open your stitches. Mind you, you've done amazingly well for someone who has been stabbed, beaten and shot. Anyway, I am sure you're thirsty, so let me get you some more water," the voice cooed.

Gluttonously, I gulped all the water and passed out again. Again, I fell into nothingness in which there were no dreams. I came to hear what I thought was a male scream. I tried to stay awake to hear more but could only make out the woman singing again. It was but a few seconds later that I fell back into the arms of sleep.

I awoke again but this time, there was no noise or warmth of a crackling fire. I opened my eyes but a heavy pain that clumsily creaked throughout my forehead told me to keep them shut. I tried to get up, but the agony was far too much so I loudly gasped. That was when I heard the scuttle of footsteps from above and then the creaking of stairs. The odd thing was that I heard every fibrous detail of the wood creak. It felt as if damn near every strand of the material that rubbed against each other under the pressure registered. When the door swung open, I was able to make out the individual noises of the wood, the metal hinges creaking, the woman's breathing, the scuttle of a mouse and an incredibly faint car alarm from somewhere outside. It was the most peculiar sensation: it was as if my brain was able to process it all at once without editing anything out for clarity. Before I could contemplate what was going on with my body and mind, the woman spoke.

"Baby monitor. That's how I heard you. Who would've thought I had such a nurturing side in me? Here, let me get you some more water."

I could only see a shadow of her movement as the only illumination was the dim street lighting that crept in through the cracks of the curtains. A few seconds later I felt the mouth of a bottle pressed against my lips and I gulped. Every part of my mouth was electrified with the sensation; it was as if every nerve was able to be heard as the liquid swished by. Suddenly, the sensation of every fibre from the woollen blanket was present all over me at the same time, as well. Then, before another split second could pass, every wound and individual stitch painfully registered in my mind. In response to this sudden influx of information, I made a peculiar noise that was similar to a ribbiting frog. When I did that, every cord in my voice box and every inflection, could be felt as well.

"You certainly are an odd one. So how are you feeling?" she asked in a soothing voice that had started to sound more familiar.

Like an explosion, all that had happened since I started my campaign to save the bumblebees came to the forefront of my mind. Uncontrolled thoughts intertwined with currents of emotion that crashed into each other. I thought about her question and quickly discovered that I didn't quite know what to feel, as the whole affair seemed composed of contradictory feeling after contradictory feeling.

I was trapped and damn near powerless as a deity's plaything, forced into degradation. My well-being was inconsequential to Little Dog's goals. Yet somehow, this went in tandem with the fact that I did actually have some sort of influence on this being of immeasurable power and had been given the ability to influence the world in ways I never had before. It was disconcerting to feel so weak and strong at the same time. Such ruminations came without also adding Satan and the megalomaniac into the mix, both of which I am sure would have just added more contradictory feelings. My mind simply could not rationalise a narrative that gave me comfort, as any conclusion that almost brought solace also ended with, "You still might be eaten and digested for aeons upon aeons", or, "You still might be tortured in hellfire for eternity."

I was oblivious to my host, who patiently waited as my thoughts zoomed on in my mind. Through this reflection, I forced myself to remember that I had started this campaign to save the bumblebee with the utmost good intentions. I felt, perhaps in desperation, that this battered part of me was the only thing that might be able to keep me afloat in the storm that I was in and that at whatever cost, I mustn't let go of it, as there was going to be so much more to come. I had just about moved back onto thoughts about constructs of power and whether such a thing existed, when a polite cough brought me back.

"You look quite lost in your own world, there. Anyhow, I fancy a bit of a chat. I suppose you don't remember me?" the lady asked.

By the time she finished the sentence, my brain had already conjured up the image of who she was. It was odd, as the memory seemed palpably distorted and blurred, as if I was watching a badly damaged but restored film clip.

"I think I do," I just about croaked out.

"Really? I am quite flattered," the voice gushed.

"It's quite dark in here, which is how I prefer it, but I imagine you cannot see much. Here, let me switch the lamp on so you can see me better … there we are. Come on, open your eyes."

For the longest of seconds, I refused to, as I didn't want to acknowledge who it might be.

"Come on. Don't be silly, open your eyes."

As she spoke with so much sincerity, I felt powerless to resist her order, so I opened them. It certainly was who I thought it was — but the most peculiar thing was that every muscle that twitched in her face, every pore, hair and dilation of the pupils was processed in sync and in high definition. Also, every aspect of the decoration of the room shone with magnificent detail, from the sinews within the wooden floorboards, the moon-like craters in the brick walls, the hypnotic splash of flame in the lamp, the shadows that danced along with the light, to the intricacies of the many polished human skulls that sat along shelves all around the room. My stomach immediately sank down to the bottom of an abyss within me.

"Please excuse the décor. I know it is quite macabre, but I thought it would be silly to hide my trophies. I am surprisingly happy that you recognised me ...".

There was then a long pause and if I had been able to, I would have jumped up and run out of the house as fast as my legs could carry me.

"So, do you remember when you robbed me?" the woman jabbed.

I simply nodded, knowing I could only hope for the best.

Author's Note:

If you've reached this point then you've probably read the book. Hopefully, that means you like the story and if you do, then that means the world to me. Quite seriously, if I could smoke or inject such sentiment, then I would and I'd also do this to quite the unhealthy level. It makes me happy knowing that there are some people out there that appreciate the fucked up stuff that comes out of my brain. If you want to make me even happier then please post a review as well. It would be very much appreciated!

Anyway, to thank you for reading this book, I want to give you a freebie. It's a prologue to this story but it didn't make the cut. Hopefully, you'll enjoy it and it adds to the book you've just read. To get it and to also get an update for when the next book is coming out, go to https://louis-park.com and sign yourself onto the mailing list.

You can find the next book in the series exclusively at Amazon. Also, it can be read for free if you are signed up to Kindle Unlimited!

Printed in Great Britain
by Amazon